CONTENTS

BURNING CROWE

1	1
Document A	8
2	15
3	21
4	25
Document B	27
5	30
6	34
Document C	40
7	42
8	45
9	50
10	53
Document D	59
11	61
12	63
13	66
14	70
15	74
Document E	77

16	79
17	84
18	87
19	92
Document F	97
20	99
21	108
Document G	115
22	118
23	125
Document H	131
24	133
25	138
26	146
27	151
28	156
Document I	160
29	162
30	164
31	168
Document J	170
32	172
33	174
34	180
35	184
Document K	187
36	189
37	196

38	203
39	208
40	210
Document L	216
41	218
42	222
43	230
44	234
45	236
46	245
47	248
Document M	252
48	255
Document N	257
Document O	259
49	260
50	266
51	269
52	278
Document P	281
53	284
54	288
Document Q	293
55	295
56	305
Document R	307
57	309
Author's Notes	314

BURNING CROWE

a hardboiled crime novel

Geoff Smith

Front cover image is The Turner Centre in Margate, photo by Geoff Smith. Cover design by Geoff Smith (geoffsmithbooks.com)

Copyright © 2019 by Geoff Smith. All rights reserved. Cover Design by Geoff Smith (geoffsmithbooks.com) Proofing and general cleverness: Chris O'Shea and Bill Booker Smith, Geoff. Burning Crowe (A Bartholomew Crowe novel) . Geoff Smith Books. Kindle Edition. No part of this book may be reproduced in any form or by any electronic or mechanical means including information storage and retrieval systems, without permission in writing from the author. The only exception is by a reviewer, who may quote short excerpts in a review. This book is a work of fiction. Names, characters, places, and incidents either are products of the author's imagination or are presented as fiction. Any resemblance to actual persons, living or dead, events, or locations is entirely coincidental.

1

Traffic pumped through the one-way system like cells through the heart of a bodybuilder. Muscular developments squeezed the pavements. Half-timbered houses re-sculpted into outlets for major high-street chains. Coffee everywhere. Costa. Starbucks. A Pret. A latte in front of him now.

He pulled the beanie from his head, roughed up his thick black hair. He sat with his coffee and his muffin, watching yummy mummies guide babies in buggies to fashionable shops, and elderly couples drifting past like harmonised notes.

A woman stood with her back to the window. Red hair draped down her back in crafted waves. She carried shopping bags, a bunch of them, waxed paper and roped handles, cursive script. A mild day, but still November, and she wasn't wearing a coat. Her phone to her ear, she tilted her head to keep the hair out of the way.

Brushing chocolate from his chinos, he tried not to look nervous as he pushed outside to meet her.

'Bartholomew Crowe,' he said and he held out his hand

She stopped him with her palm, turned away and slid her thumb across the screen of her phone. And she wore an expression of disgust or irritation, or some toxic mixture of both as she made the call.

'Listen, babe -' The accent was full estuary, London and

Essex all at once. '- No. No. No. I don't care what the bitch says. You get her out, next plane okay. Home. Yes, babe. You got it? Sure?' She waited. '- Great. Bye then.'

And she looked at him and smiled like she'd woken in a meadow of daisies and rainbows.

'What was your name again?'

'Bartholomew Crowe.'

Once more he offered his hand, but she kept hers to herself, giving him shopping bags instead.

'Take these.'

She turned on her heels. He stumbled as he tried to keep up. The shopping bags bumped on his knees. She was in good shape. Old enough to be his mother, sure, but still.

At the multi-storey she ignored the stairs and went for the button that called the lift.

'Lori Cole?' he asked.

She said nothing, thumbs like lightning, texting. The lift pinged. They stepped inside, a fat, middle-aged man on crutches following.

'Nice day for it,' the fat man said.

And she made a face - half a smile, half a wince - a face that said, Please don't speak again, babe.

'Follow.'

In the car park, the four-by-fours and SUVs squeezed into spaces two sizes too small. And Bart's Mini was parked opposite, a red Cooper S, Union Jack roof. Dad's weekend car before he wrote off the Merc - and himself in the bargain. The car had come in the will. Bart loved it. It was big and brash and bright and it made him want to cry.

He wondered how she knew it would be there? It turned out she didn't. She didn't stop at the Mini, and then he saw why.

Her Audi R8. Pearlescent white, five-spoke wheels and tinted windows. Sleek, cool and almost practical, it was a car you'd see reviewed on TV or centre-spread in the magazines they had on airlines.

The doors opened. Her smile said, Get in. This won't take

long.

Cream leather, black plastic, brushed aluminum. All mod cons. She looked good in it too, long red fingernails reaching into the glove box, a red-checked blouse unbuttoned just enough to notice, eyes intense and small and blue.

'So I want you to find someone,' she said.

With six shopping bags stacked on his lap, he wished he'd asked her to open the boot.

'Bartholomew Crowe,' he said, 'of Crowe and Son Investigations. I'm the, erm, son. Pleased to meet you. We're quite new. But Dad's had a lot of experience, important people and the law and stuff - he did personal PR. So Dad's out of town right now, but we, erm, we do consult. I mean like we check in. Every day. You know?'

A half-truth at best.

He guessed she was thirty-seven or thirty-eight - young to have a near grown up son - but have one she did. Her boy, Zack, was a kid with a ton of potential and a wild side that made sure it stayed that way. She showed him a photo and she placed her hand on his knee. He jumped at her touch. But she didn't take the hand away. Instead, she leaned in closer, gazing into his eyes as if expecting some immediate revelation or Holmes-style deduction. The weight of her expectation made him feel strange - her eyes all glitter and blue.

The picture she showed him was of a young man, a boy technically, seventeen - eighteen, Bart's age. He was on a skiing trip. Good looking with white-blonde hair - unnaturally white - and big, healthy looking teeth. He had a slanted smile and his arm around a pretty blonde with an even bigger smile, even better teeth and a prominent nose that reminded Bart of his own. He went to take the photo but Lori held on, tightening her hold on the photograph, squeezing tighter on his knee.

'The boy is my son, Zack Richards.' And she twitched and broke eye contact. '- My stepson, Zack. He disappeared from school, four days ago.'

'And the girl?'

She pulled her hand back to her chest. Her fingernails danced.

'Oh, she's a girlfriend. Lilly or Lyla, Lilith. I don't know. He has so many, I lose track. I can't tell you anything about her. I think she is from the school.'

'And the police?'

'No police. That's important by the way. I've told the school he's gone to the States to be with his dad. Made out Zack hadn't given them the note. Look,' she said. 'We have reasons for keeping the police out of this. It's important babe. No police. No media. No paps. That gonna be all right?'

'I'll do my best.'

'Sorry, but you'll have to do better than that,' she said. She pulled two red plastic envelopes from her clutch bag. Five thousand in cash. Fifty pound notes. More to be made available if needed. More cash than he had ever held. He hadn't asked for payment up front. He slipped the envelopes into the pocket of his coat as casually as he could, shopping bags snagging on the cuff. 'You see, my husband's famous. A star. Like a proper one. A-lister? And well, Zack - he aint a saint at all. And I don't want - well - we don't want any -'

And she turned away, staring at nothing through the window.

Bart said, 'I understand. So what have I got to go on Mrs. Cole? You know, if I'm -'

'It's just Lori. Okay babe? No 'Mrs', definitely no 'Ms', just Lori. The boy's called Zack, as I said. And my husband is Mickey Richards.'

She smiled brightly. She was dentally perfect.

Bart said nothing. She sighed and shook her head.

'Mickey Richards -' she continued, her tone rising at the end of each phrase. 'The singer? The Bullfighters – you know, the band? – music? The Frozen North? Are you laughing at me?'

She play tapped his knee. She was flirting.

'No. No, Mrs. Richards,' he said, adjusting himself in the seat. 'I mean I do know Mickey Richards. Of course I do. I mean I know of him. I like him. His stuff I mean. His music. But I need to know about Zack?'

'Okay - good. So Zack - well he's supposed to be at school in Ramsgate, down on the East Kent coast, yeah? The school's called St Stephen's. It aint all that, but it's better than state. Anyway, Thursday, two in the afternoon, I get a call from the office asking why Zack's not in school? And that's when I say about his dad and the States.'

'You and Zack, are you close?'

'Close enough.'

She sat back in her seat and she pulled a silver cigarette case from a clasp bag. She lowered the electric window and breathed blue-grey smoke into the cool air of the car park.

'Look. Stepmothers and stepsons,' she said. 'Things can be - well - difficult.'

The words stung. He remembered Mum, or Julia, or whatever she wanted him to call her now. At least Lori wanted Zack back again.

'Look, babycakes,' she said, ash falling from her cigarette. 'This fame – privacy thing. It's a balancing act. One that we - that I do very well. I spend a lot of time and a lot of energy making sure my life is just the way I want it, babe.'

And she blew more smoke through the open window.

'Have you been in contact with his friends at the school?'

She sighed.

'I kind of thought that's what you would do,' she said. 'It's what I thought when I saw your ad in the email. That maybe his friends might talk to you. You know, with you being, well, being so young. But I don't want any screw ups.'

'Screw ups by me?'

'Well that'll be a start babe. But I mean no screw ups. By you. By Zack. Anyone.'

'You're not that keen on the school?'

She ignored him.

'Mrs. Richards, why is Zack at a school you don't think is any good? I mean I'm sure you can afford better – the best I would think. So it must be Zack - he's been in trouble before, hasn't he?'

'Very smart!' she said. She looked pleased, either with him or with herself for choosing him. 'Yes, yes he has been in trouble. He's always in bloody trouble.'

And her hand returned to his knee.

'What kind of trouble?'

'Bart,' she said. 'St. Stephen's is Zack's third school in three years. The first was Honours, in Year 9 he brewed beer on site and sold it. He got caught. We made a donation. All smiles. So he does it again and they expel him. Then, school number two. And we thought we'd try him somewhere more remote. We sent him to bloody Wales of all places! Redhill. Caught smoking there. They were good about it though. They let him come back to take his exams. But they didn't want him to come back for sixth form. So when St. Stephen's took him in Year 12, nobody else would, except state of course.'

'You said 'smoking'. You really get expelled for that – one offence?'

'Depends on what it is you smoke."

'You -'

'Don't make me spell it out.'

'Dealing?'

'They couldn't prove anything.'

'Or didn't want to.'

She leaned across him and she slipped a hand around his neck and she whispered, 'Listen. I just want you to get down there and find him for me, babe. Wherever he's hiding, whatever he's mixed up in, you find him and get him back, in school, by the end of the month. You think you can do that for me? You've already taken my money.'

Bart tried to think straight. Five thousand was a lot of cash. And the job didn't seem too tough. He felt nervous, sure, but anyone would.

He swallowed hard. Until now, the whole private investigator thing had been a fantasy, an obscure revenge against his absent mother. Now it was real. Turn a good job down and he would look like a fraud. Feel like one too. And Lori's eyes were candy and blue and her voice just tingled with sugar. Her hand slid an inch up his inner thigh. He squirmed in his seat and the shopping bags rustled.

'Okay,' he said. 'No problem. I'll find him.'

DOCUMENT A

A journal entry by Bartholomew Crowe, 15th October, 2019, 19:34 p.m.

The Baikal automatic pistol is the most common handgun in the UK. You can buy one for about £1000. So you see I've been looking at stupid stuff online. Police and intel and spies, close-protection courses. I don't normally write journals and I'm only writing this one because I've locked myself up in my room, where I'm going quietly mad because I can't quite believe what I just did.

I told my mum to fuck off.

I don't normally even swear that much, but that's not the whole of it.

I told my mum to fuck off and she fucking well did, and she isn't going to fucking come back.

So that's the thing.

Fuck.

So this is a journal entry about Mum.

Looking back to the funeral, like three days ago, she hardly spoke to me, you know, even after I did my speech. And to be fair there was no shortage of other people to talk to. She could have sold tickets. And you can understand someone not being themselves at their husband's funeral. I mean if you are ever going to not be yourself. I mean, I'm pretty sure I wasn't myself either.

But looking back, I think I knew something was wrong even then. Anyway, that funniness continued on into Sunday, then Monday and today.

She'd got some removal boxes out of the garage. She'd taken them to her room and she'd shut herself away. And I'd see her around the house every now and again. But she'd be gone back to her room in seconds. And I tried a bunch of times to catch her, but mostly I was too late and she'd escape. And when I did see her she'd say she was 'sorting a few things out' - like that meant anything at all.

So I knew something was wrong.

But even then I never actually went into her room.

Thinking about it now, I wonder why I didn't do that.

I think part of it was that I've always been so grateful to her. You know, in the past. I felt like Julia (Mum) saved me and Dad from some horrible end. I was like ten back when we met. Me and Dad had been on our own for two years. My other mum, my 'natural' mum, had run away with my football coach, Kyle. And people thought I was okay but I wasn't. I was going psycho. Child-minders (I hate calling them nannies) were dropping me off here and picking me up there, waiting in the car while I played hockey with Facebook on their phones (I'd given up football). They were nice girls, most of them. But Dad paid their wages, didn't he, so of course they were nice to me. It was just economics.

That's how I saw it at the time, anyway. And whatever way you look at it, it is partly true, isn't it?

And Dad was away the whole time, in London, or other glam places round the world, sorting out media stuff for rich people. And when he went to London it might as well have been a foreign country, because he always stayed over, or he got back late.

But the day he brought Julia home everything changed.

We started going out to restaurants, the three of us. Sometimes just the two of them, but at least half the time it was me as well. Julia was in publishing, so the three of us talked about books and stuff. And we went to the theatre and we went to the ballet. We even did the opera once. It was all right.

And that was that. Julia brought my dad back into my life. I was part of a proper family again. I hadn't had that for ages.

I could remember being, like five or six, when Dad and Helen (my natural mum) were still together. We had holidays in Devon and also in Spain. And when it ended, Dad said sometimes people grow apart. I'd nodded and said I understood, but I didn't understand, not really. What does that even mean, 'grow apart'? You know, if Dad was alive and here today I'd ask him, 'How can you say grow apart like you're a pair of begonias or something?' People don't grow apart. Somebody always chooses.

But when Julia came along I stopped thinking about all that. I had a proper family again and I was grateful. And we were a perfect family too. So, you know, why would I question it?

Why would I question anything?

Dad and Julia married fourteen months later. I was thrilled.

And it was on the day of the wedding that I said, 'Julia, I was wondering, can I call you Mum?' or something like that.

'Come here, Boo,' she said (which is what she calls me sometimes), and she held me tight for what seemed like ages. 'I love you, Boo,' she said. 'You're my little angel aren't you?'

And I know that sounds cringe, but it was actually all right.

I started calling her Mum the next day.

Geoff Smith

After they got married Julia gave up work. She did a second degree. She went out and about and she met people for lunch. She took me to school and picked me up and drove me to hockey. We got really close. I told her everything. All the problems, all the little bullyings, all the shames and the embarrassments that kids have to deal with. I even talked about hockey and cycling and girls. She was a great listener. She'd offer advice when I asked for it, and sometimes when I didn't. But she always seemed to know the right thing to do.

Except like I said, on Saturday, at the funeral, we didn't really talk at all. And on Sunday she was still acting distant. Granddad was staying with us, like because of the funeral and stuff and I'd gone to bed to play video games. Maybe meet up with Noah and Sophie online. So I was laying there on my bed and I heard Granddad and Julia arguing downstairs. Granddad's voice was raised and that was weird. But to be honest I'd had enough of people that day, and all of their petty bullshit. So I put on my headphones and I shut it out.

But this morning (Tuesday) I was having breakfast in the kitchen, and I was looking on Snap, and this truck pulls up on the gravel out front.

Julia was at the door, talking to a man.

She says to me, 'Bart. Can I talk to you?'

And I say, 'Okay.' I shovel some cereal into my mouth and I follow her into the study. 'There's a truck on the drive,' I say, talking with my mouth full. 'Have you bought something?'

And she says, 'Bart. I've got something to tell you.'

And nothing good ever comes after, 'I've got something to tell you.' So I start to think. Has she met somebody? Is she turning vegan? Is it heavier than that? God, maybe she's gay?

'Boo,' she says. 'Listen. Your Dad and I. What the three of us had these last eight years. They've been good years. Incredible years.

Good friends. Good times. And I've learned so much. And I've really grown, as a person too. I can feel it. And you know. Well, Bart, you've grown too. You've become this fine young man, and I want you to know I'm proud of you but-'

'But?' I say.

'But, when your dad died, I felt things. New things. I felt how things truly are. And how sometimes things just end. And that - well, new things begin.'

I say, 'Are you pregnant?'

She laughs, but it's not a nice laugh. It's sort of hollow. She says, 'God, I hope not!'

'So?' I say.

She composes herself and I see her shoulders hunch and she takes this really deep breath, and she says, 'Look, Bart. Your dad dying, it's like a message from time. Time for a new phase, a new beginning, for us both. There's a truck outside because I'm leaving. Not for good, not forever, but for a while - I don't know how long - and you mustn't worry. The house is paid for. There's more than enough money and your Granddad's going to stay and look after you while I'm gone. And of course I'm not saying that you need looking after. You're eighteen. You're a man.' And she takes a step closer to me as if she's going to touch me but she stops and she doesn't. 'Honestly Bart, it won't be forever. I just need. I don't know. I just need something. Maybe it's just time. Maybe something else - something other, I suppose. That's all.'

And I can barely process what she's saying to me.

So I say, 'You're just going? Just like that? Where? Where are you going, Mum? When are you coming back?'

And she says, 'Cambridge. At first. I'm going to stay with Christine.' (and I have no idea who Christine even is!) 'After that, I don't quite know. I haven't decided.'

And I can't even look at her. I'm turning from side to side, and I want to run away. Lock the doors. Stop her from leaving. I want to smash holes in walls.

'Are you saying -' I say, and I can't even string my words together. 'Are you saying that you don't want to be my mum anymore?'

And she does that sad face she does with the eyebrows raised, her there-there sad face that used to be exactly what I needed, but this time it's a mockery of itself and of my whole fucking life to boot.

And she says, 'No. Of course I'm not saying that. Look, I don't quite know what I'm saying, but something isn't right for me, Bart. And it's something big, something important. And I need to go away and find out what it is.'

And I say, 'We happy few.'

And she says, 'What?'

And I say, 'We happy few. I read it at the funeral, didn't I? 'We happy few', from Dad's favourite Shakespeare. I thought it was the three of us. You. Me. Dad. And when Dad used to say that, 'we happy few', that was what he meant wasn't it?

And she says, 'Look Bart, I loved your Dad. I love you too. It won't be forever. But can't you see that's what makes it all so difficult? We're not a few anymore. We were, and we needed each other. But it's different now. I need to change. And so do you. I just need to reconnect with the world. To figure out some stuff. You can understand that can't you?'

And I say, 'No, I can't. I don't understand it.' And I say, 'But you know what I do understand? I understand you. I understand that you've been a self-centred, manipulative, narcissistic, gold-digger. And that's what you are now. You're selfish and you're a narcissist. That's what I understand.'

The sad face hardened at that.

She says, 'I think it's best you don't contact me for a while.'

And I say, 'Well go on then. Fuck off, Mum! Fuck off to Cambridge and don't come back.'

And then she left, and she didn't come back.

And she closed the door softly behind her.

And I wish to God she'd slammed it.

2

They ran through the long grass, leaping over walls and bustling down paths at speeds amped just beyond reality. A biplane buzzing overhead, not shooting and not bombing yet.

At the flinted farmhouse, they burst through the gate and into the fray. Enemy tracers stitching the spaces between them, and soldiers with dayglo tags firing and falling in the courtyard. And Bart waiting by the wall, hoping he couldn't be seen from the first-floor windows. The tag of Connor's avatar disappeared behind the boundary wall. He was up to something. A tank rattling by, diamond-shaped, like the ones they had in The Great War. The tank was tagged Blue and that made it dangerous, Green soldiers falling in its wake. Bart had to move fast. If he waited were he was, the tank would spot him, or some psycho twelve-year-old would bundle around the corner and spray him with machine-gun fire without a second thought.

Noah said, 'Dude. I'm running to the barn. Cover me okay?'

'Sure. Where are you?'

'Right behind you, dummy.'

Noah was always asking for cover. Too many films. 'Inglorious Bastards'. 'Fury'. Bart thought the whole idea of cover was flawed. With little to lose and a short time to win, these games were gung-ho craziness. Unlimited shots and unrestricted confrontation.

But Bart did as he was asked, firing at any Blues around Noah.

And Noah's avatar reached the wall and turned.

'Go Bart! Run. I'll try not to shoot you!'

'Get me killed, and I'll hit you for real.'

A Blue appeared to Bart's right. He hadn't seen it and his screen flashed red, but his virtual momentum and superhuman constitution pulled him through, the virtual soldiers bumping past each other like dodgems at a fairground.

'Ouch!' said Noah. 'Missed that one!'

And when Bart reached the barn he bounced off Noah's avatar and around the side of the building. There was a double door at the back. Easy to enter but tough to defend. The four of them could make it a pretty solid fortress. There could be others already in there though, just waiting for a mug like him to show his face. But with nothing to lose and nothing at stake, you just had to go for it. There was no cause, no right or wrong. Puppies play-fighting in a pen.

A Green walking towards them.

'Come on then boys,' Sophie said. 'There's two ladders to the loft. Let's take them both.'

'All right guys,' Noah said, reasserting himself. 'The opening up there looks right out across the courtyard. We get up there and we're made. So if there's Blues up there, we clear them out. Go!'

Sophie was already climbing the narrow ladder in the corner.

'So I guess that's you and me up here then,' said Noah. 'You first bro.'

Bart climbed the wide ladder and leaped into the loft. Two Blues. Both were busy firing on Greens in the courtyard. They had left the ladders unguarded. Bart had one free shot. He missed first, but still had time to fire again and score a good hit before the Blue turned to face him. Noah opened fire and took the Blue out for good. Sophie, from the other side of the barn took out the second - but not before Bart had taken another hit.

One more and he'd be finished.

Noah and Sophie whooped.

'Me and Soph will take the guns, bro. You guard the barn.'

So, with heavy machine guns, Sophie and Noah fired freely, taking out Blues in the courtyard below. And pretty soon the whole yard cleared, other players knowing that to cross it was suicide. So Noah began to fire off pot-shots at windows of other buildings where he thought Blues might be hiding.

'Where are you Connor?' Noah asked, reveling in the confidence of his position.

'Nearly with you,' Connor replied. 'Got a little held up.'

'Grenade that tank, Soph,' Bart said.

As the Blue tank rattled past, all three of them hurled grenades. The impacts didn't seem to affect the tank at all as it rolled on.

'It can't have much left, surely?' said Noah.

'Keep the front covered, you guys. I'm coming in the back,' said Connor.

Not a lot seemed to be going on now. Most of the foot-soldiers had found cubby-holes in buildings that they didn't want to give up. Biplanes buzzed overhead now, carrying bombs that would start to flush them out into the open.

'What do you say we go out there?' Bart said. 'Take down that tank or something?'

'No way, bro,' Noah said. 'Everyone's holed up . We step out there we're dead - and Jeez bro, what are you, like eight percent? You're a dead man walking.'

'He's right,' said Sophie. 'Don't get impatient Barty Boi. Let's just sit tight for the win.'

Then gunfire.

Loud, rapid gunfire.

Sophie's screen flashed red and then faded, Noah turning just in time to see a Blue with a heavy machine gun taking him out at point blank range, his own screen gone red and fading quickly.

Then the Blue was standing over Bart. It put the machine gun away and switched to a pistol.

And Connor said, 'See ya Bart.'

Bart thought about shooting, but at eight percent there wasn't much point. Connor took his time, raising the pistol until the crosshairs centred on Bart's forehead.

He fired a single shot.

And the screen went red and faded.

*

'Dead man walking,' Connor said and he grinned, a wide smile with perfect teeth.

Noah stood, pushing his long hair back, and for a moment he seemed paralysed. Then he wheeled round and threw his controller at Connor. Threw it really hard. Connor got up to face his friend down.

'You're a fucking dick!' Noah said, and he left the room and he slammed the door.

Sophie looked at Connor's screen.

'Oh - my - God! Are you still playing?'

'Yeah,' said Connor. 'Erm... I'm not dead.'

Sophie pulled the power cable from his console.

'Better?'

Connor fell backwards. He was grinning, mischievously, but with genuine affection.

'Come on guys. It's just a game, Soph.'

Sophie gasped and she crossed her arms and her dark eyebrows dropped and her wide mouth pursed in judgment.

'It's just a game. Right Bart? Tell her.'

And Bart said, 'He's right Soph. It's just a game.'

*

Later, placing the slice of pepperoni pizza back in the box, Bart said, 'Guys? I've got an announcement.' Two seconds of silence. Then, 'I've got a private detective job.'

'No! Way!' Sophie pushed her hands into her dark wavy hair, shook her head and did an exaggerated cartoon surprise face. 'No fucking way. No! My little Barty! You can't go! Who am I going to patronise without you?'

She moved to embraced him but then she stopped dead still, and only her eyelids moved. And then Connor patted him on the back, grabbing his shoulder, shaking.

And Connor said, 'Well done, mate. You can do this, yeah.'
Sophie was still staring.
Noah, who had calmed down since Sophie had applied the pressure and made Connor apologise, looked up, mouth half full of pizza.

'So, go on bro,' he said. 'Tell us what the case is.'

'I got to find a lad, like our age, make him go to school.'

Noah almost choked on his pizza.

'Yeah. I know, okay,' Bart said. 'Irony. Anyway, I reckoned you lot all thought that I was BS-ing you with all this P.I. stuff. And maybe I'd have thought that too if I was you, but there you go. I got a job! It's a real one! And I'm going to take it. I'm off to Margate tomorrow. So, there you go. What do you guys think? Like truth.'

For a moment no one spoke.

Then Noah approached him and placed a hand on Bart's shoulder.

'Okay bro, I'm gonna be completely honest,' he said, 'I think you're crazy. You're totally mental dude. I mean, you are so smart, you could do literally anything, bro. Private Investigators don't even make that much - and have you ever met one? So, jeez Bart - I mean you know we're proud of you and everything, but -'

A muscle spasmed in Bart's cheek.

He said, 'Look Noah, I just want to do something. Like something important, you know, something good. Not make the world right exactly. But I do wanna make it a little bit less wrong. I know you don't understand.'

Then Connor stood up. He put his arm around his friend. And his arm was strong and his grip firm.

'You can do it. I know you can. You can do anything, mate. And we're all totally on your side. No tricks in real life, yeah, no bullshit. Just friends. On your side man.'

He offered Bart his fist and Bart pumped it. And he did the wink. The wink he knew was charming. The one the girls loved.

But Sophie was shoveling things into her bag.

'Soph?' said Bart.

'What did your Granddad say about this?'

'Soph?'

Bart reached out for her but she shook him away.

'You heard me,' she said. 'What has your Granddad said? You know, about this? What you're doing -'

Bart stepped back.

'I - I haven't told him.'

She snorted and she shook her head, filled her rucksack and pulled the cord tight.

'My God, can you boys even hear yourselves?' And she spoke with a raised, tremulous voice. 'Private Investigator - You can do this, mate – it's macho bullshit, all of it, and you're all idiots! All of you. Sorry Noah. Not you. You know, I do actually care about you Bart! I really fucking care. A lot. And you're going to throw away your exams, ruin your whole future - and for what? To go on some stupid quest because your mummy doesn't love you? You need to grow up! Everybody's family stinks. Everybody's does!'

And Sophie Dean left the building. She didn't slam the door and she didn't come back. The boys heard her car start, its little wheels spinning on the gravel drive.

Connor looked at Bart.

He said, 'We're going to need a lift home, mate.'

3

Barbara didn't give her surname but she photographed his driving licence and his debit-card twice. She could have been anywhere between forty-five and sixty-five and she had the unstable gaze and herky-jerky movements of the serious drinker.

'The website said there was wi-fi?'

'Best not to trust the agents,' she said. 'Everything's in the book.'

The 'book' was in fact three crumpled sheets of A4, stapled, with a coffee stain in one corner and no mention of wi-fi. But the room was big, and the bed was big and ugly, with a varnished pine headboard and a salmon pink throw, a quilted cover and floral cushions. Topping it all off was an improvised four poster frame, draped in what looked like net curtains. In the corner of the room, a TV, wires sprawling out like the legs of a drunken spider.

'Remember,' she said. 'I can't guarantee the room beyond Friday. I've got families coming in.' Her voice fluctuated between bullish aggression and fawning politeness. 'You here for work or visiting?'

'Just visiting,' he said. 'A friend of mine. Zack Richards. I doubt you've heard of him.'

'No. Can't say I have. Still, that's nice, isn't it? Nice to have friends. I've got a boy about your age myself. So hard for you young people nowadays. Don't forget, if you want to have breakfast, you need to fill out the form.'

The line of her underwear was visible through her green leggings, and he averted his gaze, searching his pockets for his mobile. The stairs creaked as Barbara descended and Bart wondered if there was a man on the scene. The dark stains on the carpet made him think that if there was a man, he probably drank even more than she did.

There was a child running about in the room upstairs, feet like a bass drum at a speed-metal gig, so Bart went down to try and sort the wi-fi.

When he reached the desk, Barbara was nowhere to be seen. He rang the bell but there was no response. Shouting. A man's voice. Something about money. Money owed or lost or not lent. The man sounded young and he sounded mean. And there was Barbara's voice too, a hysterical wail. Bart ears strained to separate the words but he wasn't able to make them out. He pushed his face close to the glass that separated Barbara's flat from reception.

There was a crack.

A crack like the beginnings of an avalanche.

Bart backed away from the door as the banging grew louder. The stud wall vibrated. The door opened, swinging so hard that it rebounded from the wall and rattled and wobbled like a diving board. It crashed shut and was kicked open for a second time, a young man thundering out. Tall and gaunt, he had pasty skin and greasy hair dyed black, clumped on top like Johnny Rotten. He wore a biker jacket and grey jeans and he shoved Bart in the chest as he passed.

At the entrance, the young man turned back and shouted, 'Go fuck yourself! Stupid bitch!'

Then he was gone.

Barbara appeared at the door. Green leggings, grey slippers. Her hair was a mess. Her left cheek was redder than her right. There was a cut above one eye and tears were streaming from both.

'Are you all right, Mrs. -?'

She was high on nerves. Her face twitched.

'Feathers,' she said. 'Barbara Feathers! It's in the book!'

And she broke into a flood of tears. Bart touched her on the shoulder and she threw her arms around his neck and she pulled him close.

'You're such a good boy!' she wept. 'Such a good, good boy!'

She held him tight. He was surprised to find that soon he was crying too. Tears were welling on his cheek as Barbara Feathers collapsed into his arms and he guided her back into the flat, to the spongy maroon armchair in front of the TV.

'Can I tidy up for you, Barbara?' he asked.

She shook her head.

'Really,' Bart said. 'Look. I'm going to tidy up a bit. Really. You're in no state -'

She turned away and she wiped her tears on her sleeve as Bart went deeper into the flat. It looked worse than it was. The young man's anger had been as much theatre as rage. Most of the ornaments scattered on the carpet, were still in one piece. Crystal and china figures. Cats and ballerinas. Photos too - cracked glass in only a couple of the frames. The young man himself was in most of the pictures. Various stages of boyhood. He had one of those smiles that always looked forced, and his eyes were dark and blank. Papers were strewn about the hall. School reports, utility bills and medical appointments.

The school reports were about a boy called Raymond Feathers, and they weren't exactly glowing.

He stacked the papers as neatly as he could on the sideboard. And then Barbara's wet breath was in his ear. He jumped with shock. Her lower lip protruded and her head was bowed. And her eyes were big, soft and comfortable.

'You are good boy!' she said again.

She didn't hug him this time although a part of him wished that she would.

'It's all right, Mrs Feathers,' he said. 'You know, if there's any-

thing else I can do. I mean if you want to call the police - or -'
Her eyes hardened, and her lips became taut.
'I think you had better go now,' she said.
Bart photographed the wi-fi code on his way out.

4

At Westwood Cross shopping centre, busy mums, reluctant dads and groups of Eastern European guys in sportswear drifted from one shop to the next. Young men and young women peacocking about, searching for better versions of themselves on the racks and rails of the airy stores.

Bart bought a couple of things, absent mindedly, not thinking much about the cost. In truth he rarely did. He'd always had a generous clothing allowance, more for special occasions. And anyway, since Dad died, money felt like a limitless resource. He was rich, at least he felt he was. And with the five thousand in cash he had from Lori on top of that, the managing of money seemed a rather hazy and distant idea, like the blue outline of some far-away hill.

He tried on a shirt in H&M. It was a slim fit, narrow collar and a black arrow print. He wasn't sure - too 'prisony'. Placing the shirt back on the rack, he saw a short woman in black leggings stuffing a cream coloured something into an over the shoulder bag. He did his best to look as though he hadn't noticed, slid his phone from his pocket and set it to video. Then he returned to browsing the clothing on nearby racks, looking at the floor as much as he could. She did it again. A black cardie this time. And he had it on video. Evidence. He felt sick. It felt sleazy, and yet the woman was a criminal. And theft was theft.

At customer services, he asked for security. A young man approached – twenty one or twenty two – and very tall – six foot five at least, with an acne pocked complexion. Bart described the woman and the tall detective scanned the store. He was so tall he didn't need CCTV. Bart didn't mention the video. He didn't want to surrender his phone. And the store detective seemed happy to take him at his word. He nodded when he saw her, and he gave Bart an appreciative half-wink.

Outside, he passed the shop-front once, then again five minutes later. On the third pass he saw the detective accosting the woman as she tried to leave the store. The detective grabbed her arm. The woman spun away, shouting and angry. She beckoned to a young girl, who ran to her mother and embraced her, crying loudly. Nine or ten years old, young enough to be afraid, and old enough to be secretly thrilled.

Bart sat on a bench outside, checking his phone and genning up on local news and the latest in small-town violence. It was near to an hour before the woman and the girl left the shop, escorted by police.

And as the little girl passed she gave the finger to the world.

'Fuck!' she shouted.

The mother was hunched, and ushered her away. She glanced at Bart and stopped, staring for two clear seconds. She knew he was a snitch.

DOCUMENT B

*An email from Colin Crowe
to Bartholomew Crowe.
10/11/19. 23:18 p.m.*

Dear Bart,

I hardly know where to start. I don't know where you currently are, or what you're up to, but by Christ, you had better bloody well tell me or there'll be hell to pay for it. That's guaranteed.

You're probably not much interested, but I've spent the last two hours on the phone, trying to work out why you haven't come home tonight - do I need to point out that it's nearly half past eleven? And thanks for not answering your phone. That was helpful. It didn't help either that I had no-one else to call! I phoned the hospitals of course. At least I could find their bloody phone numbers!

Eventually your friend Sophie got back to me on Facebook. Thank God she did, or I'd have stayed up all bloody night. I still will of course, but at least I don't have to think you're dead at the same time!

Sophie tells me you're very much alive, and I hope she's right. She tells me that you have set yourself up as some kind of private investigator! I thought she was winding me up at first, but I've been through your room (sue me) and she's bloody well right. I found that box under your bed. By Christ, you don't do things by halves. All those packages and envelopes. Not video games or UCAS at all, were they? Quite the little sneak aren't you? Well, I suppose at least you've done some research.

And I see you've called yourself Crowe & Son Investigations.

Now, I'll tell you this for all the good it'll do. Give this up now, Bart, before there's a mess. You're a smart kid, and being smart's good - but you're not tough. You're not P.I. material. If you were tough you'd be here, with me, toughing it out in the real world, not trying to escape it. And I'm sure you know by now - if you've done your research - that most private investigators are ex-police or ex-military.

There's a reason for that.

But the most important thing is we both know you're doing all this for the wrong reasons, don't we? You can't change the past, boy.

Simple as that.

And the thing that annoys me the most - and I am very bloody annoyed right now - is the blind cowardice of it all. Too scared to talk to me, were you? Well maybe you were right to be scared. I'd have tried to talk you out of it.

But that doesn't stop you from being a coward.

Let me be blunt. Your dad's dead, Bart. It's painful. I understand. My bloody son's dead. And car accidents are tragic, but they happen. And okay, your mum's gone too. And that's a shame, I admit. But really, you need to take a second and calm down, because she isn't dead. And she'll likely be back. She's made her decision, and it's a shitty one, it's true, but I'm afraid that's just life. Accept it. Deal with it. Get on with it.

One final thing Bart. Whatever happens, whatever you decide to do, you email me back by 9 o'clock tomorrow. Give me your address. Then email me again the day after that, and then again the

Geoff Smith

day after that. And so on and so on.

If you don't do that, I'll call the police myself, and I'll report you missing, and you'll become the subject of an investigation.

And by the way, I still expect a bloody apology.

Private Investigator – bloody hell!

Granddad.

5

The approach to St. Stephen's School was lined with sycamores and it was high and square and ivy climbed the walls of its crenellated towers. It looked like a fairy castle. Big too - not intimidating big, but big enough to get your attention and big enough to hold a secret or two. He adjusted the jumper of the uniform he'd got from Lori. It was a little tight across the shoulders.

He had hoped to get lost, to become anonymous in a crowd of uniformed students, but, with only three hundred and fifty kids and a generous campus, there wasn't much of a crowd to get lost in. The few students there were milled about in small groups and some kids stood alone here and there, staring at miniature screens. He pulled out his own phone and he pretended to look at it, and he followed the path around the outside of the main building, through courtyard areas and across a patchwork of mismatched paving. And he eavesdropped where he could, trying to catch any stray snippets of conversation. But it was tough to get close enough to hear anything. And when he did, all he heard was who wore what to where and when, and who was out of order to who, and who was just so like *so* totally embarrassed right now. Standard. Just a school.

And just like school at home nobody was in a hurry to move. They were killing time and taking their time doing it.

And there weren't even many of them around. Nowhere near three-fifty.

Then the bell sounded.

Long and loud and more of a rattle than a bell.

And then, from every gate and doorway students began to spill in - the boarders. And they merged with the day kids and they swelled and drifted towards the breeze-blocked building on the far side of the field, boys of fourteen or fifteen running at tangents, stealing rucksacks and kicking and jeering, making themselves conspicuous around the slow moving mass.

The main buildings and dorms would be more or less empty now. Just a skeleton staff, maybe some non-Christian students who had opted out of assembly. So, as the final flurries of students drifted away, Bart slipped back through the main gate, and across the road to the dorm.

No-one stopped him and no-one asked questions.

The dorms were two storeyed, square and featureless, ugly sisters to the school itself, a piped metal fence in front with bicycles chained to it. The front door had a combination lock. Lori had provided the code and it opened on Bart's second attempt. A long, grey corridor, double fire doors at the back and a staircase where two sixth formers stood guard.

A girl and a boy.

He bowed his head and drove forward as if leaning into winter rain. But he was moving too fast and he looked suspicious. He had intended to push past the pair at the stairs, but instead he collided with the large chest and belly of the prefect.

'You can't go up there.'

He was big in all three dimensions. A floppy haircut and a cable knit sweater. Bart stared blankly at him. The other sixth former was a girl, soft-faced and tawny. And she looked up at the boy, happy to let him take the lead.

'It's ass-em-bly.' The boy spoke slowly, and enunciated every syllable. 'You need to go to the gym.' And he pointed and he shook his head.

He seemed to think Bart was foreign.

Feigning an Eastern European accent, Bart said, 'I - uh - need - um - passport -' He pointed towards the main building. 'For - um - head-master -'

The boy and the girl looked at each other and the girl shrugged.

'The head-master is in the assembly, with everyone else,' the boy said, 'over there.'

But Bart was not to be put off.

'Head-master - he say - passport is required - I am required to fetch.'

The girl shrugged again. Bart switched his gaze to her and he shrugged also. She certainly wasn't a natural guard, and her instinct was to smile, but she had the self control to stop herself before she got there.

'What's your name?' said the boy.

No response. Bart was looking at the girl.

'Your - name?' the boy repeated.

'Name is Leo - Leo um - Leo Demidov.'

He had lifted the name from a book he hadn't enjoyed. It was a stupid risk.

The girl looked up.

'Okay,' the boy said. 'You've got ten minutes.' And the prefect tapped his watch twice. 'Ten minutes,' he repeated.

Upstairs a series of varnished doors stretched down the full length of the dorm. Thirty rooms in all, Zack's at the far end, a yellow plastic trolley outside it. The room opposite was open with cleaners at work. As Bart walked down, he saw most of the other doors were decorated with stickers - boy bands, football clubs and sports stars - but Zack's door was plain, just a chromed number seventeen. A frame for a name tag but nothing inside it. A cylinder lock was built into the handle, and Bart took his pick set from his pocket. He'd been practicing around the house at home, and he thought he had it sussed. He eased the tension wrench into the lock and raked it gently.

'Having problems, Love?'

A woman in the door across the corridor, the cleaner. Her arms were crossed and she was frowning. Bart jolted up, hiding the the picks behind his back.

'I - I can't find my key,' he said. No accent this time. 'My books are stuck inside.' He tapped the door. 'Never mind. I don't suppose you could,' The muscles around her mouth tightened and Bart said, '- No. Of course you couldn't. I suppose I'll have to phone the caretakers.'

He took out his phone and wandered down the corridor towards the stairs. As the cleaning lady disappeared into the next room, he slipped back to the door and raked the mechanism as quickly and as quietly as he could. The pins moved, which was very, very good. Then, as the movement freed, the vacuum cleaner went quiet in the room across the hall. He twisted the handle and the door opened. He went inside and closed the door behind him and he stood, with his back against the door in Zack Richards' room.

His heart thumped hard in his chest.

6

The room was tidy. The bed was made and the desk was clear. Music posters lined the white walls and personal photographs covered the wardrobe doors. Group shots of dorm rooms, pubs, clubs and holidays. The blonde from Lori's photo was in a bunch of them. Big smile. Great teeth. And a few other faces appeared more often than most - a slight lad in slim-fit jumpers with heavy eyebrows and an elfin face.

He pulled a picture down from the door.

The back was labeled in pencil - *15th May, Kay's Party, Off our faces!!!* Bart took down another, and another, then he just took all of them. He checked the notes and stuffed them in his pockets. Not one of the photos was more than a year old.

The wardrobe itself was full of patterned shirts, jackets, and jeans - all new or nearly new, and all of them expensive. He checked the linings and the inside pockets of the jackets and the fleeces but there was nothing, just a crumpled receipts and a couple of used train tickets, London. Bart took it all, just in case. The bookshelf was stacked with text books - business studies, media studies and music - and CDs by world artists, mostly from South America. A suit-case under the bed contained aftershave and underwear and condoms and cigarette papers – but no tobacco and no lighter and no weed - and no electronics in the room. No mobile. No lap-top, no tablet, and no chargers. And that changed things. It meant there had probably been at least some planning.

The lock rattled and he jumped.

It rattled again.

The handle turned and the door opened. A girl came in. A blonde, uniformed, black blazer and long, checked skirt. She closed the door and walked to the desk. She opened the drawer and put something inside. Then she climbed on the bed and looked out through the window at the traffic on the street. She took her phone from her blazer pocket and turned and sat on the bed, and when she saw Bart, she jumped but she didn't scream.

'Who are you?' she said.

He recognised her immediately as the blonde from the pictures. But he didn't answer. He didn't have a good answer to give. He thought about it some more - then gave up and told the truth.

'I'm looking for Zack,' he said. 'I'm a friend. Are you Zack's girlfriend? Are you - Lilith?'

She took her time, looked down at her phone and smiled.

'It's not Lilith. It's Lola. And I don't recognise you,' she said. 'Have you been at St. Stephen's long?'

Bart felt a flush of embarrassment. She didn't seem at all afraid and that made him nervous. He sat on the chair by the desk and he leaned forward.

'My name's Bartholomew Crowe,' he said.

'Well that name's made up,' she said.

He gave her his card.

'Truth,' he said. 'You see my name really is Bartholomew Crowe and I really am a private investigator. And I am trying to find Zack Richards. Your boyfriend I think. I can't tell you who's paying me, but honestly, I think we both want to help him out. And we both want to keep him safe.'

'And I'm supposed to take you seriously?'

'Why wouldn't you?'

She gestured at his clothing.

'Because you're wearing a school uniform.'

He winced at that.

'So do you know where Zack is?'

She looked at the card. She looked at it for a long time, turning it over in her hand.

'How did you know my name?'

'I didn't, remember? Anyway, I'm an investigator. So I guess I investigated.'

'I don't know where Zack is,' she said. 'And by the way, if I did, I wouldn't tell you. I'm Lola Golden by the way. Hi. You know, you really shouldn't be in here, should you? I mean, you're not a student here. And you are in an actual student's room. And you're in a stupid disguise so I'm guessing you don't have permission. I suppose that makes you a *criminal* doesn't it? And seeing as you've just told me who you are and you've given me your card, I suppose that I could tell the police or the school about you being here and -' She looked at him directly, and her eyes were big and blue and calm. 'What I'm thinking is, that you should probably tell me everything that you know, because if you are a friend it would be a real shame if you got arrested, so -'

Bart ran both hands through his hair and pulled it forwards.

He said, 'Okay, so what about you? Why are you skipping assembly? And why are *you* in another student's room? And what did *you* just put in the drawer of Zack Richards' desk? I mean, you're not supposed to be here either, right?'

She raised her eyebrows and she gave him pitying smile.

Bart said, 'Okay. Okay. Look, I'll tell you what I can, but honestly, I've only just taken the job and I reckon that whatever you know, you probably know more than I -'

A noise. A clump. Something hitting the door.

They froze. Someone in the corridor.

The handle rattled.

The door swung open and a cleaners' trolley clattered

in. It was followed by a tall man, young, with dark, spiked hair, grey jeans, a tabbard worn over a biker jacket and a mop in his hand.

'On the floor!' the young man growled. And he came at them with the mop, jabbing with the stick end. Bart raised his hands. He dropped to his knees. Lola followed suit. And then the two of them were lying there side by side on the thin carpet.

'Now don't you move! Don't either of you fuckers fucking move okay!' And he shook the mop and he kicked Bart in the ribs. 'Hands out in front where I can see 'em! Both of you. Now stay!' And he pulled off the tabbard and he threw it at Bart's head but the impact was disappointing so he kicked him in the ribs again, just for good measure.

And the young man turned the room over. He cleared the shelf, emptied the cupboard and the wardrobe. Folders, books and clothes raining down on Lola and Bart, who found himself on the receiving end of several more kicks as the young man clomped about.

Then Lola said, 'Ray, go home! We can still fix this if you go now, okay?'

He stopped. He thought for a moment. Then he shoved the mop in her face.

'You're a silly bitch! You don't fucking know anything! You don't know fucking shit! And if I hear you talk again, I swear down, I am going to crack your fucking head.'

He pulled the drawer from the desk. Paper spilled out. Receipts, a notepad, a calculator and hundreds of red foil hearts.

So, Lola was a romantic.

The young man in the biker jacket tore at the paper lining on the the underside of the drawer. Then he stopped. He dropped the drawer to the ground. The wooden corner came down on Bart's head. Gritting his teeth, he moved his hand to check for blood.

There wasn't any.

And for a moment the room was silent.

Then Raymond said, 'Get in! Oh get in! Oh yes! You - fucking - beauty!'

He knelt down and he grabbed Bart's hair.

'Do I know you?' he said, inspecting Bart with suspicion.

It had already clicked for Bart. Ray was the lad from the hotel. Barbara Feathers' son. He tensed, anticipating a thump to the jaw that never came. Everything went strangely silent. And then, from his position near the ground he saw two big feet in expensive trainers. And the voice that went with the shoes was deep and sure.

'All right you three lummocks, line up! Come on now. Stand up. In front of the bed and looking this way - now, thanks.'

He was a hulk of a man and he filled the doorway, blocking the exit. Seriously built, like the guys you saw on YouTube, his shoulders broad and his neck so thick that it blended into his head with just his ears protruding.

Raymond let go of Bart's hair.

'You two as well now. Get up! Come on. Let's find our way to the bottom of this madness shall we?'

Bart and Lola stood up, and the three of them lined up in front of the bed.

Raymond dropped the mop and his fingers tapped at his pockets.

Lola's hair was badly messed and Bart had a carpet burn on his left cheek and a cut behind his ear where the drawer had hit.

With a black Nike track-suit, black trainers, and a gold chain necklace, the man moved slowly, like a rapper onstage, psyching the crowd. Just looking at them for near to a minute. His eyes were puddle green and his dark hair was cut short.

'All right then, Lola,' the man said. 'How about you tell me just exactly what's going on here, and whether or not I should be calling the police.'

Lola half-heartedly fixed her hair. She didn't smile, but

looked serious and honest.

'Yes Mr. Hasland,' she said, and she paused. 'I'm afraid I was skipping assembly, Sir. You see I wanted to leave a message for Zack. For when he gets back, you know?'

Hasland lifted a single eyebrow, the rest of his face unchanged.

'And who the Hell are you then?' he said to Bart. 'You got anything to say there, fella?'

'No Sir,' Bart said. 'Nothing to say, Sir.'

'Really?'

Bart had hoped the uniform would be enough. Hoped there wouldn't be too many questions. Hasland leaned in close to Bart, sensing something was amiss, trying to place the boy. And Raymond saw that Hasland was distracted, he took his chance and bolted. Reacting fast, Hasland reached out to block him, and he grabbed the collar of the biker jacket. But Raymond was fueled by desperation and blind panic. He writhed free of the thing, and he barreled down the corridor at break-neck speed. Hasland threw the jacket to the floor and bounded out after him into the corridor. But Raymond had gone. His footsteps drumming down the stairs.

'Shit!'

Hasland took his phone from his pocket, and started to dial.

Lola followed him out, and she reached across him and she laid her hand across the phone.

'No, Sir,' she said. 'Wait. Please.'

DOCUMENT C

An email from Bartholomew Crowe to Colin Crowe: 11/11/19. 10:58 a.m.

First off Granddad, you're 100% right. I am 100% not dead.

Right now, I'm standing outside a private school in Ramsgate. I'm meeting a girl who can help with my case. I would tell you more, but I don't think I can, and you know what? I don't think I want to.

And you want to know why I didn't tell you what I was doing? Well okay. I'll tell you. I wanted to hurt you. I still do. I definitely want to hurt Julia Crowe, or Julia Spence, or whatever it is she's calling herself now.

Except she's the one person I can't hurt, isn't she?

She gets to mess me up, and she gets out of it, scot-free - and that pisses me off. I'm not going to lie.

And yes, I am pissed at you too Granddad. Because you KNEW, didn't you? You knew - about the whole thing! What Julia was going to do. You must have known. But you didn't stop her. And you didn't even think to tell me.

You say I'M selfish. You say I'M a coward. Well I say what about YOU?

Geoff Smith

Did it make you feel important being in Mum's confidence? Was it good for your ego?

Tell me I'm wrong if you like, but don't expect me to believe you.

So you know what Granddad? I've decided. I'm not going to be a passenger in my own life anymore. I'm going to get involved. And I'm not playing at being a P.I. I am a P.I. My business card says I am. The law says I am. And most important, I say I am. So I'm done with school. And I'm done with family too. Families lie. Grades mean nothing. You know, I could work really hard for the next three years, four or five. I could go to university, do a graduate scheme or a law conversion. I could use Dad's contacts to hook me a job I don't deserve. And then at the end of it, what? I'll get a nice little pension like you - or maybe a car crash, like Dad.

No thanks.

Thanks for your mail.

Bart.

7

He pressed send and stood outside the school and he stared at traffic and waited, his head filling with emptiness, cars passing, a white van. He jolted when she tapped him on the shoulder. He spun round, and then she was there, grinning on the other side of him, Lola.

'Good work detective,' she said, checking her phone.

He tried to laugh it off.

'Thanks for meeting me.'

'That's okay,' she said. 'Listen, Bart. I'm sorry, but I have to ask. You don't want to do anything bad to Zack do you? I mean, you are on my side, aren't you - I can trust you - can't I?'

'I don't - I mean yes - yes - yes you can trust me. Satisfaction guaranteed!'

And he tried a cheesy smile.

'Don't joke,' she said. Her heavy eyelids fell as she scanned his face. 'Yes. You know what, I think I can.'

'So what did you say, to Mr. Hasland?'

She looked back at the screen and shifted her weight as she spoke.

'Just that it could be bad for me if the police arrest Raymond. That's all. I've had some dark times. People here, well they're sort of protective of me, I suppose.'

Bart tried looking over at her phone but she sensed him snooping and she slipped it into her pocket.

'What kind of dark times?' he said.

'Not today,' she said. 'But another time, really, okay?'

A wry smile on her lips, and her big eyes looked up as he fumbled around in his pockets, pulling out the photos and rifling through, looking for the right one.

'How do you know Raymond Feathers?' he said. 'Does he work here? At the school I mean?'

Lola laughed. Her face lit up and her teeth gleamed.

'No! God no! Ray doesn't work.'

'What does he do?'

'Well that's the question isn't it? I suppose Ray's a sort of a sole-trader. That's Business Studies.'

He showed her the photograph, a group-selfie from a night out - Zack and Lola and the lad with the big brown eyes like a deer in the headlights.

'Can you tell me about this guy?'

It was almost a double take. She paused and gave Bart an evaluating look.

'Okay,' she said. 'Well, obviously that's me and Zack, and the other boy is Torin Malone.'

'Can I meet him?'

'No. No, you can't meet him.'

'Listen I really would appreciate your help -'

'He's dead, Bart.'

'I'm sorry I -'

'There was a fire - at a casino where Torin worked. You know Torin did dumb things, drug things, all the time. But he was a lovely boy. Always had a smile.' She was welling up. 'I'm sorry. Can we talk about Raymond now?'

He nodded.

She dabbed her eye with her fingers.

'Well,' she said. 'You probably know Zack does a bit of dealing, weed mostly. Trust, remember?'

'Trust,' Bart said. 'So Ray is what? Like a business partner?'

'I suppose he sort of is, yes. He knows the area really well and he stores the stuff and sells some on. Listen, the Ray you saw today was a total thug but - he can be quite sweet. He's just not very bright. Not too good under pressure. I wonder if Zack's being away is getting to him?'

'Do you know what he found, Raymond I mean, under the drawer?'

'Oh God,' she replied. 'Something small! Honestly I don't know Bart. I'm sorry. I really don't know. I can tell you where you'd find Ray now though if you like.'

She took out her phone, thumbing the screen.

'Do you know why Zack has disappeared?'

She blinked and she blanched slightly.

'Everybody wants to disappear sometimes, Bart. He did send me a text you know, after he left. Like five days ago.'

She held out her phone for him to see.

[Keeping a low profile. Be in touch babe. Zack. Xx]

A string of text messages followed that one. All from Lola. None had a response.

She said, 'At the end of the day I don't know why Zack does half the things he does.' She smiled. And it was a big, bright, honest smile. 'I suppose it's a part of his charm.'

8

Athelstan Road was ragged and tough. Victorian terraces lining the road like a beige and brick militia, a frontier-land where decay met gentrification, crisp redevelopment ebbing in from the coast. The Bel-Air Hotel was stubbornly holding to the decay of years past. Its sign was yellow and blue, but smashed with its innards exposed and its light bulbs removed. The ground floor and basement were boarded, and every window was boarded too. The double doors were fitted with a heavy metal brace.

There were four young men in Bart's wing mirror. Track suits and slip-ons and a dog on a string. And one of them banged the Mini as he passed. He swore loudly and made an obscene gesture. He laughed as he walked on, and his mates laughed too. Bart got out of the car. But he didn't follow and he didn't shout. Cowardice, not wisdom.

He crossed the street to the main doors. The brace was fastened with heavy bolts, so he took the stairs to the basement until he was ankle deep in drink cans and fast food containers. But the window was boarded and the door was blocked.

'Ya get in round back, mate!'

Another young man in a track suit and cap stood at the top of the stairs. He held a rollie in his left hand and the smoke lingered round his fingers and wrist.

Bart looked up.

'Okay. Thanks.'

The lad didn't move but his top lip curled, showing his yellowing teeth.

'Show ya if ya want.'

Bart squinted upwards.

'Great. Thanks.'

The young man's eyes were glazed and there were red spots around his chin. As Bart climbed the stairs he touched the wall, as if he were worried about losing his balance.

'S down ere,' he said.

And he set off up the street at pace until he came to an alley between the houses. It was neat and wide and it had an overhanging first floor that made a kind of arch. The young man rested his hand on a nearby wall and he hunched over and he breathed deeply until he could toke on the cigarette.

'And this goes all the way down?' Bart asked.

'Yeah yeah.' He pulled up one leg of his tracksuit trousers, a grey tag beneath. 'I'd take you down mate, but I got this thing on an I gotta dash.'

Bart said, 'Okay, well, thanks.'

The young man leaned back against the wall and re-lit his fag.

'Thing is mate,' he said, 'I gotta get down Westgate, meet my parole officer. Only I really need a few quid, for a taxi, or I'm gonna miss it.' And his eyes opened wide with urgency.

Bart took out his wallet and gave him a twenty. The young man held it, staring at it, open-mouthed as if waiting for the punchline. Then his nose twitched and his little eyes narrowed.

'Yes mate!' he said. He broke out his best toothy grin. 'Laters, yeah?'

He patted Bart on the arm and he set off on a staggering walk towards the shops at the end of the street.

*

The alley divided the gardens of two adjacent streets. It was wide, and it was overlooked from both sides. Someone must surely have seen him already.

He looked into the gardens and he tried to work out which one was the Bel Air. One of the gardens contained a trampoline and coloured toys. Another had pot plants and pergolas. So that only left one. A plastered wall, high, with broken glass cemented on top, and a solid looking wooden gate with two padlocks. One was a combination lock. A pick wouldn't help there. He noticed the house next-door had a wheelie bin and the glass didn't continue down the side.

He landed in the walled yard, knees jarring. The space was paved with chequerboard slabs, weeds sprouting through the gaps. In one corner of the yard was a potting shed with a hatch on one side like an ice-cream kiosk. A conservatory extended along the width of the building and every window was boarded with a thick rectangle of nailed on ply.

A metal bracket had been fitted to the door and another padlock to keep intruders out. He knocked on the door. Waited. He knocked again. Then he set to work with the picks and the rake. It took longer than he expected, and he dropped the rake twice. He was about to give up when the lock sprung.

Bart paused.

Was breaking into a squat even a crime?

It shouldn't have bothered him. But somehow it did.

'Hello?' he called, not too loud. He didn't want the neighbours to hear. 'Zack? Zack Richards? Raymond Feathers? Are you in there?'

Nothing.

The conservatory contained mouldy sofas and mustard yellow throws, discarded packets of joss-sticks, stained cushions, countless cigarette butts. Bart picked his way through to the double doors that led to the foyer. A reception desk, stairs, and a bar. With the boarded windows it was pitch dark, only the light from the opened door creeping through, so he flicked on the flashlight of his phone. There was a small lift. He tried the door but it wouldn't budge. There were battery powered lamps all around the place, all switched off now, but all of them were new, expensive-looking rechargeables. He followed them through to the bar. He saw pizza boxes stacked beside a bean bag under the boarded bay window. And beside the boxes a kitchen bin overflowed with cans and plastic bottles, and, in the far corner of the room, a single armchair, and underneath that, a wooden box.

Bart sat in the chair and he slid the box out between his legs, unhooked the catch. Three trays inside. The top tray contained a set of scales and brass weights. One compartment was neatly filled with sealable plastic bags. The second layer contained a block of greenish brown hash wrapped in thick film that had been whittled down a bit but was still substantial - about fifteen centimetres by ten. The bottom tray was split into six sections with two types of weed in separate compartments and some rough, white crystals. He wondered if this was Zack and Raymond's main stash. If it was, then these guys were strictly small-time. Even if it was, they must have portioned bags somewhere too - their eighths and quarters and grammes. He considered ditching the stash, just taking it, dropping it in a bin somewhere. If nothing else it would piss Raymond off and after what had happened that morning, it would feel good to do it. But as he tucked the box back under the chair, and the temptation passed.

The walls in the bar were covered with luminous posters of cannabis leaves. Bart checked behind them. Nothing. There was a bong on the bar and three bottles of bourbon. All of the bottles were open. And there was something odd there too. A football trophy. Under 14s regional champions. Out of place in a hotel. Out of place in a squat.

Bart flashed the light at it. He picked it up. Lighter than he expected. The figure was plastic. The plinth too. It only had the illusion of weight. He used a butter knife to move the screw under the plinth removing the figure on a hunch. It loosened, then wobbled. Something small dropped from the gap. He scanned the carpet with his flashlight. And he found what he was looking for - a micro SD card. He stashed it in his wallet. He re-tightened the screw and placed the trophy back where he'd found it.

His pulse quickened, feeling strongly the need to get out. He pushed his hands deep in his pockets and he stretched, extending his neck. Then he began to make his way back through the mess. He tripped on a lamp and he kicked it away.

Outside, he refastened the padlock and made his way to the wall. Too damned high! No climbing it. On the other side of the yard there was a big pot, a stump of something dead inside. He began to scrape the whole thing over the paving slabs towards the wall, cursing every inch of the way. It was achingly heavy work, and worse, it was excruciatingly loud.

He should've thought of this.

Should've thought ahead.

9

Detective Sergeant Simmonds was a plain clothes detective with a 1970s moustache and thick-rimmed specs. And if it was possible for a man to look so much like a policeman that he didn't look much like one at all, then DS Simmonds was the living proof. At his side was a uniformed WPC, lumpy faced and heavily built. And beyond her, in the bay window of the Seaview Hotel, Bart could see Barbara Feathers' multi-coloured cardigan, hovering behind the nets.

DS Simmonds introduced himself and named his colleague as WPC Stock. The WPC said nothing and her cold stare had Bart squeezing at the edges of his wallet, checking on the memory card inside, as if the mere presence of the police officer might somehow magic it away.

'I don't know about you, Mr. Crowe,' said DS Simmonds, 'but I could murder a bacon sarnie.'

*

The cafe was nearby, on the main road into town. Bart and DS Simmonds sat next to each other at a bench table with a view of the sea and the patrol car where WPC Stock was waiting. A podgy young man with bleached hair and an earring place their plates in front of them. The bread was crusty and lightly toasted, and the bacon was thick, and the eggs were golden.

'Looks good,' said Bart.

Simmonds said, 'Go on then. Tuck in.'

So far Simmonds hadn't mentioned a crime. He'd asked about Margate, how Bart was finding it, about whether he'd ever been to Dreamland or the shell-grotto, and about the weekend's football. He didn't seem to be under arrest. And the detective couldn't possibly know about the Bel-Air, could he? Hasland could have reported what happened at the school. Or Lola maybe? Either way, he felt that Simmonds was toying with him, waiting to see what he would let slip.

The podgy lad with the bleached hair passed with a tray that he carried out to the WPC. A cup of tea and mushrooms on toast.

'WPC Stock is a vegan,' Simmonds said.

And Bart took a mouthful of coffee.

'Am I under arrest?'

Simmonds smiled, his grey-blue eyes peeking over his thick lensed glasses. It was a smile that didn't look as though it got out much.

'Oh dear, Mr.Crowe. I've been putting off the business-end of things again, haven't I?'

Bart's nostril flared, and his forehead tensed.

'Tell me, why exactly are you in Margate, Mr. Crowe?'

Bart swallowed down some bacon and eggs.

'I'm a private detective. I've got a job to do.'

'And what would that job be - exactly?'

'I'm looking for someone, a young guy. He's at school near here.'

'And when was this *young guy* reported missing?'

'He hasn't been.'

'Okay. And you'll forgive me here,' said Simmonds, 'but you were at the school, were you not, quite recently?'

'No comment,' Bart said on instinct, and he bit enthusiastically into the bacon and bread and hoped it hid his nervousness.

'Yes,' said Simmonds, pausing. 'I think you might have

been there, and I think that you might have been in this young man's room - let's call him Zack, shall we? Hypothetically of course. And let's not go into the hows or whys - but I wonder if you might have had an altercation with another young man, and for the sake of argument, let's call him Ray or Raymond. Does that sound like something that might have happened, hypothetically?'

'Hypothetically. I reckon that's something that could possibly have happened, hypothetically,' Bart replied.

'Good, good,' Simmonds continued. 'I thought perhaps it might've done, hypothetically. Because of course there's been no crime reported. So while we're talking hypotheses, I'd like to say that were such a thing to happen, and you were to learn anything relating to this hypothetical young man, Zack, from any further enquiries you might make, then er, you might like to get in contact with me.'

He slid Bart a card - his direct number and an email.

Bart had loaded his fork but stopped. He looked at the card.

'Are you threatening me?' Bart said.

Simmonds looked affronted.

'No no, Mr. Crowe. No, no. Not at all - well - look I'll be honest here. I don't enjoy talking to private detectives, but I want to suggest to you that it might be in everyone's best interests if we proceed co-operatively.'

'Are you offering me help?' he asked.

Simmonds looked uncomfortable.

'No. I don't help private investigators. But I am here - for support, let's say. Look Bart. You're just a k-, I mean you're a young man, Mr. Crowe. What are you? Eighteen? Nineteen? I don't think you know what you're doing with this at all, do you?'

Bart sipped the black coffee and said, 'Being honest DS Simmonds - you're right. I really haven't got a clue.'

10

The music in the bar was too quiet to dance to but too loud to ignore, and the snares rattled in his head as he slotted the micro SD card into the laptop. The card was loaded with images. Hundreds of them. He opened the first and began to flick through but nothing stood out. It must have belonged to Zack Richards though. He was in most of the selfies. But the pictures were nothing special. People out and about, people in town, the same people at gigs, at parties. Skewy pictures of PowerPoint projections from school. There were a bunch of pics of Zack Richards with his side-swept blonde hair and thin, flat nose - posing with a girl he didn't know, whose hair was an unnatural red, almost pink.

She looked sort of familiar.

'If you buy me a drink, can you put it on expenses?'

Lola was standing beside the table in a pink v-neck and a white t-shirt. She had friends at the bar. Two boys and a girl.

'I'll give it a try,' Bart said. 'What can I get you?'

'Vodka and Coke, thanks. A large one. Lots of Coke. Lots of ice.'

And as they flicked through the pictures, Lola named all the people that she could. She didn't know everyone in the early pics, but the further they got the better she did.

'Where did you get these?'

'They're pictures from Zack's phone.'

He wanted to see her reaction.

She leaned back and folded her arms.

'So I suppose you're working for the family then?'

'That's a direct question - you should have my job.'

'Maybe I should.'

'You know,' Bart said. 'I reckon you must be pretty sure that Zack still has at least one phone with him or you'd have asked how come I'd got your boyfriend's phone. You've had some contact since this morning haven't you?'

She smiled a slow smile.

'Maybe.'

And she slid her phone across the table. The same string of messages he had seen at the school. But there was a new box on Zack's side of the conversation.

[Don't worry babe, all good. Thnx for all the texts!
Pls don't reply to this. I'll be back soon. Love. Xxx]

'And you're sure this is actually from Zack?' Bart asked.

'Is that supposed to be helpful?' she said.

And she turned to the glass and looked at her reflection in the window.

'Sorry,' he said. 'Listen. Do you mind if we keep looking through these? I mean, you're really helping, and I'd like to know about all the people closest to Zack, and I can't think of anyone I'd rather ask to help me.'

Her eyes softened a little and Bart felt a tightness in his cheeks. He took a sip of his beer and scrolled to the next image.

'I'm afraid - I mean I'll warn you I haven't checked through these,' he said. 'So if there's anything weird on here, okay?'

'Go back to that last one,' she said. 'The selfie. Yes. The girl with the red hair. That's Franny. It's from before I met Zack. You know he's only been here since April?'

Bart said, 'April. You're right. But you have met Franny, haven't you? She was in that pic with you I saw in the dorm.'

Her lips thinned and her eyebrows furrowed.

'Franny's a singer. You know she's actually really talented, and she's just got a contract, a proper one. And Zack helped her get it. You know Zack's dad is famous?'

He nodded.

'Good. So you should. Anyway, Zack's been doing music management for about a year and a half. And he's managed Franny since last Summer. He's had such a crazy life because he knows like, a *lot* of people in music and art and theatre too. So cool. And he's *really* determined as well. When Zack sets his mind to something he doesn't stop. He manages a couple of other acts, but Franny's the biggest by far. She and Zack are actually quite close. She's been down here a few times and he goes up there too.'

'Up there?'

'London. She's got a flat. I suppose London's where you have to be for music, isn't it? But she's from there too so - sometimes we go up at weekends. Like I said, Zack knows a lot of people and being there feels a bit like being famous. We get free entry to places and I get to watch Zack being, like super confident with all these amazing people. And there's clubs. And we eat out like *all* the time.'

'You think Zack might have gone to Franny's place?'

She sipped her drink.

'I don't think so. You see I phoned her up after Zack had been gone for like a couple of days. I didn't tell her anything exactly, but I dropped loads of hints about Zack. But it was like she didn't even know that he was missing. I was listening for any clue he might be there but I couldn't hear anything, so -'

'So you and Franny aren't that close? Because in the pictures -'

'Anyone can look that way in pictures,' she said.

She leaned forward and she put her hand near to his. Her wrist was slim and her nails matched her jumper.

'Honestly,' she said. 'I don't actually like Franny that much. It's just jealousy really. I won't deny it. Zack insists that he isn't sleeping with her. Just music buddies. But I think I don't like her anyway. She's cold, you know? Like she doesn't need anybody. And I don't think you can trust anyone that self-sufficient. Everyone needs somebody, don't they?'

Bart said. 'I don't suppose you have her phone number? And an address?'

Lola tapped through the apps on her phone.

'Yes. Sure. Here's the number,' she said. 'I've got the address at home somewhere. I'll text them to you.' She moved her hand over his and she fixed him with a shot of her pale blue eyes. 'You will let me know if. Well, if he's there, won't you?'

'I will,' Bart said. 'I Promise.'

She moved her hand to the laptop and scrolled back to the first image. As the carousel passed in front of them, Lola visibly relaxed. St. Stephen's. The East Kent Coast. And herself in more and more of the pictures. And it was she who was closest to Zack now, and Franny was relegated to the edges of the frames. Other than Lola and Francesca, and Zack himself, it was Torin Malone who was in more images than anyone else.

'At the school this morning, you mentioned Torin Malone,' Bart said.

'Yes, I said he was a beautiful person.'

'What happened? I mean what do you think happened when he died, in the fire?'

'Torin was a beautiful boy,' she said, 'and a loyal friend. He was popular at school and funny, but he took too many drugs. He was a boarder at the school, like Zack was, and I suppose that sometimes he felt a bit forgotten, by his parents. I mean, he'd see his grandma a lot. They were close. But I don't think he ever saw his parents in term time, not even once. Bart, you should know that Torin was on stuff for so much of the time that even the teachers thought it was normal, just what he was like. I think we all did too. But he was sweet even so. But he had this habit of falling asleep, like wherever, like narcolepsy, I suppose. Just click, and out like a light. I suppose all that speed and ket and the weed and the coke, it has to do something to you in the end, right?'

Bart nodded. He wasn't sympathetic. After all, he'd been forgotten by his parents too, but he wasn't going off the rails like Torin Malone, the self-indulgent druggie.

'So what happened at the casino?'

'Well Torin had a job as a croupier. He was good-looking and well spoken - military family - he could be firm when he needed to be. So anyway he was working there -'

'Where? I mean what was the casino called?'

'The Ten-Ten Casino. And Torin had been there for a couple of months. He was only seventeen. I don't know how he wangled it. So he was near the end of his shift and he goes off, but he falls asleep on the toilets. At least that's what we think. It wouldn't be the first time. And I suppose everyone thought he'd gone home because they locked the place up. Well that night a fire starts in a waste paper basket, from like a cigarette or something, and the whole place burns down with Torin inside. People at school think Torin probably started the fire himself, like by accident, lighting a spliff, but -'

'You don't think that's what happened?'

'I don't know. I suppose it's the most likely thing isn't it? Zack never thought so. Thinks there's something we're not being told.'

'And what did he think that was?'

'Listen. What happened to Torin, it was awful. It was really, really bad. But going over it's not going to bring him back, is it? No one ever comes back, do they? And some mysteries don't get solved.'

She looked round at her friends at the bar, who were pointing at their watches and phones and beckoning her to come.

'C'mon Lola'

'Time to go.'

'Taxi's waiting!'

She looked at Bart, a tear on her cheek.

'Sorry,' she said and she brushed it away with a finger.

'Listen. We're all off to a club. Canterbury. Come along if you want. It'll be fun.'

Her blue eyes had an energy that showed that she meant it. He was tempted. And it could be good. But there was so much more to ask, and he was pretty sure that talking business about Zack Richards was not what Lola had in mind for the night ahead.

'Thanks,' he said, 'but - you guys have fun.'

He scrolled forward to the next image. It was a picture of a man, taken from a low angle. But the shot was dark and blurry and he couldn't make it out.

DOCUMENT D

An email from Colin Crowe to Bartholomew Crowe: 11/11/19. 21:13 p.m.

Dear Bart,

Thanks for texting me that address. Your hotel looks interesting. Mixed reviews is an understatement. I Googled it.

Of course, you must know that I'm tempted to drive down there and bring you back. And I'd like to think that's what your dad would've done if he were still with us. But I'm not your dad and I know that - and that changes things - so I won't. Not yet.

I've told the school you won't be back for a while. I've said you're struggling to cope with you dad's death. They've been very polite and very understanding. But remember, they won't keep your place open forever. I know you have this fire inside of you right now, but remember, school is a game like everything else, a game you're lucky enough to be good at. And it's a game you have been winning. But still, it's a game you will lose if you're not playing.

And I'm not saying you won't make a halfway decent private investigator one day. Maybe you will. Time will be the judge. But you should be sure you know what you're throwing away.

Okay, so bad things happen to good people and good people

suffer all the time, often through no fault of their own. It's true. But Bart, think about it - and tell me where to go if you want (and you probably will) - but you really haven't had it bad. You've had opportunities and experiences in your life that most kids can only dream about, and many that most of them couldn't even imagine. And you've had love too. And you still have it. And maybe you can't see that, but I know it's true.

But now you're 'pissed' at me. Well, all-right. You know what. I admit it. You were right. I did know that Julia was going to leave. Guilty as charged. And yes, I agreed to stay on at the house, to look after you. Guilty again. I argued with Julia about it. Of course I did. I thought it was the wrong decision. But sometimes you have to let people do what they have to do. And if the same thing happened tomorrow, I don't think I'd do much different.

The way I see it, Bart, you have to let people make their own mistakes, at least, if they insist on making them. So, if you're going to insist that this private investigation business is what you want, then do it. Fine. But I do have one condition: you make me a partner. Now I won't try and tell you what to do, but I want you to tell me everything. And you will contact me every day. This is a non-negotiable, and I am deadly serious about it.

Like it or not, Bart, we're family, and Christ knows, you'll need to talk to someone sooner or later.

And Crowes should stick together.

So I'm afraid you're stuck with me.

Love Granddad.

11

The grey-gold town buzzed with morning traffic as he walked down the front, past the arcades and past Arlington House - the cold, grey tower block that imposed itself so definitely on the Margate skyline - a reminder of a time before the new nostalgia. Beyond the tower block, the neo-Georgian facade of the railway station, and the cafe where he ordered his breakfast.

Googling the fire at the Casino gave him plenty of results. The local online news site carried several stories, all following the same line. The fire had taken place on a Thursday night in July and a young man, employed as a glass-collector, had died in the blaze. The police hadn't commented directly, but the reports implied the young man may have started the fire himself, perishing in a blaze of his own making. The articles contained interviews with Malone's family and comments from the school stressing the boy's friendly and outgoing nature, his popularity, and how deeply he would be missed. The school had brought in grief counsellors and Torin's funeral had been attended by over two hundred mourners, which, apart from the glass-collector thing, was pretty much just as Lola had said.

And then he found something that Lola had not told him. The Ten-Ten Casino was owned by a Mr. Glenn Golden. And it didn't take much to work out that Mr. Glenn Golden was Lola Golden's father. Maybe she was embarrassed, or she just felt sorry for her father, who maybe felt terrible about the whole mess himself. Or perhaps her father's involvement had caused tension between herself and Zack, tension she wanted to keep private, or tension between Zack and her father?

He pushed the plate aside and ordered more coffee.

Francesca Da Souza's Twitter feed had links to a ton of different magazines and TV appearances. They documented a number of London shows and prestigious support slots. She had recently signed to a major label. And though Zack's name was absent from the mainstream articles, the social media posts and tweets had plenty of pics with Richards in-frame. He was name-checked a bunch of times too. One photo had Francesca with Zack and his dad Mickey. All were beaming at the camera - the three of them happily drunk. He tried her personal Facebook. It was private, but her artist page had a couple of thousand likes and a whole bunch of fan comments. Things were looking good for Francesca Da Souza, and for Zack Richards too. It made the small-time dealing and the secret photos harder to fathom. After all, Zack wasn't a hopeless drifter like Raymond. In fact for an eighteen year old kid, exam results or no exam results, it looked like Zack Richards was doing great things.

His third coffee and the cafe had gotten busy. Smart guys and smart girls dressed up like estate agents, white-van guys and misfit males. And Bart felt a weird swell of happiness, like somehow he belonged in this place. He was a part of something good, and if not good, real at least.

He folded the laptop and left a tip at the counter.

On the cold walk back to the hotel he looked out across the Margate sand, stretching to the distant sea. The clouds were torched meringues and the sun a low red. A couple paddled in the water - difficult to age - and pair of black dogs chased a yellow ball, writhing and wrestling, each hoping to grip the thing in its jaws and be the one to return it to its master.

12

From the basement window of the Seaview Hotel he watched, waiting for white trainers and skinny grey jeans. Raymond Feathers was over an hour late.

'Should I just go?' Bart said.

Barbara was stacking a cupboard with hot crockery. She spoke with drawling vowels.

'Well, you could. But you wouldn't want to go and then miss him would you?'

Bart didn't respond right away. Missing Raymond Feathers was, in a way, exactly what he wanted. He didn't fancy getting his head stamped for a second day in a row.

'I'll give it ten.'

Fifteen minutes later, and Bart was folding his coat over his forearm and tucking his laptop away. Barbara didn't look round.

'Mrs. Feathers, Sorry but do you know anything about Raymond's friends at all? I mean, can I ask, do you recognise these people?'

He touched her on the shoulder and held up the picture of Zack and Lola that Lori had given him.

Barbara glanced at it.

'Pretty girl,' she said. 'But I don't know her. Or the boy. I can tell you more about Raymond if you'd like to hear it. Obviously I'm busy but -'

She looked at his coat pocket, the one where he had put his wallet.

'So you don't recognise them, the people in the photograph?'

'No, but there's lots to know besides. He used to be very athletic, you know? Football. Played for the county.'

And her eyes strayed to his pocket again.

'Thanks, Mrs Feathers, and thanks for arranging this,' he said. 'But I won't take up any more of your time.'

He slipped her a twenty.

'If he does get in touch -' he said.

And he went up to his room, all alone, to look through the photos again, the party shots, the good times, and the blurry man. There had to be something. Even if the card wasn't what Raymond stole - and it had to be - hidden inside a trophy like that. There had to be something.

In frustration, he phoned Steve Hasland. Maybe he would have some insights into Zack and the Torin Malone thing. But it went straight to voicemail. At this time of day he'd be teaching of course. So Bart left a message. Just his name and number. He called Lola. Got voicemail again. He didn't leave a message. He started typing her a text - something light and friendly - but he couldn't find the words and gave up.

Then he fired off an email to the contact address on Francesca De Souza's website. He figured that as her manager, the note might go straight to Zack.

> [Hi Zack, I'm a private detective and I need to speak with you. Pls call 07907231888. Just want to talk. Thx]

Then he checked the Internet, where he found Glenn Golden through Lola's Facebook. A personal page and one for his business, Golden Enterprise. He scanned back through to the posts in July, from around the time of the fire. Nothing of interest on the business page. Just a link to an online news article and condolences to the Malone family. His personal page made no mention of the fire at all. The casino had burned on the thirteenth. Golden had posted pictures of himself and a couple of other guys at a hotel in Dartmouth. All men in their fifties, all holding drinks. They looked to be having a good time. The next day, on the fourteenth, and the same men were playing golf, no mention of the fire even in the comments. No posts at all on the fifteenth, sixteenth or seventeenth.

Golden Enterprise had a few other local interests besides the casino. A bar in Broadstairs, an amusement arcade on Margate seafront. Bart tried to work out which number to call. It was too early for the bar so he rang the arcade. A woman answered. She sounded like she didn't get many calls.

'Golden Enterprise, Golden Arcade,' she said.

'Hi - I - I mean, my name is Bartholomew Crowe, of Crowe & Son Investigations, private investigators. I wondered whether it would be possible to come in and speak to Glenn Golden?'

'What's it concerning?'

'Okay, um, well it's about a missing person. I really need to talk to Mr. Golden.'

There was a pause. She'd put him on mute. Then she clicked back.

'Mr. Golden's not in. You'll have to leave your number.'

He left his number and the woman hung up.

13

Murky brown pebble-dash and broken signage, heavy steel-braces and boarded windows, rubble and cans and boxes and glass, and no sign of anyone at the Bel Air Hotel. There were kids playing football in the street. On a Thursday, they should have been in school. The ball bounced off the wall where he stood. He controlled it with one touch, dribbled lazily across the road.

'Gis it mate!' the smaller boy shouted.

The boys were twelve or thirteen, and he held the ball out to the small lad. But as he came to take it, Bart dropped it, trapping it under his foot.

The bigger boy came over, and Bart backed up and turned taking the ball with him.

'Ah mate!' the boy said.

Bart flicked the ball up, caught it and grinned.

'All right lads,' he said. 'Just wondering how long you've been on this street? You seen anything unusual? Anyone odd?'

'Just you bruv,' the smaller boy said.

'No mate. We've seen no-one - you got skillz tho. Who d'you like? Arsenal?'

The bigger boy was the clown of the two. Bart liked him. But it was the smaller one who stood in front of him, squaring up like a terrier.

'Gi' us the ball mate, yeah, then fuck off.'

Bart swung the ball behind his back.

'Anyone gone down that alley?'

'Aint seen nothing,' the bigger boy said. 'I like your hat. It looks cosy.'

Bart tossed the ball up to the bigger boy and gave him a wink. He ruffled the smaller boy's hair and walked away towards the alley.

'Beanie Prick!' the smaller boy shouted.

And Bart pulled the hat down over his ears.

At the entrance to the alley he looked back as a car pulled up outside one of the smarter houses, a guy getting out, leaving the engine running and barrelling up the steps. And Bart saw the two boys close in on the car. He doubted they would actually steal it. And whatever they were planning, he didn't want to get mixed up in it. It would definitely interfere with his breaking and entering. So he took a photo. And he ducked down the alley and left them to it.

An old guy in his garden, leaning on a spade said, 'Nice day for it!'

Bart faked a smile.

'Yeah,' he said. 'It's lovely.' And he bowed his head and walked on quickly. He had to sort himself out. People were noticing him, and when people notice, they remember. He took deep breaths, coaching himself. *Don't talk back, don't talk back.*

No padlocks on the gate this time. And he figured it for a sign Raymond might be home. It could even be Zack, or both of them. The gate swung open - it was loose, off the latch. He crossed the paved yard, past the heavy pot that still stood against the wall, where he'd left it the day before.

The lock was gone from the side-door. Odd. It wasn't even properly shut.

'Hello!' he called. 'Raymond? Raymond Feathers? This is Bartholomew Crowe. We were supposed to meet earlier.'

The call bounced back off the walls.

The silence worried him. Perhaps someone, Raymond maybe, would be asleep somewhere in some drug-induced fug. Perhaps. But still he was nervous. He looked around for a weapon, anything, but nothing stood out - same old mouldy sofas, the same old dirty cushions, books and trays, Rizlas and baccy. There were two pint-glasses on a side-table. The dust inside them glittered as he shone his flashlight on them. Then, standing back from the door, he beamed light into the foyer. Some of the lamps were on, some quite bright, others only a glimmer.

The floorboards creaked as he walked.

'Hello? Raymond Feathers? Hello, this is Bartholomew Crowe. We were supposed to meet.'

He peered around the reception desk, shining the flashlight into every gap. But he found nothing. No-one. Some pictures had fallen from the walls since his last visit. Photos of a family and photos of a boat. The door to the bar was closed. He shivered. He pulled his hand back into his coat and pushed down on the door handle. He didn't want to leave a print. Then he cursed. He had been here just one day before. His prints would already be everywhere. He didn't know how long fingerprints lasted but it was a sure bet they lasted longer than a day.

In the bar, chairs were turned over, plastic bottles on the floor, pizza boxes ripped apart. The lamps were on here too, but were covered in rubbish, where they glowed like embers under coal. The wooden box was on the bar. It had been flipped wide open. Little plastic bags scattered on the floor. Bart knelt down. Loose weed, the large block of ganja and the grainy white powder that looked like sea-salt and smelled of soap. And in the middle of the room, a mustard throw, and Bart didn't need the torch to see that there was something substantial beneath, or to see that it was darkly stained at one end, and that the dark stain wore the gloss of wetness.

A lump rose in his throat, a convulsion in his chest. Long, deep breaths, and taking care not to touch the throw with his skin, he lifted the clean end.

White trainers, grey jeans.

He pulled the throw back from the head of the corpse. It was Raymond Feathers. Or at least he was pretty sure it used to be. It had the same build. The same clothes. It was lying face up - if lying face up was something you could do without a face. A cushion had been held over his head. A gun had been fired into it at point blank range, probably more than once. Fragments of skull and brain were mashed with synthetic stuffing from the cushion, and he thought he saw clumps of Raymond's dark hair, but really it could have been anything in all that blood and darkness.

Suddenly giddy, Bart stood up. He looked around for something to throw up into. He saw the plastic kitchen bin. He grabbed it and he vomited.

And he stood, taking long, rasping breaths. And more breaths again, and more, until he came back to himself - Bartholomew Crowe, private detective, leaning over a plastic bin in a dark room, with a faceless corpse with brains mashed into the carpet.

And then he laughed.

He laughed at the grotesqueness of it all, while on the bar, the chromed plastic figure, frozen forever, kicked an invisible ball into an imaginary net.

14

The interviewing officer was in his early twenties with thick black hair and skin that was paler than pale. He had a deep voice for a young man and he liked to show it off.

'So, let's just wind this back a little,' he said. 'Are you saying Zack Richards is involved with this shooting or not?'

'No. Look, I don't know. I mean, what I know is that this guy, Raymond Feathers - I saw him running away from Zack's dorm when I went to look in at St. Stephen's School. I talked to people and showed around a few pictures and I found out that Zack and Raymond knew each other. I got a tip off that they were working out of a place on Athelstan Road - which turned out to be the squat. I went there yesterday at about two o'clock but it was locked and I couldn't get in. You see, by coincidence I found out that Raymond was the son of my Landlady at the Seaview Hotel. She arranged for me to meet Raymond this morning. He didn't show, so I decided to pay him a visit. This time the gate was unlocked. I went in and I found the body. And that's when I felt sick and I threw up in the bin. After that, I left, came here. That's it. So I've got nothing on Zack Richards. Nothing but hearsay. I'm sorry Officer, but someone was going to find this body eventually. It just happened to be me. With the business they were running there, maybe you should be glad it was me, and not, well, someone else.'

The statement was dragging. But Bart had wanted to go in, get it done quickly, but instead they had kept him waiting for nearly an hour before they even made a start. And now this guy was dragging it out, questions, questions, making him repeat himself again and again, and always about Richards. He'd been honest where it mattered, but all that waiting, they'd given him too much time and he'd self-edited. He'd cut down on the incident at St. Stephen's, turned yesterday's visit to the Bel-Air into a mere knock at the door. He'd not mentioned the SD Card either. It felt weird, misleading the police, but somehow not as frightening as he had expected. He wondered how much of this stuff would end up in the actual statement? How much would be recorded in searchable text? He knew they had computers now that shared stuff like that, but did they transcribe everything? He'd have to ask.

'And you mentioned Miss Golden. Had she been to the Athelstan address before?'

'No. Look, I don't know. She just said that Zack had given her the address. That he and Raymond were there sometimes. I assumed she'd been there but, no she never said she had.'

'And she didn't say how she came to be in possession of the address she gave you?'

'No. I'm afraid that didn't interest me at the time. I'm really sorry Officer but honestly, I can't help with that one. Is there anything else?'

And the vampiric officer curled his lip, Bart's formality appalling him, as if it were disrespectful somehow.

He turned off the machine.

DS Simmonds was waiting in reception. Brown corduroy jacket and beige slacks. The flashback cop. Simmonds nodded at the constable. When he saw Bart he opened his arms wide in fake welcome.

'Mr. Crowe!' he said. 'I'd heard you were here. Let's do lunch. You like Thai?'

*

Seven minutes past three and Simmonds knocked on the glass door of the cafe, just as the owner of the cafe was turning the sign to closed.

'Kenny!' Simmonds had this way of sounding simultaneously sarcastic and sincere. 'Any chance we could um?'

The owner, a stocky Asian guy, five-five at most, but tough and compact, not someone Bart would want to mess with. He nodded from his waist, and he looked up with eyes that were dark and intense, like the black eyes of a boar.

They sat in wooden chairs at a small table. Bart made small talk and Simmonds listened, giving only the briefest of responses, seeming somehow to hear more than was said to him, or maybe just knowing more than he let on.

'So, Mr. Crowe, we have been in the wars, haven't we?'

'Yes we have,' said Bart. He smiled. 'I'm surprised you don't already know all about it.'

Simmonds looked quizzical.

Bart said, 'I mean, last time we spoke. You made some good guesses. Why did you come and find me?'

Simmonds leaned back in his chair. He looked at Bart, evaluating, staring for several seconds.

'So tell me, Bart, one investigator to another. What do you really think is going on here? Just lay it out for me will you, as you see it.'

'You mean the murder?'

'If you like.'

The dishes arrived. Simmonds announced the names proudly. *Yummy Yama curry and Pad Prik Ghang*. Kenny placed them down, and he patted Simmonds on the shoulder. Simmonds thanked the man and slipped him a twenty.

Bart leaned forward.

'I think the Raymond Feathers murder has got something to do with that fire, the one in July, at the Ten-Ten Casino. I don't have any proof, except that Torin Malone was tight with Zack Richards and Lola Golden, Richards was tight with Raymond, and Malone was a user, so he probably knew Feathers as well. I know the story is that Malone started the fire himself, but I think there's more to it than that. The Ten-Ten was owned by Lola's dad. And she didn't tell me that, so -'

'Would you have told someone if you were her?' Simmonds asked. 'I mean you'd tell a stranger?'

'I'd like to think I would.'

Simmonds did that slow nodding thing he did.

He said, 'The Ten-Ten's been investigated, Mr. Crowe. A fire in a waste paper basket, possibly a discarded cigarette. What do you think about the idea that Zack Richards killed Raymond Feathers?'

The directness of the question surprised him.

'Well, maybe,' Bart said. 'I know they were dealing and I know drugs can get people very uptight about money. Except Zack has money, pretty much as and when he wants it. He deals for kicks. So I don't know. Maybe he kills for kicks too - but it seems a big step.'

Again Simmonds paused.

'Lola Golden? She's a good-looking girl from what I remember.'

'Yes. Yes she is.'

DS Simmonds leaned forward, stuffing curry into his mouth, and chewing as he said, 'You're blushing Mr. Crowe. Eat up or your food'll go cold.'

15

Lola's hair was tied back and her eyelids had that heaviness he liked. She was dressed in navy and black and she supped on a vodka and coke.

'I'm sorry I had to bring you into it,' Bart said, 'but I expect the police will want to speak with you.'

She touched her neck and looked thoughtful.

'That's okay,' she said, 'seriously. Anyway, I was at home or at school the whole time I suppose, so -'

Bart said nothing.

'What about you though?' she said. 'You found Ray's body. So that makes you a um - I mean, I suppose you haven't been with people all the time, have you? You must be - a suspect.'

Bart's eyebrows rose in the middle and his brow furrowed.

He said, 'A policeman came to see me before I even found the body.'

Lola reached out to put a hand on his.

'What? Why?'

'I don't know. He met me yesterday at the B&B. Detective Sergeant Simmonds. Looks like a refugee from the seventies but seems a nice guy. And he knew something about the break in here at the school, but he didn't seem to want to make anything of it. And he didn't arrest me or caution me about anything. But how he knew what he knew and how he knew where I'd be, I don't know. The only people who knew where I was staying were my Granddad, Ray maybe, and well -'

There was a second of silence then Lola pulled her hand away.

'Oh my God. You want me to deny it was me, don't you? You want me to tell you that I didn't set the police on you, that of course I could never do that to someone like you. That's what you want, isn't it?'

'Well - yes,' he said. 'Yes, okay. I would like that actually. I would.'

'Well I won't deny it. There. That's it. You can think what you like. You know, I am sharing quite a lot with you here, and I don't have to talk to you. And I don't suppose Zack would want me talking to you. But here I am, talking to you, and I'm trusting you. You have heard of trust, haven't you?'

Bart took a mouthful of his pint and he wiped his mouth with his sleeve.

He said, 'Trust is something you earn.'

Lola stood up and she pulled on her coat, her vodka and Coke half-finished.

'No Bart,' she said. 'Trust is something you give. Look. Sorry but I have to go. Got to check in with someone about a Psychology assignment. Someone at school will drop me home.'

She headed for the door. He followed, hurriedly pulling on his coat.

'I'll walk with you.'

'Do what you like.'

He bumped the table with his thigh, turning to steady it.

'Lola - will you just wait.'

But she did not wait, and he had to run to catch her, and when he passed her, he walked backwards with his palms out until she came to a stop.

'It's cold. Let me past.'

'Look,' Bart said. 'I'm sorry. I shouldn't have asked you that, okay. It was stupid. I trust you. I do.'
'Okay, well that's really great, Bart, but I have to -'
'Wait. Okay, can I tell you something, Lola?'
'Bart, I-'
'It's about my mum.'

DOCUMENT E

An email from Bartholomew Crowe to Colin Crowe: 12/11/19. 23:02 p.m.

Dear Granddad,

Have you spoken to any policemen about me and what I've been doing?

Sorry to ask, but I need the truth here.

And I've thought about what you said, and I'm still pissed, but, I'm going to trust you anyway. Just don't start thinking you've earned it, that's all. So anyway I'll tell you everything (well nearly, probably). And I'll be honest here Granddad, I'm only talking to you because I <u>have to tell someone!!</u> - and I'm going a bit mad here. So I need someone who's not in the middle of things, and that's you. And like you say, we Crowes should stick together.

So, are you ready? It's your trial period, partner! If you're not ready, stop reading now.

You have been warned.

So I found a dead body today. Found it in a squat. A murdered, dead body with its face blown off - the most disgusting thing I've ever seen in my life.

And this afternoon I spent with the police. There's a guy there called Detective Sergeant Simmonds - I think he's called Wayne (???). He seems decent. At least, he doesn't seem to hate me yet, but he does seem to know a lot about me - hence the question at the start of this email.

The body is (was) a guy called Raymond Feathers - complete coincidence, but he's the son of my landlady here at The Seaview (awkward!). Feathers was a sort of business partner to Zack Richards - and it's Zack I've been hired to track down and get back on the straight and narrow.

So that's going well then(!).

I've got to tell you Granddad, that I know I should be scared. And I am scared. But there's a part of me that isn't. There's a part of me that's actually excited. Like I know it's illogical but I totally feel like if I can sort this out there will be some kind of a knock-on effect, you know? Like if I can sort this out then somehow that will make Dad's death feel more - well - just - make it more like it meant something - you know? I know it sounds crazy. But it makes a weird kind of sense, in my head at least.

And then, if I can get Zack Richards back with his mum - well, maybe that will have some kind of a knock on effect too.

You know, I was going to use this mail to write a load of stuff about you and Julia, about you guys playing God with my life. But my brain is so totally buzzing with everything that's happening here, that I really don't care about that right now.

So, thanks for dealing with the school for me.

Bart.

16

'**M**y first lesson's at ten so I can only spare you twenty minutes, and in all seriousness, I have got a ton of stuff to get through. So - how are things Mr. -'

'Bartholomew Crowe.'

'Oh yes. Of course. I do remember. Anyway, you called me, so?'

Hasland handed him a black coffee in a white mug. It was good china. And they faced each across matching settees, Bart leaning forward.

'I want to talk to you about Zack and Lola, and Torin Malone. I thought you could help me get to know them a bit better.'

'So what? I should just talk then?'

'About Zack. Please.'

Steve put his tea on the table. He leaned back and spread his arms across the cushions, tilting his head back, gathering memories.

'All right - well - okay so - Zack Richards arrived at St. Stephen's in April, year before last, just before his GCSEs. And of course that set alarm bells ringing in my head straight away. You know, who changes schools a month and half before their exams? No one. It's madness. Anyway for whatever reason the school let him in, and Zack rocked up, giving it the big *I am* right from the get-go. Pure bravado. Incorrect uniform. Asking daft questions of staff - all swagger and show, like he wants everyone to see that he really couldn't give a toss about being here. And I thought to myself, well, his parents must have some serious money for the school to take him on like that. And that haircut - dyed and swept like a blonde Justin Beiber. In all confidence, I didn't like the lad. And that *is* in confidence, Bart. Of course you know his dad is an actual rock star! I suppose you can understand why a kid like that thinks school isn't worth the effort. The girls loved him of course.'

'And Lola?'

'Mr. Crowe, you're a young man, right? You know how it is. Good-looking new boy in town, almost famous to boot - the bad girls compete for him and the good ones stand around a lot and wait to be noticed. I'll tell you, Bart, Lola's a good girl at heart, but she isn't always good in practice. I'm sure you know what I mean.'

Bart touched his cheek. He really needed a shave.

'I could see it from the off,' Steve continued, 'those two getting together. Like I say, Lola's a good girl but she makes some bad choices. But you know what's most frustrating? Can I call you Bart, by the way?'

Bart nodded.

'It's that Lola's one of the cleverest girls we've got. But deep down, she's far too much like Zack to make the most of it. It's the example they get from home isn't it? They can see how their Mums and Dads are doing - plenty of money - not much education, and they think, well, what the bloody hell do I need one of those for, then? Can't see the point, can they? And you can understand it, can't you? It's just common sense when you think about it. And that's Lola and Zack to a tee, both of them. But you Bart, you're not like that at all are you?'

'No,' Bart said. 'I'm not like that.'

'As it goes, Bart, I think that someone like you is exactly what Lola needs.'

Bart blushed. Steve's mouth curled into a smile.

Bart said, 'You mentioned parents. I mean everyone knows Mickey Richards - artistic set, drug issues, all that. But what about Lola? I've read a little bit about Glenn, but mostly it's just quotations about the fire. The one that killed Torin Malone.'

'Ah yes. A tragedy. I had to guide Lola through that one. Things got pretty dark. It's part of why I feel protective of her I think. You know, Torin had been her one constant friend since he arrived in Year 8. He worshipped her, pretty much. And she mothered him back, the way these girls do sometimes, you know? And Lola's very popular, but she flits between social groups, never really settles. So Torin was her one constant, her anchor if you like. Even after Zack arrived. Her and Torin, it was just one of them relationships that worked. Poor old Torin, eh. All alone and starved of attention, and then look what happens to him, poor fella?'

'So you agree with the papers then, that Torin started the fire?'

Steve's grey-green eyes were focused and intense, and he leaned forwards, elbows on knees.

'I don't think we'll ever get the answer to that one. Lola told me after the fact that he was taking a lot of drugs. I mean, obviously, Bart, I'm a teacher here, and I hear things, but there's a lot I don't hear about. Off the record though, I had overheard a few references to Torin's drug habits, so -'

'And what about Glenn Golden? You said you had to guide Lola through it right? How did Glenn Golden deal with it all?'

Steve stood, and he tipped back a mouthful of tea, and he stood in the doorway, his big frame filling the space, then he disappeared back into the kitchen.

'You really think any of this stuff is going to help you find Zack?' he called back. 'You know, he's probably on the other side of the world by now.'

Bart put his mug down and looked up.

'It might,' he said. 'And I don't know. I've got a feeling that Zack won't be far away. He's got too much going on here. Anyway, it's not just a missing person now is it? There's a murder too.'

There was a clink of china and Steve swung out on the door-frame.

'Whoah, whoah, whoah - hold on there - nobody's told me about any murder.'

'Yes,' Bart said. 'Remember the lad who we definitely didn't see ransacking Zack's room. Turns out he's dead.'

'Christ!' Steve's jaw dropped and he stood there, open mouthed. 'You know, Bart, if the police do ask me, I'm going to tell them the truth.' He came into the room, hurriedly collecting his teaching stuff - keys, a whistle, a lanyard. He bent down and picked up a magazine from the coffee table, Christiano Ronaldo on the cover.

'And you do know, investigating a murder is the police's job, Bart?'

'Yeah I know. But I am kind of involved now. And anyway, I think the murder and Zack's going AWOL, well, I think it might be connected. So I'm going to find Zack. It's what I've been hired to do. And so I'm not really investigating a murder unless he did it, am I? Look. Before you go, Steve, can you just tell me about Glenn Golden and the fire. Please. I'd really appreciate it.'

Steve had his bag on his shoulder.

'Okay. All-right but ground rule - you do not tell Lola about this conversation, and I mean any of it. Plus, I'm only telling you for her sake. So don't you go bothering her with any rudeness. Okay, so Glenn Golden, he's what used to be called a self-made man. Working-class lad - like me, and you know I think part of the reason that I can get through to Lola is because of that. And he's driven too, like me again. Except of course, that I took the more conventional route through school and university, and Glenn, well he went in for business - buying and selling and that. Came down here from Birmingham about fifteen or twenty years ago. Opened up a nightclub, a casino, an arcade, bought a whole bunch of properties. And he's done very well. But Glenn's never really been a hands on sort of dad. And, after he divorced his wife a year ago, and probably before that too, being honest, Lola's not had a great deal of what you'd call parenting.'

Bart leaned back and put his hands behind his head.

'And so you've filled that parenting gap?'

'No Bart. I'm a secondary school teacher. I don't have the time to fill those kinds of gaps in these kids' lives. You know, all this lot here, at St. Stephens, they've got money, but that doesn't mean they don't have problems of their own, does it? So I do what I can - just listening really - and not enough of that.'

'And after the fire?'

'Well, that was where the problems came from, you see. Her dad wouldn't talk to her about it. You know, her best friend had just died, but whenever she mentioned it, he shut her down or he went out, and if you ask me that's no way to behave towards your own kid, is it? So Lola, she did talk to me about it. She doesn't blame her dad, you know, for the fire. She just wanted to talk about Torin, about feeling alone. And God knows, everyone needs to talk about feeling alone sometimes, don't they?'

Bart felt the muscles tense around his mouth.

And Steve said, 'This is the thing, and I don't feel bad being the one telling you, as you'd have found this out eventually -'

'Go on.'

'Glenn Golden's ex, she was Lola's step-mother. Lola's birth mother died about ten years back. She was shot. A random killing. They never found the gunman. And what with having a dad who's distant at best, well that's got to screw you up hasn't it?'

And Bart ran his hands through his thick, black hair.

'Yes,' he said. 'I reckon it has.'

17

The red-ribbed frontage of The Golden Arcade resembled the hull of a ship, its unlit bulbs glistening like raindrops. Water streamed down its sides and dark figures moved beyond the rain-streaked glass.

At a loose end, waiting to hear from Glenn Golden or Zack, or Francesca De Souza, or anyone, and with nothing better to do, he pushed hard on the heavily sprung door and entered The Golden Arcade, waves of retro-electronica rushing over him, the clunking of consoles and claw machines.

A skinny lad in a black polo shirt appeared to be running the place. He had a mullet haircut and acne and was standing by the fruit machines talking to a couple of teenage boys. They did not look like nice kids. The rest of the customers were fifty-fifty, tired-out wasters in tired-out clothes and tourists in flat-caps and trench-coats, here for the nostalgia and kitsch.

The skinny lad went back into his booth, but the boys didn't leave. And the two boys began hawking from machine to machine. One of them stopped to text and glanced sideways at the other boy, who checked his phone and looked up. Bart followed their lines of sight to a bobble-hatted couple, fishing for toy dragons at a claw machine, an iPhone on the shelf. The boy in the middle moved first, a spiel about a friend who had left with his train ticket and all of his money and, as he spoke, he slid a magazine over the phone. The couple shook their heads as the other boy began his pass.

'Thanks anyway, yeah,' the first boy said, peeling away, Bobble-Hat's phone concealed under his magazine.

The second boy passed, and the first boy handed off the phone, moving off in opposite directions. The second boy was halfway across the arcade when Bobble-Hat realised what had happened.

'Little shit!'

He chased the first boy to the door and outside. But the boy had gone and he stood helplessly looking up and down the street.

On the other side of the arcade, the second boy was surprised when his trailing foot was hooked back. He felt a sharp jab in his back and he fell forwards, his head smacking on a Pac-Man console. A hand grabbed tight round his collar. And a knee came in. His face was forced onto the carpet. His pockets were being turned out.

And Bobble-Hat came back, breathing hard.

'Hey!' called Bart. 'Any of these yours?'

There were three phones on the floor and Bobble-Hat came over, picked one up and balanced it in his hand.

'Little shit!' he said. 'Should I call the police?'

Bart pushed down on the thief's back and leaned in close to the boy's ear.

'Listen to me now, okay. What are you, like thirteen or something? Year 9? I see you've got your school tie on the floor there - so I'll tell you what. I think you and your little friend should get back there before afternoon registration because I'm here all day, and if I see your ugly face, I'll call the school and this guy will call the police. And maybe I'll rough you up a bit more too, eh?'

He gave the boy's head a firm push into the carpet.

'All right,' the boy said. 'All right! I'll fucking go! Okay?'

Bart got off his back, and the boy stood, bending down to take one of the iPhones from the floor.

'That's mine,' he said, tucking it in his pocket. He turned slowly towards the exit. Then he spun and launched himself at Bart. His fist made only a half contact with Bart's chin. And then he walked quickly off. And he stopped at the door. He brought his hand to his mouth like a megaphone and he shouted.

'Cunt!'

He gave Bart the finger and left, speed-walking down the street.

Bart steadied himself, rubbing his chin, a grin forming on his face.

'Kids, eh?' he said.

But Bobble-Hat was not smiling.

'For God's sake!' said Bobble-Hat. 'You had him pinned! Why didn't you wait for the police? You actually had him pinned!'

Bart stared at him blankly. The words barely registered. And to be honest he didn't have a clue how to answer the question. Fortunately he was distracted by a tap on the shoulder. It was the skinny lad from the booth. He put an arm around Bart's shoulder and steered him to the back of the arcade where a middle-aged man stood beside an open door with his arms crossed.

The man was overweight. He had dyed black hair and a black leather jacket. The puffy kind with the elasticated waist. The euphoria of his triumph made Bart feel strange, and he moved towards him without thinking. And it was as if he were only watching himself as he disappeared down the dark passage at the back of an amusement arcade.

18

The middle aged woman in the small office dismissed him with a glare and the man in the black leather jacket shoved him forwards into a second office, a bigger office, with a functional looking desk, a Macbook Air and a stainless steel in-tray.

At the window, a tall man looked out through venetian blinds. He was broad shouldered and balding, checked shirt, navy chinos, suede loafers. The man stretched. He could touch the ceiling with his palms and looked like he did so often, just for fun.

The door closed. The man in the leather jacket no longer followed and Bart imagined him leaning against a filing cabinet and flirting with the woman in the office over milky mugs of tea.

The tall man didn't turn around.

'Take a seat, young man, take a seat.'

There was a black three-seater Barcelona chair and Bart flopped onto it. He regretted the move immediately. It made him look petulant and immature. And when the man turned, he towered over Bart. The man reached down and they shook hands. The big man's hand dwarfed his own. A big rough, hand, the kind you could really put some force behind. The man leaned back on the desk.

'Young man.' He looked amused. A noticeable brummie accent. 'You appear to have been throwing your weight around in my arcade.'

Bart nodded, trying to smile.

The man said, 'You know, I watched your little display out there on this thing.' He patted the Macbook gently with his fingers. 'Amazing what these things can do nowadays. You can see everything. Very impressive. My associate wasn't much taken with your technique, but you know, I thought you got the right result.'

'And you are?'

He shook his head theatrically.

'Oh come along, Sherlock. This is the Golden Arcade. I'm Glen Golden. Get with it. And my associate outside, before you ask, is Mr. Graham Cameron. Don't worry. He'll grow on you - like mould.'

He grinned at the joke.

Bart leaned forwards on his elbows, feeling no less like a silly kid than he felt before.

'So do you know who *I* am?'

'You're Bartholomew Crowe, private investigator, no less. I erm - I *googled* you when you called, Mr. Crowe. And look, next thing I know, here you are, in my arcade, in the flesh, coming in on a wet Wednesday morning and roughing up my clientele. All very intriguing.'

Bart took off his hat and stuffed it in his pocket. He moved across to the window, peeking through the blind at a brown brick wall.

'I have a proposition for you Mr. Crowe.'

'That's great, Mr. Golden, but I wondered if you might help me out first? Can I call you Glenn?'

Glenn Golden nodded.

Bart said, 'I'm afraid it's all a bit sensitive and I don't want to cause offence.'

Glenn Golden straightened. He put his hands on his hips.

'Go on son. I'm a straight talker. Say your piece.'

'I'm looking for a young man. He's called Zack Richards -'

Golden Snorted.

'He was in a relationship with your daughter, Mr. Golden.'

'And what? You think *I* can tell you where to find him?'

'Amongst other things,' said Bart.

'Oh! Amongst other things! The intrigue, Mr. Crowe! Well, all right. I'll throw you a bone. I don't like Zack Richards. I didn't like him when I met him and I don't like him now. And you know, if he's vanished, I hope it's permanent. And I don't care how much money his daddy's got. How's that for straight talking?'

'Where do you think he'd go?'

'Oh I don't think he'll be far, much as I'd love to think otherwise. That boy loves trouble. I'm sure he's having way too much fun annoying the school, upsetting my daughter. He'd love to know we were talking about him now, probably. You see the boy's an attention seeker, a shallow show off, nothing more. That's my opinion. What else do you want?'

'Torin Malone.'

Golden opened the drawer of the desk. He pulled out an ash tray and a packet of cigarettes. He offered one to Bart.

Bart held up a hand and frowned.

'Please yourself,' said Glenn. 'And I'll please myself too if it's all the same to you.'

And the cigarette fizzed.

Bart said, 'I want to know about Torin Malone. He worked for you at the Ten-Ten, didn't he? What was he like? I mean it's probably nothing but-'

'I didn't know the boy,' Glenn said breathing smoke. 'He was an employee. That's all. And a cheap one at that. I employ a lot of people, Mr. Crowe. Lots of staff, low wages, high turnover. You know how it is. Now this boy you talk about, he burned down my casino from what I can gather, but I didn't know the kid. I'd never met him. Obviously, it's a shame the boy's dead you know. Tragic. Are you done with this now, Mr. Crowe, because I'll be straight, you're beginning to get on my nerves.'

'You said you had a proposition for me?'

And Glenn breathed out smoke in a long, slow plume. He gestured towards the desk and Bart sat as Glenn lowered his heavy frame into the chair opposite. He stubbed out the half-smoked cigarette.

'It's simple enough, Mr. Crowe. I am concerned for my daughter. I've heard about what happened with you both at the school the other day. And now I hear the police have found a dead body. You know frankly, I don't care about what happens to Zack Richards - but I do care about my daughter, and I do not want that little toe-rag bringing my daughter down into whatever he's involved in.' The left side of his face twitched. 'Now, I appreciate that you've got your job to do, Mr. Crowe. But I really need someone close to my daughter, for her own protection. And I want that person to report back to me if anything dangerous should happen.'

Bart ran his hands through his hair. He looked up.

'Did you know Raymond Feathers, Mr. Golden?'

Glenn took a deep breath and Bart leaned forward.

'No. No I didn't know him,' Glenn said. 'Would you like me to check through my records for him as well?'

He tapped a few keys on the laptop and Golden's eyes widened a little, just for a moment.

'What did you find?'

A short pause.

'All-right, so he did used to work here briefly, as it goes. In this very arcade, about a year ago. I sacked him. Smoking on the premises. What can I say? Low wages. High turnover. I'm afraid I don't remember the lad.'

Bart drummed the desk with his fingertips.

'I'm sorry Mr. Golden. I mean, I'm busy. And anyway, I think there's a conflict of interest here. You know, I'm might need Lola's help for the case I'm already working. So I really don't think I can.'

'There's no conflict, Mr. Crowe. You don't have to tell me

anything about Zack. Just be there for her to call on, you know, if you're needed. I'd like you to report anything that could put her in danger back to me. Nothing more. It's not surveillance, it's protection. Look, I'm a single parent, Mr. Crowe. This is what fathers do. And of course if I can help you in return - in any way at all.'

And he slid an envelope across the desk. It was stuffed with twenty pound notes.

19

The door of the BMW whumped shut. Graham Cameron stepped on the accelerator and he whooshed away on the wet tarmac.

Bart was glad to be back out in the rain, water soaking into his coat as he stood on the steps of the Seaview, taking the air, while inside, Barbara's TV blared out a daytime antiques show. He could see her through the window, her untidy spaghetti hair spilling over the side of an armchair, a supermarket bottle of whisky on the side-table, three-quarters gone.

He went in, pushing the door to her apartment, the handle creaking.

'Hello?' he called in, not shouting, but loud enough to stir her. 'Barbara? Just wondered if there's anything I can do, you know, to help out?'

Her head slumped in the chair and she started to snore. Bart didn't want to frighten her, so he closed the door and left.

As he climbed the stairs to his room his phone buzzed. A text from Lola. She'd sent him an address for Francesca De Souza to go with the number she'd given him already. He began to tap out a reply but he deleted it. He didn't really know where he stood, and the envelope of Glenn Golden's cash felt stiff and bulky in his pocket. He started the text again.

[thanks]

The best he could manage. Not gushy or snarky, just flat.

In the dark bedroom, dust glittered in the light that filtered through the curtains. Barbara's already low standards had dropped still further since the shooting. Understandable. And the bed had, at least, been made. In the middle of the duvet was a sheet of A4 paper, and on it, Barbara had written in red felt-tipped pen, 'PLEASE LEAVE!!!' He was taken aback. She couldn't know that he was the one who found her son's body, could she? Maybe the police told her enough for her to add two and two together and, well, she had known that he'd wanted to see Raymond that day. Maybe that was enough.

Beside the scrawled note was an invoice.

She'd overcharged.

Bart sat on the bed and he called Francesca De Souza's direct number. It went to voicemail. He rang again. On the third try someone picked up.

'I swear down, if this is another sales call you better hang up or I'll stick this hand right down this phone line and throttle ya.'

The voice was female, young sounding, a strong London accent. It was low-pitched for a girl and a little rough around the edges.

'Francesca De Souza?'

'How about you tell me who you are?'

'I'm Bartholomew Crowe -'

'Cool name.'

'Thanks. I'm a private detective -'

'Cool job.'

'Yes. And I'm trying to find -'

'True happiness?'

'No.'

'True love?'

'No.'

'The lost city of Atlantis?'

'No. No I'm looking for someone who doesn't interrupt all -'

'Bummer,' the voice said and she hung up.

He rang again.

'You're persistent.'

'Thanks. Hi. So -'

'You're welcome.'

'Okay. Listen. You're going to have to stop doing that or maybe I will enter this phone number on every seedy marketing list that I can find and you can spend your time interrupting them instead.'

At the other end of the line the voice laughed.

'Ah mate!' she said. 'I'm sorry. It was funny though. Who are you again? I'm afraid I'm in one of them moods. This is Francesca,' and she switched into a cheesy American accent. 'So what can I do for ya, Detective?'

'Can I start from the beginning, please?'

'Shoot.'

'Okay. So my name is Bartholomew Crowe. I'm a detective. I'm trying to make contact with a Zack Richards. I believe you know him quite well?'

'Y-e-s.'

'So. Well I was wondering. Have you seen Zack Richards at any time in the last week to ten days?'

'Who gave you this number?'

'Lola Golden.'

Pause.

'Look. No offence - Bartholomew Crowe - but I don't know anything about you. Are you in London?'

'No, but I can get there.'

'Good. I'm going to hang up now. And I'm gonna check you out. And if I think you look all right, I'll text you a time and place and we can meet, yeah? One condition though.'

'What?'

'You're paying.'

'Sure.'

'Oh, and if you don't hear from me, don't bother to call again. Cos I'll block your ass and I'll report you. Ta-ta now.'

And she hung up.

Emptiness filled him. Nothing to do once more. Golden's money in his pocket. He buttoned up his coat and headed into town for a takeaway and a four-pack of lager.

*

'Yea-he-ello.'

It was dark and he held the phone awkwardly, the empty cans and takeaway boxes crunching under his feet as he swung upright.

'Bart? Is that you? Were you asleep? You sound weird.'

'Sophie!' he said. 'Ah wow, it's good to hear from you. I was just thinking about you guys actually.'

'Were you? What were you thinking about us?'

'I was just thinking - all right I wasn't really thinking anything. I might be a little bit drunk.'

'And you hide it so well. It's quiet there. Are you on your own?'

'Yeah yeah yeah. All alone. Completely alone. A bit drunk. Did I say that? And guess what, Soph? Someone's been murdered!'

And he laughed.

'That's not funny, Bart. What really though? Actually murdered?'

'Yes. Murdered. Shot in the head. About as proper as a murder gets! And guess who found the body? Ah God, it was totally disgusting. I'm not gonna lie. And I don't know who did it but it looks like -'

'And is investigating the murder your job?'

'No, but -'

'Well I'm glad to see you've always got room for a bit more macho bullshit in your life. Have you found the person you were looking for? Remember him? The one you're being paid to get back into school?'

'No. I haven't found him yet. But -'

'Oh Bart, will you get real? Murders are dangerous! And

murderers are really, really, really dangerous. And I know it's like stating the obvious, but they actually kill people. We're just kids, Bart - you and me, Connor, Noah. And you're my friend, you're not Jack Reacher. I care about you, okay? So find this guy of yours. Do what you've been paid for. But please, stay away from murders and stay away from murderers. Promise me will you?'

Bart grunted something that sounded a bit like a yes.

'You're not listening to me. I can tell. Look, I'm scared for you, Bart. I think you should come home.'

'Ah, Soph. You know I can't. I can't just carry on like before. Things are different now. It's like Julia said, you know, old things end, new ones begin.'

'And what about us, Bart? What about me, and Connor and Noah? Are we old things? Are we supposed to just end? Are we from before too? Is that a part of your grand plan? Well I'm sorry, but we're not letting you go - none of us. You know the reason I actually rang was to tell you that we're coming down to see you, the three of us. Connor's driving. Saturday morning, then overnight. Now you'd better promise to stay away from murderers until then, or I'll be chewing your ear off the whole time.'

'Okay.' And Bart felt suddenly dizzy. 'All right I promise. Almost certainly, I mean definitely. No murderers.'

'You sure?'

'Sophie?'

'Yeah.'

'Thanks Soph. For calling, for everything. You're a proper mate.'

DOCUMENT F

An email from Colin Crowe to Bartholomew Crowe: 13/11/19. 23:35 p.m.

Dear Bart,

I read your email and frankly I'm a little frustrated.

First you say you'll tell me everything and then you give me only the parts that will make me worry, and none of the details that I might be able to work with. Here are my immediate concerns:

1. How are the police viewing this death?
2. Are you a suspect?
3. What about this 'Zack'? What's his situation? Do you need to get him back with his mother? Has he run away?
4. Is Zack a suspect for the murder?

Now you say in your email that Julia and I played God with the truth. Well, okay. We did. I apologise. It turned out to be the wrong approach. But now - and I want you to think about this one - you're doing exactly the same thing to me. You just can't give out these snippets of information and then just stop. Either we're full partners or we're not.

And no, I have not spoken to any police.

Let me give you some advice. And I know you won't want to hear this, but you're confusing facts with feelings. I know you're in pain. But if you start down this road of acting on your feelings, taking crazy risks, there will end up being Hell to pay for it. And if that's not a fact, then it's pretty damned close to one. If you can fix things in this case then great. But don't expect it to mend your life.

Life's already dangerous enough.

Let's talk. Phone me. I think that would be best.

Granddad.

20

Eight forty five a.m. and Bart was dressed. No shower. No time to eat. He'd weather the hangover. He didn't feel up to moving out just yet, so he left a note at the desk asking for Barbara's bank numbers. He'd pay by transfer later.

He'd received a text from an unknown number:

[Zack Richards will be at the Turner Centre this morning at 9]

He didn't want to be late.

The Turner Centre was a big, white wedge of modernity, stuck to the coast, jutting out against the skyline, striking and powerful, like an invader from another dimension.

It was perched on a steep incline and you could stand beyond the far wall above it and look down - a good view of the piazza without being seen yourself. He paced up and down on the concrete. It was half past nine. Nothing had happened and he was hungry. He eyed the cafes on the other side of the street.

Time passed.

His confidence diminished.

And then, there she was. Lola Golden. Her blonde hair, her navy coat and her black wool beret. He backed from the wall a little and turned up his collar. If Lola saw him she'd think he was spying on *her*. Simple as. Golden's money was in his pocket and though he'd decided he would give the money back, and it made him feel sick when he looked at her.

But he had a job to do, and so he edged back, closer to the wall.

She was looking down at her phone the way unaccompanied people do in public places. According to the text she was half an hour late and still no sign of Zack. Maybe she was confiding her frustration to friends or sending Zack the news that she'd arrived. Whatever. If she was looking at her phone she wouldn't notice him.

And it must have been Zack she was texting because two minutes later, there he was - Zack Richards - thin, average to tall, almost-white hair worn in a broad diagonal stroke across his face - just like in the photographs. And his skin was tanned and he was handsome - dark eyebrows furrowing to form an aquiline 'v', dark skin - Latinate. He wore black jeans and shoes and an over-sized Parka. Black, or a green that was almost-black. It's colour changed with the light.

And for a moment, Bart forgot to breathe.

And then he took pictures.

Zack had a loose, swaggering gait. He crossed the piazza. Lola threw her arms around Zack's neck and she kissed him repeatedly.

The hangover was making Bart queasy.

With his arm around her shoulder, Zack and Lola headed for the entrance. Bart followed, jogging down the hill, up the concrete stairs. At the tall glass doors, he stopped and looked up at the building. It resembled a row of futuristic beach huts, just on a massive scale, like leisure space for hi-tech giants. He shouldn't go in. He should find a secluded spot and wait. If he found a good spot, then Lola and Zack would eventually come out and he could introduce himself, explain to Zack that whatever he thought of his mother, she cared enough to hire a detective to get him back on track, and maybe suggest that he owed her at least a small amount of, well, something anyway. He had the feeling it wouldn't work, and the more he rehearsed it the less viable it seemed. Still, it was better to wait. Wait and follow. Find out where Zack was staying - but his actions contradicted his thoughts, as against his better judgement, he tucked himself in behind a group of European students, and followed them inside.

The foyer felt like the hollowed out inside of an enormous sugar cube. Zack and Lola were at the far side by the glass. He watched them with the self-facing camera on his phone, silhouetted by grey sea and sky. An enormous, spider-like installation hung from the ceiling - all tubes, grotesque angles. Zack was looking at it, gesticulating, and Lola was laughing. She continued to laugh as they made their way to the lift.

And Bart followed.

Close, stupidly close.

'Come, come. Follow me. Enter my cave! Enter the glorious world of art!' Zack's voice was all mock theatre. 'Follow me, my darling. Follow me!'

'Oh my God!' Lola laughed. 'You are such a dick!'

Then the lift doors closed.

Taking two or three steps at a time, he bounded up the stairs, where he heard them again. Her laughing. And his voice, deep and languid and not very rock-star. And when the voice faded he poked his head around the top of the stairs and he peered down the spacious, white corridor. He must have looked comical. The openness of the space lent a cartoonish quality to his snooping.

The exhibition was called 'Entangled'.

'Yeah, yeah,' Zack said. 'We met her - the artist - in this country actually. London. She's pretty wild. Hit the town with us, clubbing and shit. She's really cool. Not like an older person at all. You know, she's not even that old! She does likes her gin though. Kinda crazy seeing her stuff here. Small world, man.'

Lola held onto his arm, her head on his shoulder.

'You like it, then?' she asked.

'Oh yeah, yeah. It's totally brilliant. I mean I wouldn't exactly buy something like that. Nowhere to put it you know - but she really is very talented.'

Their voices faded into the dirge and Bart edged out nervously from an alcove. Following and hearing them again, but not so distinctly. Their voices mixing and mingling with the rest. Zack was still talking most - art, all the stuff he'd seen, the people he'd met or knew something about. But he was paying attention to what he saw. He evaluated each piece he came to, and he was enthusiastic and generous - not the sneering arrogance Bart had imagined. He heard Lola say that she missed him and she asked him to promise to stay close.

'Maybe we should go back to yours,' she said. 'I'll cook.'

He didn't hear Zack's answer.

And then their voices were gone.

A table of tiny sculptures in the centre of the next room, delicate frameworks, arcs and arches, all constructed entirely from grass, inter-weaved and airy and beautifully complex. Bart stared at them. He stroked his cheek and he kneeled down to get close. So small, so fragile. He stared until Lola's laugh snapped him from reverie. He got up and crossed to the next space.

But when he reached it Zack and Lola weren't there - just a bunch of deconstructed Peruvian hats, a woollen reconstruction of Central Park and literally nowhere to hide. He felt exposed. In a gallery the visitors are also on show.

Lola's voice.

'My God, they're so weird! It's like Dr. Who or something!'

'You don't even watch Dr. Who!' Zack said. 'Anyway that's what you're supposed to think -'

At the corner of the brightly lit passage, papier-mâché models of children had been dressed as penguins and placed on a paper island, and Bart came face to face with Zack Richards and Lola Golden. He tried to duck past but Lola had blocked his way.

Zack said, 'Wait. Do you two guys know -'

Close up, Zack's appearance was even more striking. His tanned skin bled into his white-blonde hair and his flat nose and dark eyes had an almost mystical quality, eyebrows slanting down like an eagle or a witch-doctor.

Lola broke the silence.

'Yes. Yes we do know each other. He's called Bartholomew Crowe. He's the new kid at school. What a coincidence! Hi Bart. This is Zack. Remember? I was telling you about him.'

'Hi.'

Bart held out his hand and Zack shook it.

'And you two are friends?'

'Yes, we're friends' said Lola, turning to Zack. 'We're friends. I told them I'd look after him while he settled in, you know, like a buddy.'

'A buddy?' Zack said. He looked Bart up and down.

'Yeah, and thanks for that, Lola, I mean like so much,' Bart said, hamming up the new boy nervousness. 'You've been really so helpful - um - really.'

Zack took his phone from his Parka.

He looked at the screen.

'Well, time is flying guys, and it's looking kind of iffy for me to catch the next train. So hey. I gotta run, yeah. Great to meet you. Bart, was it?' And then to Lola, 'Seeya babe. Gutted but you know, gotta go. I'll call you, okay.'

He kissed her on the lips, and then shrugged elaborately and walked away at speed. And then he was gone. Bart tried to read Lola's expression without success. Her eyes were open unusually wide and her lips were wide and flat.

Bart said, 'Look, I should be going too, you know, if I'm - it's the job - um look - anyway - speak later.'

And he touched her on the shoulder.

'Stop.'

Her voice was quiet but it was steely enough to let him know he had overstepped the mark. He threw up his arms and walked backwards.

'Listen, Lola. I could find him. Right now. Where he's staying. I could let you -'

'I said stop.' She spoke slowly but with crystal clarity. 'If you go now, Bartholomew Crowe, I'll text him and I'll tell him the truth about who you are before you even reach the door. And I'll tell him that you're working for his step-mother, which I think you are. You think you'll be able to find him then?'

Bart's shoulders slumped.

'Ah Lola! Please. Look, I could end it. I could tell you where he is. I don't have to speak to him yet. I just want to know he's safe, you know, just like you do. Come on, Lola. You've got to let me go.'

'I told you to stop. If you go now, and he so much as catches a glimpse of you. Guess what he's going to think. He's going to think that it's me, isn't he? His stupid, possessive girlfriend. So you can't go. Sorry.'

Bart checked the time on his phone.

And he said, 'You already know where he is, don't you? And you won't tell me. That's it, isn't it?'

'Goodbye, Bart,' she said.

And she walked away. Bart watched her go and he shook his head and followed, but she sped up.

'Lola?' he said.

She ignored him.

Trying not to look like a creep, he stood up straight and hoped people would think they were together.

Across the piazza, down the steps, out on the promenade where the sun shone down and the sky was on the bluer side of grey and the tankers and the freighters slept off shore like dormant crocodiles.

Lola stopped walking.

'Are you serious?' she said, and there was anger in her voice. 'I mean, are you truly fucking serious? I mean, are you for fucking real or what? How are you even here?'

'What?'

'I asked how you're here. It's a simple question, Bart. Who even told you to come here today? Because I didn't tell anyone. I told no one. Not a soul. So I'll ask you again, how are you even fucking here?'

Her eyelids hung heavy and her eyebrows were raised in the middle.

Bart stared, mouth slightly open.

'I'm just doing my job,' he mumbled.

'My god, I suppose it didn't occur to you that the best person to talk to Zack might be me, did it? No? I guess not. You didn't for one second think, *hey, Lola might actually find out where Zack is staying, all on her own, and then she'll tell me! Wow! I might not even have to do any of this silly, stupid, playground James Bond stuff at all.* I suppose that didn't occur to you, did it?'

He blinked hard and stared.

Lola laughed.

'So, come on,' she said. 'Answer the question. Who told you to come here?'

'I don't know,' he said. 'I got a text. Unknown number.'

He held out the phone and she snatched it from him. She checked the number against her contacts and passed it back.

'I don't have that number,' she said.

'I - I'm - er - I rang Francesca. She's interesting. I mean she - she has character.'

And at that, Lola half smiled.

'That's one way of putting it. We're really only friends because of Zack. We're not friends, friends, if you know what I mean?'

Bart nodded.

'So. Are you going to see her?' Lola asked.

'I think so. She's *checking me out* she says. I'm not supposed to talk to her - it's a don't call me, I'll call you situation.'

He forced a out a laugh.

'I'll send her a text,' Lola said.

'That would be great,' said Bart.

Her face changed as she looked through the calls on his phone. Bart watched her. Even her frown looked good.

'Have you been talking to my dad?' she asked.

'We spoke.'

'Did you speak about me?'

He turned to the sea, counting the ships.

'My dad really hates Zack.'

'I got that, yes,' Bart said.

'And did he tell you to look out for me?'

Bart pulled the beanie tighter on his head. He played with his collar.

'Yes. Yes, he did.'

'And I suppose you're to report back to him, are you?'

'It wasn't specified. No. He never said I had to do that, but he did say to let him know if you were in any danger. So no. Not really.'

Lola threw her free hand in the air. Her lower lip dropped in disgust.

'*Never said you have to!* Jesus Bart! Did he pay you?'

Bart raised his shoulders.

'How much?' she asked.

He wanted to put his arms around her. He moved closer, half a step, a quarter. But she backed away, matching him and raising him a step each time.

So Bart turned back to the sleepy ships in the middle distance and he said, 'Yes he did. He gave me money. A grand.'

'I knew it!' she said. 'I bloody knew it!'

She threw her arms in the air and walked over to the edge of the promenade.

'I'm going to give it back!' He stood behind her. 'Look, you can have it. Here! You can give it back to him for me. Or keep it.'

There was a tear on her cheek and she pushed him away with both hands.

'Unbelievable! Just who do you think you are, Bartholomew fucking Crowe? I helped you. I stuck my neck out for you,

I mean I properly stuck my neck out and I helped you! And what do you do for me? You accuse me. You spy on me. You wreck the only chance I get of finding my fucking boyfriend. You stalk me! Who the fuck do you think you are, Bartholomew Crowe? You know, you act like you're this sweet, kind guy, the private detective, the innocent righter of wrongs. But all you ever do is stuff everything up! What are you even for, Bart Crowe? Oh fuck off!'

21

The Mini hit eighty, then ninety, then touched a hundred. The speed blocked his thoughts of the Turner Centre, his thoughts of Lola Golden. He slowed, played bad songs too loud, floored it again and forgot about art.

He reached Stratford at just after noon. Buses, cars and suits, grey high-rises and new red brick, and in among the plate glass and the concrete and the weathered wood panelling was The Pie Crust Cafe, an anomaly - Victorian brick, with flaking paint and dated typography.

Bart stood close to the window. He tried to peer inside but he couldn't see past the net curtains. It looked pretty busy. He hoped that Francesca De Souza would already be there. He couldn't be sure she'd turn up. He'd checked her social media feeds. As a singer there were plenty of pictures, and of course there were the photos on the SD Card too. He felt sure he'd recognise her even without the cerise hair.

The cafe was just as dark on the inside as it looked from the outside. There were pictures on the wall of Asian men in military uniform without names or explanation, and the diners who huddled around the thin topped tables were equally anonymous. Men and women of working age, dressed in office clothes, and media types in smart casual and converse - but no Francesca De Souza, just the clear, crisp confidence of affluent London.

There were two menus, British and Thai, the chicken and ginger mixing it with the eggs and the bacon. Bart ordered a coffee from the lady at the counter. She was the oldest person in the place. Her face was lined with experience way beyond his understanding. She muttered to herself as she placed the white mug on the counter. A group of perfectly preened guys peacocked out, all banter and back-slaps, and Bart took their table, squeezing into the seat nearest the wall. Behind him a mixed group laughed about the night before, and two women sat in front, comparing business trips, clients and short-sighted bosses.

The table had been cleared and his coffee was two-thirds gone when Francesca Da Souza walked in. Scarlet mini-dress, purple leggings, and red ballet pumps. Her bright, bright hair, was redder than expected. And a thick plait fell down one side. She was a striking woman, all the more striking in the flesh, and Bart was not the only one to notice. She turned heads. Bart tried to stand and wave, clattering the chair of the man behind. He apologised quickly, and he raised his hand from where he was. And when her eyes met his, she gave the faintest of nods.

He admired her economy of movement.

'Bartholomew Crowe?' Her accent contradicted her manner. East London, bawdy and brash. 'Well I don't know about you but I'll have the chili prawns thank you very much. You still paying?'

She turned to the counter. When he turned back she plonked two beers on the varnished surface.

'I'll have yours if you don't want it,' she said.

She tilted her head back and massaged her neck with her fingers. Then she took a short swig of beer. She laid both hands on the table. She stared at him. He looked away, but she kept right on staring. Her eyebrows were neat and thin. Her lips were turned down at the edges, giving her face the appearance of a permanent frown. She leaned in towards him and she rested her chin in her hand, and kept right on staring, eyes that burrowed into his soul.

'Are you going to stop that?' he said.

'Stop what?' she said, not stopping.

'You know what.'

She lifted a hand and slapped it down on the table.

'Ah, just screwing with you,' she said and she grinned, showing her unnaturally white teeth. 'Cheers Bart.' She lifted her beer. 'So, Lola Girl tells me that you're all right. She says you're trying to help Zack out or something. Well that's fine because I got to be honest, hun, I didn't even know he was missing.'

Bart pushed his business card across the table and she took it. She was still inspecting it when the food arrived. He couldn't read her face. She was a strange one. She showed emotion, but she kept her feelings hidden. Then food smelled so fragrant and fresh. He breathed it in, filled his lungs. God, he was hungry.

'It's even better in the evening,' Francesca said. 'They've got the whole menu on.'

The fork was already half way to his mouth when he said, 'Can we talk in a bit? I'm starving.'

*

Pushing the empty plate to the side, he leaned back and he patted his stomach, and he watched the other customers leaving, the lunchtime customers ebbing away as the afternoon traffic buzzed hazily past on the road beyond the nets. The two women in front were standing, checking their handbags, and comparing appointments.

Bart said, 'When was the last time you saw Zack Richards?'

Francesca was still eating and she swallowed before she spoke.

'Okay, and straight back into it then, I see. Well, I guess it was about a week ago, no ten days. Not Saturday just gone, but the Saturday before that. He's been my manager, but - well, you know that, yeah?'

'And you've had no contact since then?'

'Nothing.' And her face switched back into the expressionless stare she had used when she first sat down, her eyes dark and large.

'You said *has been*, your manager,' he said.

'Y-e-s,' she said.

'Does that mean he won't be for much longer or he isn't any more?'

She reached across the table and placed a hand on his. Her bracelets rattled. And she smiled and her head swayed a little.

'Well aren't you clever?' she said. 'Look I'll be honest with you - between us - and this is confidential yeah, Zack has been great. I've loved having him around. He's got great connections. But I'm signed to a major now, and that's big league innit? I mean, a thing like this, it's only gonna happen like one time in a girl's life. I only get one shot at it, and it's down to me not to fuck it up. And I'm not saying that Zack would fuck it up exactly, but well, it's a major label! A manager's got to be organised and reliable, and well, not like money obsessed exactly, but they gotta have a handle on the numbers and they gotta have strategy. And all them things, like detail and strategy - well they aren't Zack's strengths, are they? I mean he's gorgeous and all, and he's passionate - but he is so not organised. So yeah, I'm looking.'

'I think it's amazing by the way,' said Bart.

'What?'

'The music,' Bart said. 'I think it's amazing. You know? Doing you're own thing, pushing it through, making a success. I think it's brilliant.'

'Okay then,' she said. 'Thanks.'

She looked at him, amused, and her eyebrows flattened slightly.

'Are you sure you're a detective?' she said.

And his cheeks flushed.

'The card says I am,' he said. 'Other than that. Well. I reckon you'll just have to trust me.'

'I like you, Bart,' she said. 'I don't know why but I do. So come on, what's next?'

'You've got a gig in Ramsgate the day after tomorrow.'

'And someone's read the website as well! Well done.'

'Yeah. So anyway, you've got this gig. Is Zack going to be there?'

'Well yes, I mean I hope he'll be there. At the end of the day we can play just fine without a manager, and he's not at every gig, but really, we're only playing Ramsgate coz Zack is living there, so yeah, I'll be pissed if he misses it. Tickets are still available through reputable online sellers.'

She winked and she smiled.

'That's great. Really great,' Bart said, blushing. 'You said earlier that Zack isn't that organised?'

She leaned in.

'Understatement!' she said. Then she leaned back and laughed. 'I swear he literally doesn't keep a record of anything at all. And his bills, he just makes them up. I don't complain because we both know he's undercharging me, but business-wise, he hasn't got a clue. He is busy though. And don't get me wrong. He has done a great job for us - got us gigs and support slots we'd never have got without him, and he's got us studio time for next to nothing - and he got all those A&R guys down to see us an' all. But now he's got us signed. It's contracts and fine print now, innit? Zack don't do fine print. So I kinda need someone who does.'

'You said he was gorgeous?'

'What? Are you getting jealous on me now? I only said I liked you.'

She rocked back on her chair. Fake indignation.

'No,' he said. His cheeks felt hot. 'I just meant -'

'I know what you meant. Next question, detective.'

'All right then. How do you feel about Lola Golden?'

She tilted her head looking serious.

'That's the same question from a different angle,' she said. 'But all right. I'll play. She's a nice girl. We get on all right. Had some good times. I mean, we're never going to be friends exactly, yeah. We're way too different. She's the whispery secrets type, especially with - well- but I think what you're really asking me is *am I fucking Zack?* Am I right?'

Bart scratched his neck.

'Well -'

She touched his hand on the table.

'Well, let's just say, he's gorgeous, he's loaded, and I don't want a steady boyfriend. And I swear down if you can't read between the lines on that then you don't deserve to be a detective at all.'

'Are you and he on good terms. I mean right now?'

'Look Bart,' she said. 'It's casual. Just like, once every month, every two months, like five times total, tops. There's no bad feeling. And it ain't love, Bart. Not for either of us. It's just sex. That's all.'

He said, 'Just sex?'

'It is for me. Don't be a loser, Bart. I'll go off you.'

'Who decides, you know, when the two of you get together?'

'You're very nosey, aren't you?'

She smiled without teeth. Stared at him.

'Does Lola know - about you and Zack?'

'If she does know, I certainly haven't told her. Look, okay, I don't think she likes me much. But she's never said anything to my face. Listen Bart, you know, if other people want to lie and cheat that's their business. So no offence, but I'm done with that topic now. You've driven up from Ramsgate, then?'

'Well, Margate, but yes, yes I have.'

'You wanna go out tonight. Just drinks, maybe clubbing, there's a few of us going. You should come.'

He fought the instinct to turn her down. It could be

really good, just what he needed - just strangers - no pressure - no judgement - and no Lola. He thought about the B&B and how he might not have one, how he might find his things on the street when he got back. But then, he didn't have a room here either.

'I've got nowhere to stay,' he said.

Francesca said, 'I like you, Bart. You're all right. So let's worry about that later, okay?'

DOCUMENT G

An email from Bartholomew Crowe to Colin Crowe: 15/11/19. 10:13 a.m.

Dear Granddad,

Sorry I didn't call yesterday. I've been really busy - and you'll be glad to know that it wasn't all work related!

First up, I haven't heard anything more about Raymond Feathers which I figure means I am not an immediate suspect. But I reckon that the police have got Zack pegged as one, what with them dealing together and Zack's not being around.

So I didn't call last night because there's these two girls. They're both sort of involved in the case. And last night I was out in London with one of them. She's called Francesca De Souza. She's a singer. Zack Richards is her manager. And Zack's been sleeping with her on and off. Cheating on his girlfriend (she's called Lola - more on her later). Anyway, I found out that Francesca's looking to move her management away from Zack and on to a bigger company.

Francesca said she hasn't seen Zack for nearly two weeks, but I found out she's playing a gig in Ramsgate this weekend - so if Zack's going to show up anywhere, it's going to be there. Francesca thinks so too - so I've bought tickets.

But like I said, there's this other girl too. She's called Lola Golden and she's Zack Richards' official girlfriend - the one he's cheating on. Her dad owns the Arcade that burnt down - I know! Too many coincidences. Anyway I told him (her dad) I'd keep an eye on her. Which was stupid of me. I wish I hadn't done it. Anyway, she found out (I admitted it). And I don't think she likes me much right now. But we were getting on okay before that, so we'll see what happens. I actually told her about Mum - she's like the only person I've told. I don't know how that happened exactly.

Anyway, Zack's been in contact with Lola, and she's been helping me - at least she was until I wrecked things.

And all this comes from yesterday morning, when I got this tip off sent to my phone - someone who knows my number and knows who I am. The tip off was a good one. I found Lola and Zack meeting in secret at the Turner Centre. But I got caught. My fault. I was an idiot. I should have kept my distance but I acted on emotion (just like you said I would - hands up, guilty), and I'm sorry now, because she's angry with me for spying. I should tell you I took some money from her dad to keep an eye on her (£1000). Feel stupid about that too. Shouldn't have taken it. Didn't really want to, even at the time, but I just sort of did. I didn't exactly agree to anything specific, but money is money, right? And now I feel like he has a hold on me.

I'll take the money back next chance I get.

And you're probably shaking your head as you read this (and rightly too. I screwed up). But I figure private investigation is like a learning curve like everything else. And I've got to tell you Granddad, I feel like I'm closing in on something. Something that is going to make a difference - maybe not to me directly, but well, to someone at least. Time will tell.

I'll phone soon. I promise. Like I say, I didn't ring last night because I was out on the town with Francesca and her mates (it was really good - thanks for asking).

Geoff Smith

Oh, and the gang from home are coming down this weekend, so we can all go down to the gig together!

So, okay all in. Making progress. Don't worry. Everything's fine.

Speak soon.

Bart.

22

He held to a steady sixty as the road swelled in and out of focus. Mid-afternoon, and he wanted to zonk out and sleep. And, staring at the road ahead, he couldn't shake the feeling that he was somehow moving backwards.

At the services he opened the laptop and flipped once more through the photos on the SD card. Francesca De Souza. Francesca in a sequined mini dress, Francesca in jeans and a vest top. Maybe they'd meet up again at the gig tomorrow night. He scanned the other images too. Something. Some connection somewhere and somehow between the break in, the assault, the accidental death, the fire, and the murder.

Something.

Walls of glass and electric light on his right, the outskirts of town, a city of greenhouses, tomatoes and peppers and cucumbers growing the whole year through. And then the town itself, Margate, then out and beyond, the hospital and the school, and then on and into Ramsgate. He parked the Mini outside The Music Hall, and he got out and stretched. The venue was smaller than he'd imagined. It looked like a building where you might keep a fishing boat except there weren't any fish and it wasn't by the sea. It was painted white and had the name carved into the stone and it was very definitely closed.

It was evening and the sun had started to set. Shops

winding down. No one much around. Even the coffee shops were empty. And down at the harbour, the main road arced up and funnelled the traffic upwards out of town, headlights streaming like fireworks. And then there was the harbour where he had met Lola Golden just four days before, its pubs, bars and takeaways glowing under a string of white lights.

Halfway along the marina, the King's Head had everything a proper pub should, George-Cross flags, CCTV, bottle-green Victoriana. And open all day with the heating set to Summer. There was a couple in the corner, play-fighting, drinking and flirting in that way that would likely lead to sex or violence by the end of the night. You'd be a brave one to call it.

There were two guys at the bar - the first tall and fat and jowly, and the second, skinny, with a short back and sides and a lazy eye.

The fat man called out to the landlord, 'You starting up a youth club Darren?'

And his jowls wobbled when he spoke.

'Funny,' Bart said.

He sat on the stool next to the big man and he laid his driving licence on the bar.

The landlord was late thirties or early forties. He was carrying a bit of weight in his paunch. His checked shirt was recently ironed, and his thinning hair had been recently cut.

Bart bought a pint of lager.

The skinny man was talking about his neighbours and some trouble he was having with his drive. And the fat man must have heard it before, because he turned to Bart and introduced himself. When Bart told him that he was a private detective, the man didn't laugh in his face. He would laugh about it later no doubt. Still, Bart appreciated the courtesy.

'So, you on a case now?' the fat man asked.

'I've got a couple of things I'm looking at. The main thing is I'm looking for this guy.' He showed him the picture of Zack Richards. The men didn't react. 'Any of you seen him?'

The fat man shook his head slowly.

'Nah,' he said. 'Don't ring any bells.'

'Give us a look at them pics, mate, will ya?' the skinny man said. Bart passed them over. The skinny man looked at them and considered them and passed them back.

'Anything?' Bart said.

'Well, I don't know him,' the skinny man said, and he swelled like a bad comedian setting up a punchline. 'But he don't half look like that fella over there.'

Bart looked over. Blonde hair and green-black Parka, moving from table to table, laying out flyers. Zack Richards was right there! Bart turned back to the bar. He didn't want to be recognised.

'Oi! He's over here, mate!' the skinny one shouted.

Bart blushed, and he raged at the skinny man.

Zack stopped. He stared at the skinny man for a second then carried on laying out the last of the flyers. Then he headed for the exit.

'Go on then,' the fat man whispered. 'Follow him.'

And Bart moved towards the door, but his foot caught, and he fell face first onto the carpet. His heart raced and he looked up to see the skinny man standing over him.

'Nice trip?'

'Funny,' Bart said.

Out on the street Bart looked for Zack Richards. The harbour was slowly filling with revellers and the slow, winter tourists who walked and stopped, and walked and stopped. To his left he saw a shock of white-blonde hair duck into a bar. Following, he waited, standing against the railings opposite. The flyer he'd grabbed from the pub was advertising Francesca's gig. He put a note on his phone to remind himself to sort out tickets when he got back to the Seaview. You certainly couldn't knock Zack's industry. He was working to make the gig as successful as he could.

Two and a half minutes and Zack came out. On to another bar. Bart watched the boats in the marina and checked the doors of the bars with his self-facing camera. In the darkening night the quality was still good enough to spot Zack's blonde hair as he emerged from each doorway.

After ten minutes outside The Belgian Bar, Bart was starting to worry. No sign of Richards. And, becoming impatient, he pulled down his hat and he turned up his collar, crossed the street to the window - but he couldn't see beyond the condensation on the glass. He thought he saw him - was it? - someone blonde - he craned to get a better view.

A tap on his shoulder.

He jumped.

'Jesus!'

'You're Bartholomew Crowe aren't you?' The voice, languid and cool as wind on a still sea. 'I think you're looking for me.'

About an inch shorter than Bart, Zack's dark brown eyes were tough, and they oozed both confidence and charm.

'So, um, let's talk,' Bart said, and he extended his hand.

Zack's grip was neither assertive, nor weak.

'Agreed,' Zack said. 'Follow me, Bart.'

And Zack steered Bart away from town, along to the sandy beach and down, towards the lapping sea.

Zack said, 'You know, I really kind of admire you, buddy. You know, all this detective stuff, well it's really kind of wild, isn't it? It's individual. I like that. I can relate to it, you know?'

And Bart adjusted his collar and he said, 'You've been talking about me?'

'Lola's my girlfriend, buddy. What do you expect?'

'One of them.'

Zack smiled at that. A big, broad, slanted smile, malice and mischief. He looked like a pirate.

Bart said, 'What has she told you?'

Zack said, 'Can't tell you that, buddy - it'd be breaking a confidence.'

And he took his hand from Bart's shoulder and he

hopped down onto the dark sand. Bart wondered whether Zack was drunk.

'Come on. Over here, Crowe,' he said. 'Come on buddy. Let's talk where it's private.'

Bart trudged across the beach, and he hoped the wet sand would stay out of his shoes.

'I'll start,' Zack said. 'How did you know I was here? And how did you know I'd be at the Turner this morning? And don't roll out that shit you told Lola about the unknown number because I don't buy that.'

Bart said. 'The Turner was a tip off. Anonymous. Believe it or don't believe it. But it's the truth. I showed Lola the phone and I'll show you if you want. And as for tonight? Well, tonight's a total fluke. Pure and simple. So my turn. Why did you kill Raymond Feathers?'

Zack's laugh was full and rich.

'Oh my God! I was not expecting that! Fucking Raymond! Fucking shit!'

Bart's fists clenched and he said, 'You haven't answered.'

Zack said, 'I'll tell you what. How about you answer my questions first.' And he shoved Bart in the chest. 'Who are you working for, Crowe? Well? Come on. Tell me. I'm here. You've found me. What now?'

And he pushed Bart again.

Bart threw a punch, but it barely contacted, and he lost his balance and fell. And Zack was on him in an instant, kneeling on his chest, pulling off Bart's beanie. He grabbed a clump of Bart's hair. And he shook Bart's head. And his left fist thumped hard against Bart's right cheek.

'You've been following me, haven't you, Crowe?'

Saliva trickled from the corner of Bart's mouth.

'Yes!'

Zack took a deep breaths and his gaze drifted from Bart to the empty middle distance. He sounded distant when he spoke.

'Buddy, I'm asking you again. Who are you working for?'

Bart lifted his head but then the fist swung down again. It slammed Bart's head against the sand, and Zack leaned forward. He laid his forearm across Bart's throat, and he pushed.

'You're working for Lori aren't you, you fuck?'

Bart shook his head as best as he could.

'Can't say,' he rasped.

Zack increased the pressure on Bart's throat.

'Okay,' Zack said. 'Guess what, detective? I'm going to give you some free fucking information. No charge. Special offer. So you'd better fucking well be listening. Are you listening, buddy? Are you?'

Bart tried his best to nod.

'Y-.'

'Good. My mum - my proper mum - lives in Argentina, and she's a mess. Total fuck up. And guess what else? I fucking well love that woman to death. But my stepmother - Lori Cole or whatever the fuck she's calling herself nowadays - is - a - total - fucking - bitch! Got that? And if you *are* working for her -'

He released the pressure on Bart's throat but kept a hold of his hair. He scooped up a handful of sand, held it, and threw it in Bart's face.

'So, if you are working for her, I tell you, you better check, and double check and check again every-fucking-thing she tells you, because most of it is total fucking crap and you're a fucking idiot if you fall for it.'

He grabbed another handful of wet sand and pushed it into Bart's face, rubbing it in. The cold, rough sand entering his mouth and nostrils.

'You know, before that bitch married my dad, I didn't even have to go to fucking school. I had tutors. Went everywhere that Dad went, or sometimes off with Mum. And now what do I get? Poky little rooms in second-rate boarding schools in crappy little towns like this. But fuck, you probably think she's got my best interests at heart don't you?'

And he grabbed a double handful of sand from behind

Bart's head and he dumped them on Bart's face.

'Oh come on!' Bart said spitting sand from his mouth.

'You know what I think?' Zack said. 'I think Lori would fucking love it if I'd killed Raymond. And she'd love it if I didn't kill him but went down for it anyway. My fucking stepmother. Fucking joke! You know what I think, Crowe? I think she wants to destroy me. And I think that she hired you - the worst, most useless, pathetic detective she could find - so that she looks like she's doing everything she can to find her wayward stepson while all the time she's giving me all the fucking rope I need so I can fucking hang myself.' He placed his forearm back over Bart's throat and he leaned in close, until their faces were just inches apart. 'You know what else?' he said, and his speech was slow and venomous, 'She knocked it out of the park hiring you, didn't she? You are the most useless, most pathetic, all out fucking worst detective of all fucking time.'

And he spat in Bart's face.

It tingled on his cheek and then was lost to the throbbing of bruises and the sting of cold sand. Zack stood up, and he stamped on Bart's stomach, winding him. He pulled back his left foot, made to kick Bart's head - but then he stopped.

'You know how I know you're Lori's?' he said. 'Glenn Golden would never hire someone like you. He likes tough guys, not pussies. Oh and, Crowe, just so you know. If you follow me or you hassle my girlfriend again, I will come back for you, and I will properly fuck you up. Have a nice evening.'

And Zack Richards trudged away, up the beach to the road. Then he ran and was gone.

Bart rolled up onto all fours, panting heavily. He forced himself to his feet, set off in pursuit. Pain churned in his gut and sand and spit burned on his face.

He reached the main road, looking every way. A Smart Brabus drove past. Dark, metallic, new. A young guy with blonde hair at the wheel. Zack Richards. And, driving past, Zack saw him standing there, and he gave Bart the finger from the still de-misting side window.

23

Back in his room he fell into a doze and he rolled on his phone in his sleep. It had left its imprint on his cheek and its white light beamed into his eye. It took him a few seconds to register. The phone ringing. Lola Golden. Missed call. No message. A text.

> [Will be at Sheldons from 8:30 tonight. Come by if you want x]

*

With its Victorian brick and sash windows, Sheldon's looked okay. And inside it wasn't exactly what you'd call elegant, not tasteful, but it was okay. Maroon and white walls, grey bench seating, a pool table. Old school. Three guys and a girl were playing. Bart recognised two of them - friends of Lola's from The Jazz Rooms. Their clothes new and their voices crystal hard. One of the boys was staring at him. Bart looked back and the boy turned away, a comment for his friend, and they laughed and they slapped each-other on the shoulder. Then he saw Lola. She was at an adjacent table with a slim, dark haired girl in black jeans, and she touched her friend's forearm as Bart approached.

'Speak later then,' the girl said to Lola.

And the girl slid past Bart and joined the boys at the pool

table.

Lola said, 'Gin and tonic, ice and lemon.'

She didn't look at him as he placed the drinks down. She didn't speak.

Bart said, 'I'm sorry - about - you know. I'm sorry I upset you.'

She wrapped her fingers gently around the glass.

'So are you here professionally, Bart, or are you here as a friend?'

'Well - honestly, I think both.'

'But which is it first, friends or professional? You have to choose.'

'Friends,' he said and he swallowed.

She said nothing for a few seconds and he tried to read her.

'Give me your hand.'

He laid his hand flat on the table and she wrapped her fingers under his palm. Her big, blue eyes were intense and soft, and she stroked his thumb from the base to the tip between her thumb and forefinger, the gentlest grip.

'You know Bart,' she said, 'friends trust each other - and I'll trust you -' Her finger and thumb stroking his index finger, pausing at the tip. '- but - I can't have you telling my dad about what I choose to do, or what I choose to say -' Then his middle finger. '- or - who I choose to be with -' Second index finger. 'You can understand that, Bart - can't you?' When her fingers reached the end of his little finger she squeezed.

And Bart said, 'I'm going to give the money back. Honestly. And he only said I should be there for you. I only had to tell him if -'

'Don't,' she said. 'Keep it. Keep the money. Dad's relentless. If it's not you I suppose it'll be someone else -' She squeezed his hand tight. 'And I'd rather it was you.'

She stared at him then, for the first time not thinking

about what she was going to say next, and she noticed the swollen flesh, blueish and purple round his right eye.

'What happened to your face?' she said.

'I had an argument,' he said. 'But you should see the other guy. He looks much better than I do.'

She smiled.

'You want to take a walk?'

'Sure,' he said.

He took her hand. She slid out from the seat. He passed her her navy coat, black scarf and hat. She had her hair loose. It spilled down over her shoulders. He liked it. She waved at her friends, and the girl and one of the boys waved back, the other boy pulling out his phone and tapping on the screen.

The high-street was on a steep slope, and they walked downward, past the cafe where he had eaten with Simmonds, and further, across the busy road, down towards the sea-front. At night, even with the street-lights on, the town was dark, and shadows of women and men danced around the edges of his vision. And sometimes they emerged - suddenly close - real people for a moment before they vanished back into the void. Lola huddled close to him as they walked, and her shoulder bumped his upper arm. He was grateful for her closeness. Being with her like this.

And Lola said, 'Dad really really hates Zack, you know?'

Bart felt the swelling in his face and the aching of his chest and his gut.

'He seems like a person it's easy to hate.'

She took a while to answer and he thought he saw her smile.

'Yes,' she said. 'I suppose he is.'

They didn't say anything for a while, walking, her hair brushing his shoulder.

She said, 'Have you arranged to see Francesca?'

'I saw her yesterday in Stratford. Actually I ended up staying over at hers.'

He felt Lola's hand tighten on his, and he wondered if she

knew all this already.

'So you like her then?' she said.

'She's nice,' he said. 'But it's not. I mean. It's not anything really.'

Lola raised an eyebrow.

'Really?' she said.

They turned left to the bay. The sea was still and coloured lights glimmered, reflecting on the water. They walked down and onto the sand, down, until they could hear the gentle lapping of the water.

Lola said, 'The other night. When you told me about your mum. It meant a lot. I mean really. God! You must think I'm such a flake!'

'I don't think you're a flake.'

'And so I suppose - you know I thought - I'd tell you about mine.'

'Go on.'

'Well -' She paused. She laughed and held his arm tight. 'Okay. This is harder than I thought. Listen, my mum died when I was eight. She was shot. Someone shot her.'

'Okay,' said Bart.

'The thing is, though, when I think about Mum now, I do remember her, sort of, like how kind she was to me. And I can remember how she would go away a lot. You see she had to look after her sick auntie. And I remember how she would always hug me and cry when she went. And when she came back she'd always have a present. And I remember the arguments too. Mum and Dad. There were lots of those. They'd always start about something really small like the washing up or something, but then they'd be shouting about other things, things I didn't understand. And then Mum would cry and Dad would storm off. They argued a lot. But the thing was, for me, Dad was always around, and Mum wasn't. And so as I got older I started to take Dad's side on things. I didn't even know what I was saying half the time. And I just wanted Mum to show she cared about us. She was away like all the time.

'But anyway, one day, Mum went running on the coast, which she'd been doing for about six months I think, and some lunatic shot her, point blank, in the back. Then she was gone. Quick as that. But you know, and this is the horrible bit, Bart - I wasn't even that sad. Not really. I mean, sometimes I'd pretend I was. I don't really know why. For attention I suppose.

'And I've got pictures of Mum now, but without them I used to find it really hard to even remember what she looked like. I couldn't make her come alive in my head. And when I think about her now - I still can't, not properly - I sort of imagine she's another me - like it's not even her at all - does that makes sense?'

Bart put his hand around her waist. She held it there, still for a moment. Then she pulled it tighter.

Bart said, 'I can see you cared about her.'

'You know they never caught him,' she said. 'The shooter. It was like some kind of random attack, like a mugging or something.'

'Is that what you think?' Bart asked.

'I think what everyone else thinks. I suppose, you know, in the end, you have to accept that the world knows best.'

She pulled his arm around her again and Bart felt her pressing against him. He leaned down and she raised her head to meet his. Her lips were cool and soft. He wrapped his arms tightly around her and they kissed again. And then again. And he looked into her eyes but then she looked so sad and he didn't want to kiss her any more, so he pulled her head against his shoulder and he held her, and for over a minute neither of them spoke.

Then Lola eased away from him. She held his hands in hers.

'Bart,' she said. 'When you do talk to Dad about me, you will check with me first, you know, I mean can we talk about what you're going to say?'

He took a small step back, looking into her sad eyes.

'Okay,' he said. 'I promise.'

And she wrapped her arms around his neck and she pulled him close and she kissed him on the lips once more.
'Take me home, Bart,' she said.

DOCUMENT H

An email from Colin Crowe to Bartholomew Crowe: 15/11/19. 21:22 p.m.

Dear Bart,

You are making a mistake. You are conflating the murder and the disappearance. Remember, the murder is for the police. Zack Richards is for us, so you should stick with him. It's a business you're running here.

And as for Mr. Golden's money, my advice is don't return it - give it back and you'll just insult the man. It's his money. He pushed it on you. You didn't ask for it. Sooner or later he's going to want something in return, and if he asks too much, you can give it him back.

People say not to mix business with pleasure, don't they? But in your case, Bart, I'm glad you did. At the end of the day, you are eighteen years old, and I say if there's fun in life to be had then you should take it. I'm glad you enjoyed yourself.

One further little point.

Your friends. Sophie, and the boys, the tall one and the other one. They clearly care about you Bart, and you're lucky to have them, so when they visit <u>don't forget to put them first!</u>

And for Christ's sake enjoy yourselves or there'll be bloody Hell to pay.

Granddad (still waiting for that phone-call).

24

'Ah Mate,' said Connor, and he flattened his slicked hair as he squeezed into the Mini's passenger seat. 'So, what's it like then, chillin' at the beach while the rest of us are slavin' it at school?'

'Living the dream,' Bart said. 'How's life at the drive-through? You still lovin' it?'

'R-R-Roasted!' Noah called from the back seat.

Connor laughed.

'It pays the bills, mate. Funds my decadent lifestyle - mostly,' he said.

Sophie said, 'Connor's in love. Ask him about Ellie.'

'What Ellie? You mean Ellie, Ellie?'

'The very same.'

Connor grinned.

'A gentleman doesn't kiss and tell.'

'So there's kissing to tell about then?' Sophie laughed.

'And then some,' Connor said, and he laughed too, pulling out his phone and scrolling through his apps and messages.

'That means he doesn't want to talk anymore,' said Sophie. 'Just look at him, Bart. He's just so cool isn't he?'

Noah said, 'So Bart you gonna tell us about that black eye or what bro?'

'Smile!'

Connor held up his phone and clicked.

*

Bart slid the plastic tray onto the table, and the four of them helped themselves to burgers, fries and fizzy drinks.

Noah said, 'I don't think I've ever eaten at a Wimpy before. And look at this guys - it's a mega-burger!'

He bit into it dramatically. Connor took a picture.

'Ts-awll-righ!' Noah said.

'Don't talk with your mouth full. It's disgusting.' Sophie looked through the window at the misty, winter beach. 'It's nice here, Bart. I've never been before.'

Bart said, 'Yeah, I've had a rough time these last few days, but you know, I like it too. Don't know if you guys ever feel it, but sometimes, at home, it feels like everyone's posing the whole bloody time. 24/7 - the best places, the best stuff. I don't know. But it's different here. I mean there's posers here too but -.'

'I do know,' said Sophie. 'Maybe it's the sea. I mean, it's like there's something - anchoring - about it, isn't there?'

With his mouth full Noah snorted.

'Okay,' Sophie said. 'Bad pun.'

Connor put his hands on the table and pushed himself back in his seat.

'You do know how much crap you're both talking, don't you?' he said. 'It's exactly the same here as it is, like, everywhere else. It's just a place. Good for a bit of fun, sure, but you wouldn't want to live here. Not really. I mean, I wouldn't want to live here. I mean, look around. It's a shithole.'

Noah patted his friend's back and said, 'You can see why the girls like him so much, can't you?'

Connor grinned.

'And you love me too, Noah Heath,' he said. 'We both know it. I'm irresistible. How's your lentil burger, Soph?'

Sophie did her 'ha-ha' face and Connor smiled and bit dramatically into his quarter pounder.

Sophie shook her head.

'Nobhead,' she said.

'Let's go down to the beach,' Connor said. 'Swimming in November! Smash it!'

*

'So let me get this straight,' said Noah. 'You're looking for this guy. You find him. And then the guy you found beats you up?'

He was already laughing, and weirdly, Bart found that he was laughing too.

'I reckon that's pretty much right,' he said.

'Fuck man. You are seriously the worst detective in history!' And he wrapped his arm over Bart's shoulder. 'Still, it's nice to know you're not good at everything. What's it like being a loser, loser?'

And Bart launched himself at his friend, pulling Noah down into a headlock. And they wrestled and then collapsed together, laughing on the yellow-white sand.

Connor and Sophie walked up ahead. They turned. Connor took snaps of the two friends writhing about, and more as they sat up, grinning like idiots.

Sophie came back and took Bart's hand.

'Come on, Bartie-Boy. Let auntie Sophie look after you.'

He got to his feet and she brushed the sand off his coat. She picked up his hat and she ruffed up his hair, sand falling out on his shoulders.

'Such nice hair,' she said. 'You really shouldn't wear this stupid hat you know. You look like a coconut.'

He took the beanie and pulled it back onto his head.

'Thanks, Soph,' he said.

And Sophie wrapped her arm around his waist and the four of them walked down to the shore and they looked out to sea where the tankers and freighters were hazy in the mist.

'Why do they wait here, the ships I mean?' Sophie asked.

'I don't know,' said Bart. 'Maybe they don't have anywhere else to go.'

Connor dumped his holdall on the ground. He was holding a pair of red and white swimming shorts.

'Here!' he said and he threw them at Bart.

'Oh man! You have got to be joking!' said Noah.

And Connor pulled out a second pair and he threw those at Noah. Connor himself was already stripping off, removing his shoes and pulling off his jeans, navy swimmers underneath.

'It's the fucking seaside guys! Come on!'

'It's also November,' said Noah.

But Connor wasn't listening. He pulled towels out of the bag and passed them to the boys. He held out some scrunched up fabric to Sophie.

'I've got like some shorts and like a t-shirt if you want them.'

'You do know how cold it is?' Sophie said. 'It's going to be freezing.'

'We're on the beach. And I'm going in, whether you guys do or not. So come on! It'll look awesome online, man. Come on. Just do it.'

Noah and Bart eyed each other nervously.

Connor was already naked except for his swimmers. He put his arms wide and held out his phone and snapped a selfie.

'Who's gonna take the pics then?'

Connor held the phone out to Bart. Feeling the dare, Bart refused the phone, stuffing his hat in his pocket and throwing his coat to the ground. Top, shoes, socks, jeans. He pulled off his boxers and pulled on the red and white swimmers.

'All right, I'm in!'

And then Sophie said, 'Okay boys, who's going to hold up a towel!'

Noah stepped in and held out his towel, and Connor passed her the shorts, and Sophie pulled off her jeans and pants and slipped the shorts on. She pulled off her top but kept on the bra.

'Let's go,' she said.

And she ran to the sea.

Connor thrust the phone at Noah, and he and Bart gave chase, following Sophie to the water, their pale skins stark against the green and the grey.

The beach was shallow and the cold water slapped at their feet. Connor, powered past Sophie into the deeper water. He was the first to launch himself, belly-flopping in the waist-deep water. Sophie and Bart jumped in too. And the three of them emerged, swearing at the cold.

Bart looked round at Sophie. Her skin was white with cold and her brown curls were black and straightened with water. Then she saw him staring. Her eyes were a greyish brown. For a moment she stared back and their gazes locked. Then she splashed him and she screamed and she threw herself back into the waves.

Noah joined them in the water, holding the phone, the water lapping around his crotch. He was shivering visibly.

Connor shouted, 'Shit, Noah! That's seven hundred quids worth of phone you got there!'

'Pictures were no good, bro,' he said, his shivering clearly visible. 'Too far away. Jump in the water now, and I'll shoot that. Ready guys? 3... 2... 1...'

The three of them jumped and splashed and Noah captured it on camera then held the phone out in front of Connor.

He said, 'There. Now if I'm going to freeze my knackers off, you're bloody well going to take some pictures of me doing it. Jesus bro!'

And he leapt into the air between Bart and Sophie and spread his arms wide and crashed into the water between them.

'Did you get me?' he said.

25

Multiple headlights arced across the tarmac. Sophie leaned in through the open passenger door.

'Come on Bart. Let's have some fun together.'

Connor put a hand on her shoulder.

'Leave him to it, Soph. Boy's got work to do. You'll be in soon, right Bart?'

'Yeah, yeah,' Bart said. 'I will be. You guys know me, right. I love a good gig.'

'Mr. Muso - not!' Noah grinned. 'So what's on the Bart Crowe playlist right now, bro?'

Connor clipped Noah on the back of the head and Bart took out his wallet and he passed Connor a fifty.

'First round's on me then, guys.'

Connor took the money and winked.

Bart watched his friends cross the car park to The Ramsgate Music Hall, Connor whispering in Sophie's ear. Sophie turned back, and she looked sad, even at this distance.

Behind the wheel, Bart scanned the cars as they passed, looking for Zack Richards and the dark-grey Smart. Francesca would be inside already of course. Setting up, doing vocal exercises, whatever it was that singers did. Scales? Arpeggios? Two cars passed. Two cars more. He imagined seeing Francesca again, and Lola. The cars were passing more frequently. Small cars, young people all around him, drifting by in twos and threes, sometimes more. Groups of young men shoving each other, or strutting with staged poise.

The dark metallic Brabus was there.

Zack Richards driving, on his phone. No-one else in the car. Bart's heart raced. Panicked he laid across the passenger seat. He checked the time on his phone. Maybe five minutes would see him safe.

And he laid there, waiting.

And then the window banged. He twisted around and looked up. Three faces at the window. None of them friendly.

'WAARGH!' A lad in a tight tee and a short jacket banged the window again, grimacing like an angry chimp, his mates laughing.

'Ah look at him, man! He's got a shiner!' said one of them.

'Let us do the other one. Matching pair mate?' the one at the back said.

And the boys banged the window and they rocked the Mini and they left, laughing.

When Bart got out, he had a twitch in his cheek. He took a shoulder bag out from the boot. A small group of lads were still huddled outside the venue, smoking, a joint or something, and Bart held his hands up to his own mouth, as if trying light a non-existent joint himself.

He found the Smart was nestled three rows up, and he stood behind it and checked the app on his phone. All looked good. He kneeled and removed a small metal box from his bag. It was the size of a matchbox only matt-black and plastic. And laying down, and using the flashlight, he clamped the device to the bottom of Zack's fuel tank. It clunked and it held, tight as a barnacle.

*

The support act were in full swing when Bart walked in. Trendy electro-pop, accessible and quirky.

A strong hand clapped him on the back of the shoulder.

'Mate! You're here! Sit down, man. I'm watching the stuff.'

They sat, and before long Connor was showing him a million new things on his phone. Cool places, funny vids, funny stories, the whole school soap opera. Bart nodded and laughed in the right places and scoured the crowd for familiar faces. Sophie and Noah were up near the front. And then through the forest of arms and legs he saw Zack Richards, red jeans and a billowing black and white shirt. A couple of other lads with him at the table, big guys, fashionable, but conservative. And a girl with strong tanned legs and blonde hair and a pale-blue dress.

Lola Golden.

'You know I basically think you're mad.'

'What?'

'You mate,' Connor said. 'You're mental! All this P.I. stuff. You are proper mad mate! Mental as shit! I mean - I work my socks off at school. You do know that, right?'

'Everyone knows it.'

'And do you know why I do that. I mean, have you actually ever thought about it?'

He hadn't.

'It's so I can keep up with the likes of you, mate!' Connor said. 'I have to work that hard. You - you can just bloody do it.'

'I do work hard, Connor.'

'Yeah, yeah, I know - but not like me. I mean, I work fucking hard at school. Like really fucking hard. But for me, it's worth it. Because I'm going to make it. But you mate, you're just chucking it all away. You do know that, right?'

'Yeah,' Bart said. 'I know it.'

Lola and Zack were nodding and swaying and watching the band, Zack leaning over for Lola to talk in his ear.

'Is that him?' said Connor. 'That guy you're looking at? With the blonde hair and the shirt? Is that the one you're after?'

'That's him,' Bart nodded.

Connor craned his neck to get a better look.

'I like his girlfriend,' Connor said.

'Yeah,' Bart said. 'So do I.'

The support act walked offstage to mild applause and half-hearted whoops and were replaced by the road crew, doing that mysterious things with cables and plugs and the mystical pressing of floors. Zack bounded up onto the low stage and disappeared into the wings as Noah and Sophie came back. They were sweating and out of breath and grinning like musical theatre performers. Bart left them at the table with Connor, and he walked forward to watch the road crew. He swigged back the dregs of his orange juice and lemonade, watching, taking mental note of the makes of the amps and the mixer. One of the roadies saw him watching and gave Bart the thumbs up, enjoying his moment of fame.

'You shouldn't be here.'

It was Lola. She was standing behind him.

He turned and he leaned against the stage.

'Well I'd paid for tickets and my friends are down so - I see you're with Zack.'

'You're eye looks awful.'

He smiled.

'Hey, I know I said you should see the other guy, but you literally are seeing the other guy.'

She frowned.

'What?'

'Oh come on, he must have told you about it.'

'Are you angry with me, Bart?'

'No. It's just a bit of a slap in the face. That's all.'

Her hand moved towards his, a gentle touch against his index finger.

'I do care about you Bart,' she said. 'But I care about Zack too. And I don't suppose you'll ever be over the moon about that but I can't turn that off. And I don't want to.'

'Your boyfriend's a dick.'

'Okay Bart. I think you've said enough. Trust. Or don't

trust. Your choice. I'm going now. This is Zack's night, okay, so don't wreck it. That's all.'

He watched her strong legs under the hem of that blue dress and the white pumps on her feet.

When Bart walked back to his friends, Connor held out his fist and Bart pumped it.

'Ah mate!' he said. 'I definitely think she likes you. I'm getting the drinks in. Anyone?'

Sophie and Noah said what they wanted. Bart wasn't thirsty.

'Hang on,' Noah said. 'I'll come with you, bro.'

Sophie squeezed closer to Bart to let Noah out.

'You never mentioned a girlfriend,' she said. 'Who is she?'

'She's called Lola,' Bart said, 'and she's not my girlfriend. She's his.'

And Zack leaped down from the stage, bounding across the room and flopping back in his seat. Lola leaned over to kiss him, and Zack said something, making himself laugh. Bart couldn't see if Lola laughed too.

'And is that the boy you're - '

'Maybe -'

'The one who -'

He flinched as she touched his bruised eye.

'Yes. But he's no more a boy than I am.'

Then Zack looked over - he looked straight at them - and he bore his teeth in a sarcastic smile and he waved like a four year old.

'He looks like a prick,' Sophie said.

'He's a spoilt rich kid playing gangster -' Bart said. 'Thinks he's like The Godfather or something coz he sells a bit of weed and ket - you know who his dad is don't you?'

'No! Go on.'

'Mickey Richards. You know? Like Mickey Richards. The singer?'

'What him? Really? No way!' she laughed. 'Oh I'm sorry Bartie Boy, but that little prick just got *a lot* more interesting -

he really is quite good-looking isn't he? Sort of exotic.'

'You're not funny.'

She poked him in the ribs and laughed.

'Serious,' she said, squirming as he poked her back. 'I do love a back-story.'

And he pushed her away with his elbow.

'Oi, oi,' said Connor as he placed the vodka and Coke in front of Sophie.

He and Noah sat opposite, Noah stacking the old plastic glasses inside each other.

On-stage, musicians were hanging guitars on their shoulders, testing headsets and checking displays, shuffling from foot to foot. And, sensing the show was about to start, the crowd pushed forward. Only Lola and Zack's table staying put, looking at each other, confirming strategy.

Connor and Noah got up.

Connor said, 'C'mon! This is what the ticket money's for, guys!' He banged on the table, seeing Bart looking across the room. 'Come on mate. Let those dicks be cool as they want. Fuck 'em. Let's go!'

The crowd was seven or eight deep as the band struck up a groove, a good crowd, big enough for a buzz, swaying as the Latin rhythms kicked in. Drums, bongos, bass, a trumpet blaring over the top, the audience moving and swaying and cheering until the groove calmed, soft chords, and the drum-beat alone. The musicians rocked gently. And Bart saw Zack and Lola and the two lads pushing down the flank to the corner of the stage.

The drums continued, alone, twenty, thirty seconds.

Tension building.

And then Francesca De Souza came on stage to a chorus of whoops and cheers, high-fiving Zack with her trailing hand as she passed him. She moved in a half strut, half dance to centre of the stage. Silver dress and ankle boots. Red hair worn up but tumbling down over one side of her face. She clapped her hands over her head, as the keyboard and trumpet players began to chant. And when the bass and guitar came back, Francesca sang, and the audience responded, washing the rhythm in applause.

Song after song, and Francesca's London melodies gambolled over syncopated back-beats. Sophie took Bart by the hands and they danced. He tried to remember the Francesca he had met before, the Francesca ordering a Nando's, the Francesca at the club, then back at the flat and getting close. But somehow, watching her perform, she wasn't that brash and direct person at all. She was someone else. Someone more. Someone stronger, more powerful, somewhere out beyond herself.

She was incredible.

And Bart saw that Lola was dancing too, not with Zack exactly, but near him. Swaying subtle and slow. Zack was at the corner of the stage, his hand pulsing in front of his chest, the conductor of his own orchestra. Bart touched the swelling around his eye. He tried to remember Zack's fist impacting his face but the memory wasn't there. Nothing but a blurry visual and a dull ache. But he did remember the stinging, the sand in his mouth.

And his sense of injustice swelled.

Sophie was dancing with Noah now. The two of them getting all High School Musical, synchronised moves and cheesy smiles. On another night, it would have been funny. But tonight Bart wasn't laughing. He was moving across the dance-floor, slowly and deliberately, moving towards Zack Richards. There were shouts and shoves from the people he pushed past but he barely noticed most and ignored the rest. He'd got tunnel vision and at the end of the tunnel was Zack Richards.

And when Zack turned to face him, and he was shrugging and smiling and staging innocence.

The band began a calypso and Bart shoved Zack in the chest.

Zack looking about, encouraging others to notice.

Someone had grabbed Bart's wrist, pulling it back. Connor. But Bart yanked his arm free and he shoved Zack again.

'You're a fake! Two-faced posing fake!'

The band kept playing. There were voices over the music. Bart shoved Richards again, and still Richards did not fight back.

'Why don't you tell your girlfriend, Zack? Tell her! Tell her you're a cheater. Tell her you're a fake. Go on. Why don't you tell her?'

The music stopped. Francesca's voice on the P.A.

'Can we have some security at the front, please?'

And then voices were all around. Male voices. Some female ones too. They were angry. Shouting. Thick arms hooked under his elbows and pushed his head forwards. He was shoved him from behind and steered towards the exit.

A gravelly voice in his ear said, 'You don't do that round here, son. Out the door. Time to go home, son. Cool off a bit, okay.'

The bouncer's fist drove into the small of his back, and he fell, sprawled out on the street.

Sophie was shouting at the bouncer.

'Oh yes. That's really tough. You're a big tough guy aren't you? Well done. You must be like really proud of yourself.'

Bart rolled onto his back. And when he looked up Connor and Sophie were looking down, Connor's arm round Sophie. And Noah was kneeling beside him, brushing the hair from his face.

And Bart said, 'Do you think she'll do an encore?'

26

'I'm so sorry guys. You know, I think I'm going a bit psycho.'

A car drove past, thudding bass.

And Sophie said, 'God, Bart! All you had to do was enjoy the show. We all were! But you put yourself first, didn't you? Again! Sorry, I can't talk - *so* mad right now.'

Connor said, 'Soph. Now, we don't know the whole story, do we? But we're all mates, right? And mates stick together.' He put an arm round Bart's shoulder. And if you had to get that out of your system back there mate, then whatever man. And anyway, I thought it was pretty funny.'

Sophie threw up her hands. She shook her head and turned to look out across the marina.

Noah said, 'It's nice to get some fresh sea air though, right? I mean really, it actually is nice. I mean the harbour and all that, at night, isn't it?'

She ignored him.

Then Sophie said to no-one in particular, 'Let's go. I want to get back to the room.'

The pubs and bars were busy but not buzzing. So many of them that the town felt somehow sad. People spilled aimlessly out onto the streets as the four of them made their way back.

A large white van was parked out front. Young men

loading gear into the back.

Noah and Sophie squeezed into the back seat of the Mini.

Bart said, 'I'm just going to have a nose around. Ten minutes. The stereo's got Bluetooth, so -'

Sophie cursed and she smacked the headrest of the seat in front. She slumped back on the seat, arms crossed, not looking at him.

Connor grabbed Bart's arm.

'Say cheese!' And he snapped Bart's picture. 'Give us the keys, man. We'll find some tunes.'

The road-crew paid Bart little attention as he passed, and, once out of sight, he pulled in close to the wall, moving around to the back of the building. Voices. Zack and Francesca. He peeked around the corner and Lola was there too, and Zack's two mates, sharing a joint.

'Lola?'

One of the boys offering her a smoke.

'No. Thanks,' Lola said. 'So well, I suppose I should be going. Zack, are you -'

Bart couldn't make out Zack's response or even if he had said anything at all, but he imagined Zack kissing her, whispering in her ear.

Then Lola came around the corner. The hem of her dress flapped in the breeze. She wasn't wearing a coat. She must have been cold standing around outside like that. Now, she walked quickly, but as she passed him, she slowed, saw him there, lurking in the shadows. But she didn't stop and her face didn't change. Bart undid the top button of his coat and ran his thumb down the lapel. His heartbeat raced. Then Zack's voice.

'Yeah yeah, so I guess the cops are going to nab me eventually. I just want to get a few things sorted out before -'

'Pass the zoot, Fran.'

'Here.' Francesca's voice. 'So you really think it's him behind it all then?'

'One way or another. Yeah, yeah. I mean it has to be,

doesn't it? It'd be a pretty wild co-incidence if not, you know. I mean, man, who benefits from all this really? Well, it's obvious, isn't it?'

A shadow in the darkness and Bart jumped, and his foot clipped a glass bottle. Its trebly clink rang out in the cold.

There were muttering voices, too indistinct to make out the words, and then the two lads were there in front of him. Zack's two mates. Both of them tall and both heavily built with eyes dimmed with drink and dope.

He could run.

He was sober.

He knew he could outrun them.

But Bart chose not to run.

Instead he threw a punch, and it connected with the jaw of the bigger lad, Bart stepping forward as the big lad staggered back. And then he threw a second. He liked the sound his fists made as they hit. And it felt good to assert himself, get some revenge. But then the second lad grabbed him from behind. He wrapped his arms around Bart's neck and stomach, and doped up or not, the kid was just plain stronger than him. He easily wrestled Bart to the ground. The bigger lad had recovered from the punches, and he came over, kicking at Bart's side as he lay, pinned to the floor. The big lad's foot bounced against Bart's kidneys and the other lad's arm.

'Watch it, you idiot!' the lad on Bart's back said. 'You're kicking me, you dick.'

And Zack and Francesca were there. Bart could see their shoes.

Zack said, 'Hey, hey hey! Look, it's our little investigator - again. No offence buddy, but you nearly wrecked our show tonight, so I think you should probably fuck off for a bit, okay?'

'Sounds good to me,' Bart said.

Tarmac pressed against his cheek.

Zack said, 'You know, I do think maybe I didn't hit you hard enough before.'

And he patted the darker lad on Bart's back and whispered something in his ear. The lad pulled Bart to his feet and held him from behind. Zack loosened up, stretching his neck, twisting his shoulder. He stepped forward and he punched Bart in the stomach.

And his dark eyes glinted under the streetlights.

Footsteps.

Slow at first. Then faster and heavier.

Connor Stevens charged into the four of them. He shoulder barged the bigger lad in front of Bart and thudded his fist in to the lad's face, sending him staggering backwards. Bart twisted in the darker lad's grip and managed to push him back against the wall, wind him with an elbow. Bart broke free. He spun. He palmed his attacker on the side of the head. And the darker lad's face showed he was not enjoying the narrowed odds.

'Boo!' Bart feigned an attack. The lad flinched. Bart smiled and punched him anyway.

One last hit.

The darker lad staggered backwards but he didn't run.

Then Zack had squared up to Connor. The bigger lad had been floored and was clearly in no mood to continue, and the darker lad was backed into a corner, watching. Connor played rugby. He was properly built. Zack was more slight, but he had guts and pride and he was ready to lose them. And all the time Francesca stood facing them with her back to the wall. Not looking scared. Not looking interested. She looked bored. And she was texting.

And then Noah and Sophie arrived. They stood on either side of him, and Bart felt Noah's hand tapping the small of his back. Sophie kneeled and picked up his hat. She squeezed it back on his head and she touched his forehead.

Bart walked over to Connor.

'Come on. I think we've made our point,' Connor said and Bart saw relief in Zack Richards' eyes. 'Let these people enjoy what's left of their night.'

Bart looked to Francesca. She hadn't looked up. But he could see she was listening.

'Hey Francesca,' Bart said. 'I am sorry. I mean about the gig and all that. I've got to be honest. I thought you were really great.'

Francesca glanced up from her phone. When she looked down Bart thought he saw her smile.

Another shadow moved in the darkness.

And then a flash. And another.

The sound of the gunshots swallowed them all, then spat them out across the road. A flood of noise. Bart thought he saw a figure - a big male in a heavy coat - there and then gone in an instant - Zack next to him on the floor and Francesca crouched low against the wall. Zack's two friends had crawled across the tarmac to console each other and Connor was on his feet, brushing himself down. There was pain in Bart's upper arm.

He touched it.

The fabric of his coat was torn and his fingers came away, wet with blood.

And Sophie Dean was beneath him. He had fallen on her instinctively.

Noah rolled towards them and he touched Sophie's cheek and he kneeled and he stroked her hair. He put his ear to her mouth. He lifted a hand from the road and held his hand out in front of him. It was glossy and dark with blood.

'Call an ambulance!' Noah said and his eyes were full of panic. 'She's been shot. Sophie's been shot!'

27

He woke at six, the stretchers and staff, anonymous faces of the night before, flickers of memory. The oxygen mask. Sophie. He had called her name and she had moved her head. A single moment in a wash of thought. He tried to distill it, and for a moment he held the image of her still. And then it was gone, sloshed in the swell of consciousness.

His phone pinged. A text message. The phone was loaded with texts and other messages too. Connor and Noah.

[Are you okay mate? Let us know. We're worried about you man]

[Hey bro get in touch. Worried like crazy!]

He responded to both, briefly, and secretly he hoped they were asleep. He didn't want replies. He selected Sophie's number from his contacts, began to type.

[Hi Soph. If you're awake and reading this then I'm sorry as hell. If you're dead and in heaven, I'm sorry as hell too. I'm asking everyone how you are but no one will tell me. You need to know you're the best friend anyone has ever had and I am so so sorry. You're beautiful. Bart x]

He sent it. Then added:

[I really am sorry as hell. Pls pls reply x.]

And he pulled the covers up around his neck and he fell asleep.

*

A tall man loomed over him, dark at first, a shadow, then brown and grey clothes, sandy brown hair and horseshoe moustache. A second man stood at the foot of the bed, silent.

'So, we meet again Mr Crowe.'

He looked up at DS Simmonds and nodded.

And Simmonds said, 'So Mr. Crowe, I'm going to need you to tell me about last night.'

Bart asked about Sophie but all Simmonds would say was, 'All in good time, Mr. Crowe. All in good time.'

So Bart told DS Simmonds everything he could remember of the night before. He told him about the job, about finding Zack Richards. He would speak to his client. Maybe give Simmonds a name in a day or two. He told him about Zack and the black eye. And about seeing Glenn Golden. But he didn't mention the tracker he'd attached to Zack's car.

And there was something else he hadn't mentioned.

He hadn't mentioned the memory card.

'You said you'd tell me about Sophie.'

'I think you'll find I didn't make any promises Mr. Crowe, and I think perhaps you should be careful about putting words into people's mouths.'

Bart looked hard at him, and he said, 'Maybe you should be careful about playing games with people's feelings.'

The other man frowned and Simmonds looked across at his colleague before he continued.

'She is alive. I don't know much more than that. We haven't been able to speak to her.'

'Can I see her?'

'Your friend's just come out of surgery on a significant bullet wound. Now I'm no doctor, Mr. Crowe. But we can't interview her, so I very much doubt you'll be able to see her either.'

Bart shivered. Blood swirled around his brain like dirty water draining from a sink.

'Do you think, the gunman was the same guy that shot Raymond Feathers?'

'Hmmm, do you think I'd tell you if I did? Mr. Crowe, you have my sympathy, really, but don't start thinking we're colleagues in this. To be honest I seem to be talking to you rather more than I'd like. No offence.'

Sweat beaded on Bart's forehead. His right eye twitched.

'Can I talk to you for a minute,' he said. 'You know, off the record, or whatever it is you guys say?'

'We're professionals in the police force Mr. Crowe. You talk. Let us worry about the record.'

'In confidence - please.'

His voice cracked a little and the muscles spasmed at the side of Bart's mouth.

DS Simmonds nodded to his colleague. The man shrugged and took a stroll, and the D.S. sat in the hospital chair and he listened as Bart told him about the memory card and the pictures of Zack and his friends.

Simmonds scratched his ear.

'You have this thing with you now?' he said.

'No. It's at the B&B. Sorry.'

'Sorry is as sorry does.'

'What?'

'Have you altered this thing at all?'

'No.'

Simmonds scratched his ear.

'You do realise Mr Crowe that this piece of evidence, this thing, if it does matter, is now severely compromised. After all, all we have is your word that it was ever at the crime scene at all.'

'I do realise that, but I was there, and it wasn't a crime scene when -'

'But nothing Mr. Crowe. Let me be blunt. If you had left this thing there at the scene of the crime, your friend might not have a bullet hole in her side.'

And Bart said nothing.

And Simmonds said, 'And when I say *sorry is as sorry does,* I mean you'd better bloody give me this memory card - the one you claim to have found at the scene of a murder. I also mean that you're going to go home to wherever you're from, and you're going to stay there. And you'll leave crime-fighting to professionals like myself and my colleagues, because, whatever it is you think you're doing, you appear to be causing crime, not stopping it. Do you take my point?'

'Yes but that's not -'

Simmonds made his hands into tight fists.

'It's exactly the bloody point, Bart.' He stood up and made to leave but turned back. 'Do you know what a bullet does to a person, Mr. Crowe? Well do you? It rips them apart. Arteries and intestines. Stomach. Do you think that people come out of surgery, and what? They're fine? Like nothing ever happened? This isn't an action movie. This isn't one of your crappy video games. Crime brings pain, Bart. Real pain. You stop crime. You stop pain. But you - you don't stop crime do you? In fact I'd go so far as to say you're a one man crime creation enterprise. You are causing pain. And quite frankly, we'd be better off without you.' Simmonds paused. 'The people here tell me you'll be free to go today. When that happens phone me immediately. I want that memory card. Do not go back to the hotel without me. Do we understand each other?'

'Yes.'

Bart turned away, chastised, and he saw himself, reflected, hazy and flat, on the plastic surface of the pay-to-view TV. And it was like looking at a previous version of himself. Bartholomew Crowe 1.0. The empty, unformed person that he used to be, the person everybody else wanted him to be again.

And it made him angry to look at himself like that. His lip curled and he turned the screen away. He pushed it to the wall. The wound on his arm stung, pain pulsing up his shoulder and neck.

'You know,' he said. 'Sometimes, I think it's not justice at all that makes you guys tick, it's just security isn't it? You do just enough to keep everything ticking along. You're not crime-fighters. You're just guarding the shop. Well, you know what, sometimes I think doing the *right* thing means not doing the right thing, so I'm not going to school, I'm not playing the game. And I'll tell you what DS Simmonds, I reckon I'll do what's *right* if that's all right with you.'

Simmonds put his card on the bedside table.

'Phone,' he said. 'Don't text.'

And as DS Simmonds turned to leave, Bart called out, 'Why did you come and see me that day, you know, at the hotel? Who told you about me?'

Simmonds stopped at the curtain and he turned his head.

'The chief inspector suggested I have a word.'

And then he was gone.

And the curtains rustled, still settling when Granddad pushed them aside. His wispy hair was tied back in a pony tail, and half-rimmed spectacles hung from his shirt pocket.

Granddad said, 'Visitors? Already?'

28

High buildings, shuttered windows and balconies. Enemies firing down. Fighting on the streets. He took damage but he gave it out too.

In the main square, bullets pinged but he didn't take cover. He ran and he fired. He ran across the square, bursting through the double doors of the town hall. He came face to face with the barrel of a rifle.

And it killed him with a single shot.

Bart dropped the controller and lay on the bed as the game wheeled through score charts and demos. Still no response from Sophie. Noah had persuaded his parents to let him stay on at the Travelodge while Sophie recovered. But even he hadn't seen her yet. Connor, with school and work on Monday, and no one to pay his hotel bill, had driven home. Bart would have stayed in Margate too, but Granddad had insisted he come home. To be honest he was glad of the company.

His phone pinged.

[Dinner is served!]

Granddad loved that bloody iPhone. Social media too, not Insta or Snap, but always on Facebook and Twitter.

'I'm on my own a lot,' he'd say. 'So it's this thing or a bloody budgie!'

Dinner was Indian - korma and rogan josh - and Granddad was already eating. He was watching The Chase on TV, raising his fork or shaking his head, 'Yea' or 'Nup', and a high-pitched 'Nnn' when someone on the telly knew better than he did. Being home with Granddad was almost like a flat-share with a school mate. Take-aways, quiz shows and shared kitchen duties.

'I might go out for a bit,' Bart said, the plate on his lap. 'I gotta tell you, I'm going crazy without my computer.'

'Hell to pay,' Granddad said, and he chuckled and bit into a bhaji. 'You did the right thing there though, boy. The police want to check you haven't tampered with the data on that card. You might not see it for a while of course. And they probably think you'd copied it too. You have copied it, haven't you?'

Bart grinned.

'Maybe.'

'Good. You save it to a machine or to the cloud?'

'Christ Granddad. What do you even know about the cloud?'

The old man shrugged.

'Anyway I've done better than that. I made a hard copy.'

Bart reached for his wallet and pulled out a tiny fingernail sized rectangle of plastic.

'Bart.'

'What?'

'Let's go buy you a new computer tomorrow, boy. But get my old thing down now, will you. We'll have a look at them pictures. Oh, and get your art pad, and a ruler.'

And so they sat at the dining room table with the art pad and the ruler and Bart talked through the case from the very start. Granddad asked questions about everything. As Bart gave answers Granddad plotted a time-line.

'And that's when Sophie got shot,' Bart said. 'God, if there was any justice that bullet would have hit me, not her.'

Granddad snorted.

'I'm not joking.'

'No boy, I know you're not. But you're feeling sorry for yourself. Don't. It's dishonest. You don't want to be shot. You were lucky. And Sophie, well, she was unlucky - but not as unlucky as she could have been.'

Bart put down his fork. He swallowed.

Then he frowned and said, 'You don't know anything about what it was like.'

Granddad sighed.

'Maybe not. But sometimes it shows strength to be thankful for what hasn't happened, rather than being miserable about what has. Now come on. Let's load up them pictures and let's have a proper look.'

Bart clicked the card into the computer.

'We'll go through these one at a time,' Granddad said. 'I want you to tell me who's in each one. Give me the numbers and the dates, and we'll see where everything fits.'

So Bart read out the names of the people in each photograph, and he read out the dates and the filenames, and Granddad wrote them on his time-line. He didn't stop or comment. He didn't even look, even when Bart wanted to talk. And when they had done every picture, Granddad looked up.

'So which ones stand out?'

'Well there's a few, Granddad, but, well okay, that one.'

'Why?'

'Well we don't know who's in it for one. Plus the filename's out of sync. So maybe it's come from another device. And the date is the day of the fire at the Ten-Ten Casino - which - would make me think - that the picture could have something to do with Torin Malone.'

'So let's have a look at it,' Granddad said.

Bart loaded up the picture.

It was the image of the blurry figure standing in a doorway, grey and taken from a low angle. The figure was most likely male and took up the whole of the door-frame. It looked like he might be a pretty big man.

'So what do you think then?' Granddad asked.

'I reckon,' Bart said, 'that maybe this picture is from Torin's phone, and if it is, and the creation time of the file is right then we could be looking at a picture of an arsonist, or a burglar, or a murderer.'

'Do you recognise him?'

'Not from this, Granddad. It's just a blur.'

Granddad said, 'You know what boy? If I'd done any one of those things - I mean, arson, manslaughter, murder - the very idea of this picture coming to light might frighten me into doing something a bit silly.'

Granddad pushed his pen behind his ear and flattened his hair.

'Okay,' Bart said. 'So?'

'Well I was just thinking, that if someone was to blackmail me - what with modern technology being what it is and everything - I'd be rather afraid that they would simply copy the picture and come back for more. Again and again. And - if I couldn't be sure about them deleting the picture - then maybe - well - maybe I'd want to delete the person instead. That's all.'

Bart stood up. He paced the room and he pulled at his hair.

'You know what, Granddad. Scratch buying that computer. I'm going to go back. I mean I'm going back down to Margate, tomorrow.'

DOCUMENT I

Text messages from Sophie Heath to Bartholomew Crowe: 18/11/19. 09:37 a.m.

[Dear Bartie Boy. This is gonna be a biggie so get ready. It's sort of like a letter. So DO NOT REPLY UNTIL I'M DONE OKAY! I'll tell you WHEN.]

[1 I AM ALIVE! So I've cleared that up.]

[2 I am definitely not in Heaven and I definitely HATE HATE HATE hospitals! Plus I am in pain. Lots and lots of pain!!!]

[3 There's this big hole in my side. I've had an emergency laparotomy, which basically means they slit you open like a fish and they dredge out all the crap, and then they sew you back up again - it hurts like NOTHING ELSE!]

[Sophie's first rule of a happy recovery is - NEVER - EVER - FUCKING - MOVE!!!!! If you move you're so fucked.]

[Not kidding about the hole in my side btw. There is an actual hole. Seriously gross!]

[Thanks for the apology but you can stop it now. And I mean it. You didn't know that guy was there - assuming it was a guy - do girls even shoot people??? - Googling the stats on that. Oh and thanks

Geoff Smith

for lying on top of me - I've heard you did. Your - accidental ??? - attempt at chivalry was pretty much useless, but weirdly I still kind of appreciate it.]

[YOU HAVE TO COME AND SEE ME!!!!!!!! I'M DYING HERE!*]

[* I'm not dying, just in EXCRUCIATING PAIN. Jokes - ha ha.]

[Oh, and when you come, bring books. Lots of books. You know what I like. And btw I think you're beautiful too. Sophie X]

[Also check before you come - Dad's still pissed!]

[Xx -WHEN!]

29

Light glinted on the buckle of her black suede boots and Bart's eyes travelled up her legs. Lori Cole sucked elderflower cordial through a straw.

'So, what happens now, babe?' Lori said. 'You'll drop the case?'

'No,' he said. 'I don't think so.'

'Okay. It's just that I am going to need you to talk through all these photos for me, I mean for whatever evidence you have. And don't worry about the money babe, you know, if that's the problem,' she said. 'You can keep the change.'

And she rolled her head around, slow, in a catlike arc, and it was as if she saw everything and everyone, all the shoppers, the passers by.

Bart laid a brown A4 envelope on the table.

'Everything's in there. Nothing conclusive. But I'm pretty sure Zack was dealing out of the Athelstan Road address, only low level but -'

'And this is where the boy got murdered, yes?'

'Yeah. I mean yes, yes it was.'

Lori slid the prints from the envelope and inspected them one by one, then she stacked them face down on the table.

'So, am I okay?' Bart said.

'Okay for what, babe?'

'To keep looking. Honestly, I'm really close. I reckon I can give you a result in a day or so and -'

'Did Zack do that to your eye?' she said.

Bart touched the bruise.

'Oh, yeah,' Bart said. 'I mean yes. Yes he did. Sorry.'

'Why are you sorry?' she said. 'What did you do to him?'

She took her phone from her clutch bag and she photographed his face. Bart frowned.

'It's all evidence,' she said. 'I'm sorry he hit you.'

Bart said, 'I was wondering, what do you want me to do when I find him? I mean do you want just the address? Do you want me to arrange a meeting? I'll be honest, I don't think he likes me enough for persuasion to work.'

She had coloured her hair. A shade darker than before.

'Do you think you can arrange a meeting?'

'I think I can.'

'And you'll give me his address as well, yes? Straight away, as soon as you find it?'

'Yes. Of course.'

She sucked on her elderflower cordial and her cheeks pressed against her teeth. She held the straw in her mouth, deep in thought.

'Actually,' she said, 'a meeting might work for me. Okay, Bartholomew Crowe. You're on. Do it.'

30

He looked over the cliff-top railings. The murky Ramsgate horizon. The green tinged sea and the smoke grey sky. The seagulls wobbling in the wind. Tangled weeds that clung to the cauliflower cliffs. Below that, a glimpse of the promenade and a narrow beach at high tide.

'Watch it!'

Bart gripped tight to the rails. His body jolted. Steve Hasland laughed.

'Oh dear, I am sorry about that. I couldn't resist - lost to the world you were.'

Bart fastened the top button of his coat.

'Thanks for seeing me, Mr. Hasland,' he said.

'You can call me Steve,' he said. 'You're not one of mine are you? So first names is just fine. So come on fella, let's walk, let's talk. Before it gets dark.'

His grey fitted shirt was tucked neatly into his dark skinny jeans, and he wore black brogues and a jacket lined with synthetic sheepskin.

The two of them passed through the gate and into the George III memorial park where rows of trees, some bare, some evergreen, darkened in the dying November light.

'Did you get to talk to Lola?'

'I said I would talk to her and I have done. But you know, the thing is - Lola - well, I'll be honest with you, Bart. She doesn't want to speak to you right now - at least, that's what she told me. The shooting. It's affected her badly. And quite right too, of course it has. It would anyone really. But you know, with Lola's past as well, I mean, with her mother being - well you know, with her mother going out like that. Well, you can understand a bit of sensitivity, can't you? You got a hell of a shiner there, by the way!'

Bart touched his eye.

'I keep forgetting it's there - I had a little run in with Zack. Being honest it hurts less than the bullet that scraped a chunk out of my arm.'

Steve raised an eyebrow.

'Vicious little so and so isn't he, Richards?'

Bart nodded and Steve took a deep breath and looked at the sky.

'You know when I was growing up, my mum got married, and because of that I picked up these two step brothers, Jake and Kane. Jake was the oldest, and Kane and me shared a bunk. Every single night the two of them would spit on me before I went to sleep. Kane would spit, and Jake would smack me if I moved. I just had to keep still till Kane got me full in the face enough times to get bored. I was four years old. And every single bloody night they'd do it, just the same - years it went on. But then one day - and I think I was eight - I just snapped. I went for him - Kane - I pulled him right down off that bunk bed. And I picked up this little mini cricket bat we had and I smacked him, right round the head, hard too, not messing about. And you know what I did after that?'

'No.'

And Steve was staring straight ahead.

'I hit him again. And again after that.' And he mimed taking a cricket shot. 'Jake had to get my step-dad to pull me off.' He smiled. 'They made me sleep in the shed for the next three nights after that as punishment. And when I came back in, Jake and Kane had said they wouldn't share a room with me anymore - they wanted me to stay in the shed - but my step-dad was scared of the neighbours and social services, so I started sleeping under the dining room table instead. I had magazines and a couple of comics and a torch - it was the best bloody thing that ever happened to me, Bart.'

'Didn't you ever tell anyone, about what your brothers were doing?'

'And get smacked about by my step-dad as well? And get it worse from my brothers for being a grass, an' all? No way. And Mum was too out of it to care. Listen, I'm only telling you this, Bart, because, well - I rocked the boat, you see - and you, well you're rocking the boat too, aren't you? Nobody likes the one that rocks the boat, Bart. And they'll try and stop you doing it. Almost anything they'll try. But you know what? Sometimes it's worth it. I mean, in the long run.'

Steve looked at Bart and his eyebrows raised in the middle.

'I hope you're right,' Bart said. 'I'm not exactly feeling the love right now.'

Steve snorted. He didn't speak, just kept staring ahead, his gaze hardened. The heavy mesh of twig reminded Bart of the cloistered corridors of an elfin fortress.

'So did Lola say anything else?' Bart asked. 'Besides that she hates my guts, I mean.'

And Steve didn't reply and Bart began to think that maybe he would get no more from him, but then the big man said, 'Look Bart,' and his eyes were suddenly lively, engaged again. 'That bullet, it was meant for Zack, wasn't it? You know it was. I know it was. And you can bet your bottom dollar that Lola knows it too. She likes you Bart. I know she does. But she just wants to protect everyone she loves. No more bullets. That's all. That's where she's coming from. How's your friend doing, by the way?'

Bart reached up and snapped off an overhanging branch and he cast it beyond them on the path.

'Well she isn't dead, but I haven't seen her yet. I'm going in tonight. They think she's through the worst.' He hunched his shoulders, pulled the coat tighter, realising that he didn't know for sure if even that was true. 'You know, she wasn't involved in any of this shit. Hardly fair is it?'

Steve turned left, striding up the hill.

'This way,' he said. 'We'll circle back around.'

'You were telling me about Lola,' Bart said chasing again. 'What did she actually say?'

And Steve stopped and turned and he put both hands on Bart's shoulders.

'Listen. We're emotional beings Bart - remember that - we're emotional beings, that's all - emotions change.'

'So what did she say?'

And Steve placed his palms together and he took a deep breath.

'She said - that unless you could take her to Zack, or get that gunman arrested, then you should probably stay away. And I'll admit I may have toned down the language of that a touch.'

'I see.'

Steve slapped Bart on the back and he resumed his brisk walk.

'Don't worry,' he called back. 'I'll work on her. She'll come around.'

On the promenade Bart shook Hasland's hand and he watched him drive off down the hill. Then he started up the Mini, entered the hospital's postcode in the Sat-Nav. He pulled away, a grey BMW appearing in the driver's side mirror.

31

Mr. Heath whispered to his wife as Bart walked down the corridor towards them.

'Is that -'

'Yes.' And Mrs. Heath tried to smile. 'Hello Bart.' Nobody offered him a handshake. 'Sophie's sleeping right now. I'm afraid she's very tired. We're off to get lunch. I don't think you'll get very much out of her, I'm afraid.'

There was an uncomfortable silence.

'Noah's coming in tomorrow,' Mrs. Heath said. 'Maybe you should -?'

'I'm just going to drop off all this stuff I brought. I won't even talk -'

'Well, we could -'

'I promised,' Bart said.

And he ducked his head down and he pushed past. Sophie's dad made to follow but her mum held his arm. She hissed in his ear and he changed his mind.

At the ward entrance, Bart pressed the button and waited.

*

Sleeping deeply, she looked so peaceful. It was hard to imagine the big chunk of flesh gone from her side or the heavy stitching from the laparotomy that would be hidden beneath the clean white sheets. And lying there, sleeping, thick dark curls and pale skin, she reminded him of Snow White. And he hovered over her for a while, with that idea playing on his mind.

And from his bag, he took a photo, the four of them at Glastonbury, and he took out an e-reader. Bart had stuck post-its to the screen.

I've loaded up the Heartstriker series - can't remember how far you said you'd got!

And

Download whatever. Use my account - Bart x.

And he watched her and he willed her to wake, touched her hand, just for a moment, then he sat on the chair. He took out his phone and began to type.

DOCUMENT J

*Text messages from
Bartholomew Crowe to Sophie
Heath: 18/11/19. 19:21 p.m.*

[Dear Sophie, I am beginning these texts like a letter because I'm not that imaginative and I'm copying you. Plus you're asleep and I don't want to wake you - that's a lie - I REALLY WANT TO WAKE YOU UP! But I can't - so, I'm typing this instead.]

[Btw - I passed your parents in the corridor and I don't think they were very pleased to see me. I wanted to tell them how sorry I am about everything - God I want to tell YOU how sorry I am!!! I know you don't want me to - but anyway - I'm worried that if I do apologise I'll just make your parents angry.]

[So I don't know what to say here and it feels weird. So WAKE UP! I want to hear your voice. I want to see your eyes! And I know it's selfish, but I need to hear you speak before I can believe you're okay.]

[I should tell you that I'm sticking with the case. The missing person part anyway. And I know you'd prefer it if I went back to school - be a good boy - but I can't. Not yet. You know out of everyone, Granddad's actually been really cool about it - I'm starting to appreciate the old guy!]

Geoff Smith

[Anyway I'm rambling so I'm going to finish now - God I wish you were awake! Thinking of you always.]

[Love Bart-ie Boy xx]

32

Bart drummed on the bonnet of the grey BMW. The driver's door flew open, the stocky, leather jacketed driver getting tangled in his seat belt as he sprang from the car. Graham Cameron, Golden's man.

'Whatdya think you're doin' eh?' And his arms swung, tight against his side. 'Hey you! You hear me? I asked you a question!'

Bart turned. Cameron was a good four or five inches shorter than he was, but Cameron had the weight advantage.

Bart said, 'I'll tell you what I'm doing. I'm visiting my friend. She's in this hospital. She's been shot - shot by some guy who follows people around and sneaks about in the shadows. That's what I'm doing. So how about you tell me what you're doing?'

'I hope you're not accusing me of anything there son!'

'I don't know. Maybe I am. Are you denying it?'

'Ach, you! You're in fuckin cloud-cuckooland!'

Graham Cameron lifted his chin and the flecks of grey in his black stubble glinted under the streetlights. Bart tried to turn away but Cameron grabbed his shoulder. He spun him back round and he shoved his forearm against Bart's throat.

'Don't you turn away from me! Now you better fuckin apologise or I'll break your fuckin neck!'

The muscles were tight in Cameron's face and his eyes

were like stones.

For a moment Bart did nothing.

Then he twisted. He twisted and swung his palm against Cameron's head and he thrust his knee into the Scotsman's groin. More surprised than hurt, Cameron staggered back, and his dark eyebrows furrowed.

'Fuck -' and he pulled himself up, a hand on his crotch. His eyes flicking right as he tried to calculate the best response.

'See you! When my boss is finished wi' you. I'm gonny finish you my-fucking-self. So you watch your back, son. Okay? Watch your fuckin' back!'

33

The light from the landing made a silhouette of DS Simmonds in the frame of the open door.
'Come on, Mr. Crowe. Get dressed. McDonald's only serves breakfasts until eleven.'
Bart forced his fingers through his bird's nest hair.
He yawned.
'What? Okay. Oh right. Just give me ten, okay.'
When Simmonds went downstairs he left the door open.

*

Thirty-five minutes later, and the black Mondeo swung into the car park at Margate Police Station.
'Remember,' he said, 'we're just taking a statement here about that computer and those pictures. You're not under arrest and you're free to end the interview at any time. Capeesh?'
Bart nodded.
Simmonds passed Bart the waxy wrapping from his breakfast.
'Great stuff. So let's go. There's a bin over by the wall.'

*

DS Simmonds sat behind the table with WPC Stock and Bart

felt his eyelid twitch.

Simmonds highlighted the SD Card for the recording and Bart said that he recognised it, said he'd found the card concealed in a football trophy at the scene of Raymond Feathers' murder, that he figured the drugs were being sold from the premises. He said he thought the murder might be drug related. Simmonds listening and nodding and guiding him along while Stock just stared, not saying a word, disapproving of something.

'And you chose to tell us about the card on the 19th of November, following the shooting at The Ramsgate Music Hall on the night previous. Is that correct, Mr Crowe?'

'Yes Sir it is. I recognised that the case might be more complicated than I at first imagined. I wanted to ensure that you guys had the evidence.'

Simmonds snorted and Bart could see the moustache hairs vibrating.

'You do know that's not your decision to make, Mr. Crowe? You have heard of withholding evidence, yes?'

Bart took a breath.

'I deeply regret not informing the officers of the card immediately. Though, being honest, I do wonder whether you guys would have found it without me.'

Simmonds raised his eyebrows. Stock glowered.

'Sorry,' Bart said.

Stock shook her head, her expression unchanged.

'Tell us what's on the card,' she said.

'Pictures of Feathers' partner Zack Richards and of some of his friends.'

'Any of them significant?'

Bart paused. He looked at Stock, then at the wall.

'At first I thought not.'

Then Simmonds leaned forward. He lowered his glasses on his nose and looked over them.

'Go on, Mr. Crowe.'

'Well,' Bart said. 'One of the pictures has a different author. Well, a few of them do actually, but there's one dated the early hours of the morning on the night of the fire at the Ten-Ten Casino.'

Simmonds sighed.

'This is old news, Mr. Crowe. Signed off and filed away. I ask you again, did any of the pictures strike you as significant - to this case?'

Now Bart leaned forward.

'Zack Richards' friend died in that fire, maybe Feathers' friend too. A lad called -'

'Torin Malone,' said Simmonds.

'Yes. And Torin is in loads of the pictures and then, obviously, he isn't. The casino was owned by Glenn Golden. Feathers once worked for Golden. And Feathers wanted this card enough to steal it.'

'And who is it in the picture, Mr. Crowe?'

'I don't know. It's too blurred. But it's someone above average in height. Male. They're standing in a doorway. And it looks sort of smoky.'

Stock looked interested, but it was Simmonds, standing and facing the wall, who spoke.

'And that is significant, how, Mr. Crowe, exactly? And I'll say this to you again. The investigation into the fire is over. So enlighten me. Why do I need to dig up old ground?'

'Right. Okay. Well this is just a theory, but maybe - well if the fire at the Ten-Ten wasn't an accident and that the figure in the picture is Zack Richards. Maybe in cahoots with his friend, Torin Malone, who is hiding in the building till everyone goes home.'

'A robbery?'

'Yeah, maybe. So Malone lets Zack in the back. The two of them set a fire on the stairway to hide their tracks. They could leave straight away but they don't. They're having too much fun - breaking stuff, smashing things up - but Malone trips, and he hits his head, or maybe fractures a bone in his leg so he's immobile. Zack tries to move him but he can't, so he panics and he runs. He gets someone on the street to phone the fire brigade, but when the fire engine arrives it's too late and Malone perishes in the blaze.'

Simmonds looked relaxed, leaning back, smiling.

'That's a lot of maybes, but go on Mr. Crowe. You've come this far. You might as well finish.'

'Okay. Well, when Richards gets home he checks his phone and there's this picture of him that Malone has taken without him realising. It's blurry. He doesn't think that anyone could possibly identify him from it. It scares him but he doesn't delete it because he doesn't know if Malone has sent the pic to anyone else, or if the phone will be recovered from the fire, and he wants to be able to explain it if he needs to. But he does take the memory card out of his phone, and he hides it in his room. Anyway, nothing happens for a couple of months. He thinks he's in the clear. But then he gets blackmailed, electronically, by someone who claims to have the photo and maybe more besides. And that's when Zack decides he'll disappear while he works out what to do. The blackmailer sees his chance to get the photo he only claims to have, and so he breaks into Zack's room and takes it.'

Simmonds fingers drumming on the desk.

'And the blackmailer is Feathers, yes?'

'Exactly. Feathers is Richards partner in crime - if anyone would know about the picture, he would - he hadn't counted on being recognised at the school but he reckons it doesn't matter that much. Just blackmails Richards more openly. But Richards has got more guts than Feathers counts on, because he goes to Athelstan Road with a gun, and he kills Feathers to end the whole thing. Only Feathers hasn't told him the truth about where the memory card is, and Zack has to leave without it. He figures it's okay because even if someone does find it they won't have a clue what it is or why it's important. Except, then he finds out there's this Private Detective nosing around, who's showing around pictures that were taken on his phone -'

Simmonds brow furrowed.

'But how did Zack find out about Feathers? He's in hiding.'

'We don't know who he's in contact with.'

Simmonds raised an eyebrow.

'All right, go on.'

'Well Zack can't shoot me himself, because he figures it will show him up for the whole deal, so he hires someone else to track me, scare me off, maybe even to kill me.'

Simmonds frowned.

'And that's who you think fired the gun on Saturday night? This anonymous hired goon? Can you give me a name at all?'

Bart swallowed, leaned back and folded his arms.

He said. 'I can't for sure. But there is this guy called Graham Cameron who works for -'

'Can I just ask you, Bart. Do you know what a police detective does?'

Bart tilted his head back. A tiles in the ceiling had been dislodged to reveal an empty space.

'A detective investigates crimes. We prosecute criminals. And all this is based on evidence,' Simmonds said. 'You haven't got any evidence for anything. Now, Private Investigators, like yourself, what you do is find lost cats and love cheats, you see the difference?'

'Look, I know it's sketchy but come on. It all fits.'

Simmonds puffed his cheeks and exhaled a long, slow breath. And it was as if someone had flicked his irritation switch. He banged the table and stood.

'You haven't got any bloody evidence, Mr. Crowe!'

Bart looked down then back up.

'I can prove that Richards had that photo on his phone. I can prove the photo was taken when the casino was burning. And you haven't spoken to Zack either, so you don't even know if he's got an alibi. And anyway, you must think there's something important about that memory card or you wouldn't be sitting here talking to me now.'

'Standard procedure, Mr. Crowe. Thanks for coming.' He scratched the back of his neck. 'I'll drive you to the hotel,' he said. I've got business at that end of town.'

*

At the Seaview hotel, Simmonds opened the passenger door. Bart got out and the two men shook hands.

Bart said, 'Thanks, for listening back there, to all that.'

Simmonds turned and leaned against the car.

'No problem.' He paused, and Bart was about to turn away when he spoke again. 'Just one thing before I go Mr. Crowe. Off the record as they say.'

And Simmonds looked Bart in the eye.

'Now don't repeat this to anyone, but forensics are suggesting that the bullets that killed Raymond Feathers and wounded Sophie Heath could have been fired from the same gun which strongly suggests a single gunman. Now I'd say he has unfinished business, wouldn't you, Mr. Crowe? So do take care.'

34

Red-bricks and brown-roofs, net curtains and faux farm gates, rich green lawns and hedges and right angles - Roselawn Gardens was the perfect cul-de-sac, a world within the world for semi-affluent old folk, and a place where Zack Richards, with his wild youth and art, his music and excess, would stand out like a curry stain on a fresh white shirt.

The grey Smart Brabus was parked in one of several small car parks and it didn't look out of place. But the car parks presented Bart with a problem. Even with the GPS tracker, he'd still didn't know where Zack actually was.

And so all he could do was wait.

On his phone, he checked through the recent rentals and sales on the street. A couple of possibilities came up, but nothing very much, nothing to get him knocking on doors.

So there was nothing to do but wait.

And time plodded by.

Residents came slowly, and they went, slowly, and each of them eyed him with suspicion - an unknown youth in a flashy red car on a managed estate - he would have suspected himself.

It was two-thirteen p.m. when he saw Zack Richards. He came out from a door that was scarily close, and he had the hood of his parka up. Bart couldn't see his face or his hair, but the size was right and so was the walk. Bart ducked down and pretended to tinker with the music system. And he checked the tracking app on his phone and he waited for the Smart to move.

But nothing happened.

Nothing moved.

And when he pushed himself up, Richards had gone.

Pulling on his coat and his hat, he got out of the car and checked the Smart. It was definitely empty. The whole damned street was empty.

He jogged to the end of the road and he looked both ways. Nothing. Two choices. Return to the car and wait, or choose a direction and walk.

He turned left - into town, towards the sea-front. And he walked fast, hands in pockets. More people on the pavement than he expected. No sign of Zack. He paused at the top of an arching bridge, each car making a futuristic whoosh as it passed. Down the hill. His walk slowed. There was nothing, still, and he thought about giving up. There was a convenience store at the bottom of the hill and he decided he would buy a sandwich and head back to the car.

Zack would have to come back sooner or later.

He leaned against the shop window. He was sorting through the change in his wallet when Zack Richards came out of the shop.

Bart almost dropped his change. Turning awkwardly away and hunched into the cash-point next to the door, he pulled up his collar and hid his face.

Richards stood stock still at the kerb.

He held a dark green box of cigarettes and pulled off the shrink wrap and dropped it in the road. He pulled out a cigarette. He lit it. He inhaled. Exhaled puffs of grey smoke. Then he looked both ways, up and down the road, and then he turned and walked into town.

And Bart gasped and his heartbeat slowed. He hadn't realised he'd been holding his breath.

*

From the bus shelter, Bart peered through the dark windows of The Mechanical Elephant pub. His collar was still lifted and he hunkered his head down into his shoulders. Hating having to wait again and hating having to wait in the cold.

And it seemed to take forever.

Then there was a man in the middle distance, a familiar figure, a stocky man, black leather jacket and straight-cut jeans. Bart curled into the corner of the shelter. And it seemed to work, as Graham Cameron didn't see him as he strode past, all swinging shoulders and tough-guy strut. Ten metres down the road, Cameron stopped. He took a magazine from his jacket. He pushed it into a rubbish bin outside the pub. It seemed to take a fraction of a second longer than it should. Then, he took out his phone and tapped on the screen. Placing the phone back in his jacket, he zipped it up to the neck, did a 180, and headed back up the road, and towards the Golden Arcade.

Less than a minute later Zack pulled the sprung door open and left the pub. He walked straight to the bin. He put his hand inside and he prised a black plastic package from the underside of the bin lid. He tucked the package inside his coat. He spun away and disappeared around the bend.

Bart followed, reaching the corner just in time. And Bart saw Zack as he slipped down a side-street that was narrow and strewn with litter. It ran behind the shops, behind The Golden Arcade. Two men were unloading a Transit van at the far end of the road. There was no-one else, and no way to follow without being seen.

So he turned back.

And he ran.

Ran along the beach, back to the cul-de-sac and the cars and the flat.

*

Bart was recovering from the run. He was breathing hard and tilting the driver's seat backwards when Zack Richards appeared at the end of the road, hood up, the way he had worn it when he left. The sky was grey, threatening rain. Then Zack passed and moved out of sight. Bart got out of the car and followed. From the corner of the nearest block he heard a door buzz. It clicked open, and he looked around the corner in time to see the black door swing shut. He ducked in by the window and he peered in under the net curtains. And he saw Zack's dark coat on the left of the foyer. A red door opening and the coat was gone.

    Zack was in a ground floor apartment.

    A stroke of luck.

    Bart photographed the buzzers and headed back to the car.

    He clenched his fist and said, 'Got him.'

35

And so all he had to do was get Zack to agree to a meeting. He could do that - Glenn Golden or the police - one or both would be enough.

He'd wrote an email to Lori, giving her Zack's address and a request to keep tomorrow free. Then he sent a message to Lola Golden.

[You wanted me to find him. I found him. Text me.]

An hour later he was sitting in The Lifeboat pub, cool and rustic, an old-town place. A cold breeze fumbled to his seat. Lola had arrived. Her eyes swept across the tables and the kegs and the guys at the bar, and then she saw him, at table in the corner.

She smiled a moment later.

Her hair hung loose round her shoulders. It brushed his cheek when they hugged. Bart bought her a J2O. He slid in next to her on the bench and she touched his forearm, a single gold chain bracelet below the sleeve of a white, polo-necked jumper.

She leaned in close. Her voice soft, a velvet shawl.

'You need to know,' she said. 'You need to know that I couldn't see you before. Not after the shooting. You do get that, don't you?'

And she stared at him so intensely that he couldn't hold eye contact for more than a second or two.

'It's okay,' he said. And then he said, 'I missed you.'

The sentence was unexpected and it made him shiver.

Lola looked surprised, and then her eyebrows raised, she smiled and exhaled - a long, slow, relaxing breath.

'Well - here I am,' she said.

'Did you promise Zack you wouldn't see me?' he said. 'Just asking.'

And she looked down at the table.

'Oh Bart,' she said, 'I was scared. I am scared now - for Zack. And you too. But you must know me by now - I don't make promises.'

She touched his upper arm. For a moment he wanted to take her shoulder, pull her close and kiss her. But it didn't feel right. Instead he straightened his back, squeezing his shoulders together.

'Well,' he said, 'I found Zack.'

And he stared straight ahead and he tried to look professional and nonchalant.

'Where?' she said.

'I can't tell you.' And she edged away and frowned. 'But I can take you there,' he said, glancing her way, the muscles tensing on the side of his face. 'I need you - to persuade him - to meet my client.'

She tilted her head and she pursed her lips and she said, 'Well, I suppose that depends who your client is now, doesn't it?'

'His mother.'

'Mother here, or mother Argentina?'

'Here. I mean, his mother here. It's Lori. Lori Cole. The step-mother.'

There was a pause. She looked down.

'You do know he hates her guts?'

He nodded.

'So why should he see her?'

'Well I don't know - maybe because she's his mother? You know, whatever he thinks about her, she is his stepmother, and she's worried enough to pay me to find him. And she just wants to talk. That's all. I mean, I think she has the right to talk to him, don't you?'

Lola reached out. She stroked his cheek and whispered, 'Bart. You're getting a little loud.'

Bart coughed and said, 'Sorry. The thing is, I am going to tell Lori where he is anyway. It's what I've been paid for. She could just go down there and knock on the door herself if she wanted to. And she doesn't want anyone else involved - and I'm pretty sure Zack would rather keep things low key. I mean there are people Zack might not want to see.'

'What people?' she said.

'Well the police for one. Look, I can't - She just wants to talk. Okay? A meeting.'

'And you're sure she won't call the police if he meets her?'

'Yes,' he said.

'And if I go will you tell my Dad?' she said.

Bart snorted.

'I'm not telling your dad anything.'

Lola smiled at that, a confident, close mouthed smile.

She stroked his hair and said, 'You don't like him, do you?'

Bart said, 'Look, it's not a question of liking him or not liking him. It's just really important that he mustn't know what we're doing.'

Lola took a sip of her J2O, and when she spoke she didn't look at him.

'Don't worry. I don't mind if you hate him.'

Bart put his hand on hers and he looked into her eyes.

'I mean it Lola. Your dad mustn't know. Zack's safety depends on it.'

DOCUMENT K

Text messages from Sophie Heath to Bartholomew Crowe: 20/11/19. 20:45 p.m.

[Bart - can we pleeeease STOP talking about forgiveness and all that sorry stuff, okay? No more. Promise?]

[Much more important than that - I still haven't seen you! It's been FIVE DAYS!]

[So come see me! Forget about being an ace P.I. for a bit. And do it quick because - NEWSFLASH!!! - I am going home!!! Seriously, I literally can't wait! A couple of days they say and I'll be back in my room - all my stuff! I can hardly imagine it. They say I'm doing well by the way, I mean, apart from the pain from the stitches, and the disgusting wound - totally gross - and the CRUSHING tiredness! Apart from that I'm fine!]

[Anyway, I've been doing some thinking since I've been here - yes, actual thinking!!! So concentrate. Okay, so this hole in my side, it's made me think how fragile stuff is, how close the bad stuff in life really is - and I think that's why we - not you - but the rest of us - work so hard. School and education is like a race. And at the end of it the prize is the best chance you're going to get to get some control over your life, you know? School is our chance to lift ourselves out of the chaos. Except that of course there's some people can't *escape it, no matter how hard they try. And that's so not fair. But then there's you, Bart - you're throwing yourself right down into the chaos instead of getting away from it - and I think that's weird and I think it's pointless - so there!]*

[We miss you Bart. We all do. The others too. And school too. They love you there. You're their superstar. But they'll kick you out if you don't show up soon! You are depriving them of their star student! So selfish.]

[So...]

[COME HOME!]

[COME HOME!!]

[COME HOME!!!]

[Seriously Bart, come home, study hard, have a great life - just like your dad - AND I'M NOT GOING TO DELETE THAT because HE DID HAVE A GREAT LIFE, whatever you think about how unfair stuff is.]

[Big love Bart. Sophie xx]

[COME AND SEE ME NOW!]

36

A fast moving space rock collided with the ship's hull, shattering it into a jumble of fragmented lines.
'Asteroids eh? It's when you move from the middle you're screwed, eh?' A Glaswegian accent. Graham Cameron. 'They're all the rage them retro machines you know.'

Ten in the morning and Bart was one of the only customers in the arcade - everyone else in bed or at work.

'Your boss around?' Bart said.

'Do ya think I talk to the likes of you for fun? Follow me. Save your patter for the big guy, okay?'

And Bart's final space-craft exploded.

*

The heavy-earringed book-keeper looked back at him over the rim of her spectacles and Bart smiled but she didn't return it.

Golden's big frame filled the doorway to his office, and when he saw Bart he took a step forward. He held out his big hand, a firm grip and a handshake.

Blue shirt. Gold chain bracelet.

He ushered Bart into the office and closed the door. Everything was as before. The same tidy office, the dated and mismatched furniture. Bart took a seat as Golden paced slowly about the room.

There was a box of twenty cigarettes on the desk and the ash tray had two butts in it. Golden picked up the pack, weighing the dark green box of cigarettes in his hand.

'Government packets,' he said. 'They used to be gold, you know? Benson & Hedges. I always liked that gold box. But then they went and made everything the same, didn't they? And they'd do it to us as well if they could, make us all the same, like robots. But then, you and me Bart, we're not the same at all, are we? I mean, we're very different, you and me. And you and Zack Richards. You're very different too, aren't you? Me and Richards though, not so much. Me and Richards, now we're far more alike.'

He took out a cigarette and he flipped it up with his right hand and he theatrically lowered it to his lips. He lit it and inhaled. Blew out.

'Now me and Zack,' he continued, 'we're like a couple of Bensons in a gold box. We're a pair of similar individuals.' And he looked at Bart with fixed, icy coldness, 'In the end, it's just a question of who gets smoked first.'

He took another puff on his cigarette and smirked.

'Am I supposed to say something to that?' Bart asked.

'My money says you say something,' Glenn Golden said, the humour gone from his face.

Bart laid the envelope of cash on the table.

'Why are you having me followed?'

Golden dragged on the cigarette and Bart waited.

There was a knock at the door. The book-keeper came in. She put Golden's mug in front of him on the desk. Coffee spilled over the side. Golden gave her a wink. She blushed and she glanced back over her shoulder as she left.

And Bart said, 'Why are you paying off Zack Richards?'

'Well now,' Golden had smoked the cigarette down to the butt. He stubbed it out in the tray. He drank some weak coffee and smiled. 'You've heard of insurance I suppose? Of course you have. Everyone has, haven't they? Well I like insurance, Bart. You see insurance means I always make a profit - one way or another. And Graham, following you, well he's insurance of a sort - I'm keeping you safe, Bart. I'm protecting my investment.'

Bart pushed the envelope across the desk.

'Take it,' he said. 'I can't give you anything. I've got no information. Nothing. Nothing on Lola. Nothing on Zack.'

Glenn Golden sat on the edge of his desk, and he sipped his coffee and he took out his phone and he tapped on the screen.

'I'm afraid I disagree with you there. You see, I've paid for your services. It's time to deliver.'

The door opened and Graham Cameron walked in. And he closed the door behind him, and he stood in front of it, thumbs hooked in his pockets, his legs spread wide.

Golden pulled out another cigarette. He raised an eyebrow and leaned forward and lit it. He took a long drag, then laid it down in the glass ash tray.

'It's really very simple, Mr. Crowe. You answer me two easy questions and you'll be free to go and you can keep the money.'

Bart scanned the room. Window. Sofa. Blinds. He leaned back, hands on his head, and he said, 'Okay. Well I was thinking you might answer some questions for me too. Did you burn down the Ten-Ten Casino yourself, or did you send your monkey to do it for you?'

Glenn Golden slammed the desk with his palm. A heavy thud. The cigarette shook in the tray.

'Don't you get cocky with me, you shite-arsed little toerag!' And he turned and when he spoke again it was almost a whisper. 'Look, I'm a patient man, Crowe - lucky for you - but Graham here, he's got a temper. Just look at him. Look real close. Go on. Look close and you'll see his fingers itch.'

Graham Cameron took a step forward but Golden nodded sharply. Cameron stopped. His fists were clenched tight. He turned his head to the side and he spat on a pot plant.

Glenn Golden sipped his coffee.

He said, 'Where can I find Zack Richards? And don't tell me you don't know because I know for a fact that you do.'

'I don't know,' Bart lied.

Golden sighed. He lifted the cigarette from the ashtray and he nodded. Graham Cameron came forward this time and he hooked Bart's arms, held them back behind the chair, his hot breath condensing in Bart's ear. And Golden in front of him, squatting low, blowing smoke in Bart's face. It stung, and Bart winced and he tried to blink the smoke away, but Golden's big hand gripped his throat and his vision was filled with the orange glow of a cigarette. Shutting his eyes tight, he didn't dare move. He could feel the heat, searing his eyelid. And his lashes crackled and he began to shake. The prickling, clawing heat. And Glenn Golden moved closer.

'You don't mind if I please myself and put out my cigarette. It's just that I see that your eye of yours is black already.'

Bart felt the red heat, the crackle and pop of searing hair. He squeezed his eyelids as tight as he could. His whole face began to sweat and he braced.

And then the heat faded.

And the air cooled.

And he heard Glenn Golden's low laugh.

Still he didn't dare to open his eyes, but he released his breath and he gulped in air. Cameron's wet breath in his ear. And when he did open his eyes, Glenn Golden was leaning on the desk in front of him, theatrically putting out the cigarette in a glass tray.

'Don't you worry, Mr. Crowe,' Golden said. 'It's a fresh pack, so plenty more where that came from. Where can I find Zack Richards?'

'I don't know.'

And Graham Cameron's grip tightened.

'Where is Zack Richards? Don't make me light another. It's not good for me, and I hear passive smoking's a terrible thing.' And Golden slapped his palm hard into the side of Bart's head. 'Who was with you? Who was with you last night, at The Lifeboat?' He slapped him again. Bart said nothing. And Golden said, 'Okay, I'll tell you who you were with. You were with my daughter, Mr. Crowe, and you told her where Zack Richards is hiding, didn't you?'

'How do you know about that?'

'Insurance Mr. Crowe. Remember?' He cuffed him again. 'So, where - is - he?'

'Okay!' Bart said. 'I met Lola last night.'

'And?'

'She wanted to know about the shooting. She was concerned, about my injury.'

'You're lying to me. I know you are fucking lying to me!'

And Golden crossed the room, taking his cigarettes with him. He peered out through the Venetian blinds and Cameron's eyes followed him, waiting for a signal.

A moment of opportunity. There might not be another.

Swinging both legs up, Bart kicked hard against the desk with both feet. And the desk lifted, rearing like a wild pony. The back of Bart's head smacked back into Graham Cameron's skull, sending the two of them keeling back onto the carpet. Pain throbbed in Bart's head. Still giddy, he spun out of the chair, clambering over Cameron, frenzied, pushing himself up, elbowing Cameron's face as he did so.

And he stood and backed into the corner of the room.

Graham Cameron was back on his feet. Golden was moving towards him, both men between him and the door. And Cameron spat and a stream of blood trickled down his chin. He stopped about five feet from Bart with his arms poised like a gunslinger, his body spring-loaded and charged with malice and cool violence. Bart anticipated a punch but Graham Cameron surprised him with a kick to his midriff. Breath rushed from his lungs. And then Cameron came at him with an elbow. And he jammed it against Bart's throat. His fist pumped twice into Bart's stomach, and Bart writhed against the wall, then dropped to the floor. Then Cameron's knee came in. It thudded into his shoulder and knocked him backwards as he tried to stand. He tried again. But pain pulsed up his spine as Graham Cameron's foot stamped on the small of his back. And staggering forward Golden was there, his fist cracking into Bart's jaw, sending him spinning towards Cameron again.

'Doesn't want to go down, does he?' said Golden, laughing.

And Bart was steadying himself against the trestle table by the wall.

Graham Cameron said, 'I'll break his fuckin' legs. That'll do it.'

And he positioned himself for the kick.

Gripping the back edge of the trestle table, Bart pulled it from its stands and he spun it around, certificates and pictures clattering to the ground. Glass frames crunching underfoot. He held the narrow table top in front of him, and he jabbed it at the two older men.

In angry breaths he rasped, 'How do you know I met Lola last night? How do you know? Tell me! I said - how - did - you - know?'

Golden grinned.

'My daughter, Mr. Crowe, is my business. I pay attention.'

And Golden grabbed an end of the plank and he pulled but Bart shoved it sideways, into Golden's stomach. Then he swung the plank at Graham Cameron - but Cameron caught it, yanking it from his grasp. Bart made a break. He ducked under the table top and he ran for the door, and he swiped the envelope of money from the desk as he passed.

The red-headed secretary barely looked up as he barrelled out of the office. And he rattled down the corridor to the exit.

But when he reached it the door was locked.

Locked. Locked. Locked!

He backed up. He rammed it and shouted and hoped the customers in the arcade would hear him and maybe phone the police. But Cameron was behind him in the corridor now. Bart turned to face him. With his back to the door, he kicked out with both feet. Graham Cameron cried out. The door creaked behind him. A tearing sound. Beginning to give. But Cameron took a hold of Bart's leg, and he pulled him back. Gripping the flimsy steel handle of the door, Bart wheeled his free foot round and clumped it into Cameron's head with enough force to make the Scot drop his other foot. And again Bart launched himself at the door. Again it creaked. Again it bent. A sliver of light. And he rammed it again. And it clattered open and Bart sprawled, face first, on the blue carpet of The Golden Arcade. It smelled of sweat and rain.

He could make out the feet of people gathering around, taking a good look. And then Graham Cameron's hand gripped Bart's leg, and Bart, twisting onto his back, pushing himself away.

'Get off of me you dirty old man!' he said. 'I won't have sex with you! Get off me you perv! Someone photograph this bastard will you?'

And Graham Cameron let go and receded into darkness, and the broken door wobbled drunkenly on a single, twisted hinge.

37

'Flowers for Mrs. Malone.'

There was no answer and he was about to ring again when the intercom clicked.

A woman's voice said, 'Just leave them outside, love. I'll send my son to collect them in a minute.'

'I need a signature.'

Bart held the flowers up to the camera.

Another long pause.

The door buzzed, then a click. He pulled it open and signalled to Lola who hurried in behind him.

At the door of the flat, a slim woman in her seventies, hair greying but still dark. Full-round glasses with thin metal rims.

Bart handed her the flowers and he held up his card.

'Mrs. Malone, my name's Bartholomew Crowe. I'm a private investigator, and -'

The door was pushed shut, but by then Bart had his foot inside the gap. The door slammed against it and he did his best not to call out. Rumbling and knocking in the flat. Sounds of panic. And as the door swung back, a blur of blonde hair. And then up close. Zack Richards charged him, his head thumping into Bart's stomach, the two of them tumbling to the ground. And Zack was on top, ready to spring away. He looked down at Bart and he grinned and he raised his fist.

But then he saw Lola.

And the rage inside him drained away and his hand fell to his side.

Lola said, 'Hi.'

*

Bart drank milky tea from a china cup and helped himself to a biscuit from a willow-pattern plate.

Mrs. Malone said, 'So, now we're all comfortable, why don't you tell us exactly what you want, Mr. -?'

'Crowe.'

The old lady nodded the way you might nod at an insurance salesman. Bart placed his tea cup on the saucer and smiled.

Then he looked at Zack and said, 'I'm working for your step-mother, but you've already guessed that.' And trying to look conciliatory. 'She's concerned about your safety -'

Zack shook his head, eyes of a cornered cat.

Bart said, 'Look, she's just worried you might be involved in -'

'Oh fuck off,' Zack said. 'Just give it a rest, okay Crowe.'

Mrs. Malone frowned.

Bart continued, '- And, she wants a meeting. That's it. One meeting. That's all. Job done. Game over.'

Richards snorted.

He said, 'Okay. So, let me think. Oh wait, actually, this is an easy one. No.'

And Bart said, 'Listen Zack, you do know I am going to have to tell someone about this place. About this address. There's my client obviously, but - I mean, then there's the police. They definitely want to talk to you, and then there's Mr. Golden. He's very keen to know where you are.'

Lola's lower lip dropped and Zack's eyes scanned the room.

Bart said, 'In fact I had a meeting with Glenn Golden this

morning. He threatened to stub a cigarette out in my eye. That was because of you. And I've been shot in the arm - that's because of you. My best friend has a hole in her gut and a twelve inch scar down her side - and that's because of you too. And that's not even counting this.' He pointed to his black eye. 'Do I need to say I've got that because of you? So, I reckon that you probably owe me anyway.'

'I don't owe you a fucking thing!' Zack snarled. Then, 'Sorry Mrs M.'

Lola took Zack's hand.

Bart ignored him and continued, 'So anyway, you should take a moment, weigh up the choices you have. Turn yourself in to the police, or disappear again. Except if you do that, then how are you going to protect Mrs. Malone, here? I mean - once Golden gets this address -'

Lola squeezed Zack's hand.

'Zack.'

And Zack Richards looked at Lola, and his eyes searched for whatever it was she kept hidden behind those pale blue eyes.

He turned to Bart and he said, 'Look, Crowe, I don't owe you shit, but I'm going to tell you how things are, okay. So shut up, and listen.'

Bart dunked a bourbon biscuit.

'All right,' he said.

Zack leaned forward. He rested his elbows on his knees.

'Well you already know about my real mum, yeah? Emily Cruz. She's Argentinian. She and Dad had wild times in the nineties. Dad was a total superstar back then, and they'd had me before it properly took off. And when it did take off and I was all over the world, man - like New York, Paris, London and - well, everywhere. And I had these really cool private tutors. Artists, musicians. I saw so much stuff. Amazing. Like learning all the time. And not just trigonometry or plate fucking tectonics, but proper soulful stuff, you know, real knowledge, and crazy crazy people.

'Trouble was that Mum was crazy people too. She'd just disappear for weeks at a time. Argentina, Paris or wherever. And sometimes I'd go with her. And wherever I went there'd be people looking after me, you know - which was great - but after a while I began to realise I was seeing Mum less and less. Dad was cool. We'd go riding and we'd shoot and camp and all of that wilderness shit. We'd go to the cool shows and restaurants. Except, more and more, when we did, there'd be this woman there, Lori. I took her for granted at first cos Dad had loads of friends and she was nice and she asked me questions. I suppose I quite liked her.

'And around that time there started being all these stories about Mum in the papers. Like drug busts and crazy parties and shit, and the stories would have a comment from Dad, and it would read as if they were together all the time - like he was by her side and getting in all this help. But he wasn't by her side at all. I didn't get it. Most of Dad's friends did drugs too, and Dad took a load himself, but none of them were ever in the paper.

'And then we were in New York one day, and Lori and Dad tell me that they're together. And at the time I'm like, okay. But what they don't tell me is they've actually been together for like, nearly my whole life. And when I think about that, and the two of them keeping that from me, I burn like crazy. So fucking angry. Like the two of them made a lie of my whole childhood, you know. And then Dad and Lori were 'captured' together for the first time - it was all staged. Totally fake. And after that, Lori took charge of pretty much everything.

'She started putting all these conditions on me seeing Mum, and you know, Mum was so fucking high all the time that she never did half the stuff she said she would, and I so wouldn't be allowed to go. And when Mum and Dad got divorced - it was my choice who I stayed with - but then Dad and Lori would always follow that up with a list of Mum's problems - and everyone I knew told me the same. And even Mum wouldn't be straight and say she wanted me, so, you know -'

Zack turned away to the side of the settee and Lola leaned over him and she stroked his hair.

Bart said, 'So now you hate Lori Cole because she made you reject your real mother. Is that it?'

And Zack's eyes burned. His eyebrows furrowed.

'Oh yeah. I hate her. But mostly because she made me hate myself. Because it was me. Not her. *I* chose them. I chose Dad and I chose Lori. I chose that fucking bitch over my own fucking mother. And when I said I wanted to live with them, Lori was just like, so fucking happy. But, you know, she was only happy for herself. She'd tell people about it on the phone. And it was like she was gloating, like she was rubbing my nose in it. I never said it was confidential or anything, but fucking hell it so was, man! It so fucking was!'

Bart leaned forward.

'Nobody's perfect,' Bart said,

'You know what, they're not,' Zack said. 'And I look back and I think, fuck, I really did choose money over love. And I think, like, fuck, I am one mercenary little bastard. And I think, *is that all I am?* Like is that all, you know, really?' He was leaning further forward, his voice breaking.'And they never wanted me either, not Lori anyway. And her and Dad totally screwed Mum over in the divorce, considering the size of the estate. And they could do that to her because of me. Because of the choice I made. So that's what I am really. I'm a traitor, I'm an entry on Lori Cole's spreadsheet.'

Bart stood up. He looked out of the window at the perfectly ordered, silent street.

Zack stood behind him and said, 'They ship me off to fucking boarding school. And no one even asks me what I think. I'd been learning everyday before - theatres, gigs, exhibitions. But Lori took all that away - in like, one hit - and what do I get instead? Fucking public school with public school pricks and soulless fucking drones teaching me their empty little lessons. So I thought, fuck it, I'll school myself. So I did.

I brewed beer, and me and my mates just got hammered. And I sold it on too. Sold weed. I sold a lot of fucking weed. They caught me of course, and they asked me to leave. Lori was so pissed.'

He laughed.

'But they don't give up. They send me to fucking Wales! And man, they are totally starved of quality product down there, and I can get the really good stuff. So I started dealing again, and not just weed this time either. Got chucked out of there quick-smart. I told Dad and Lori exactly how I felt. And I almost got Dad on board - you know, if it was just down to him - but Lori wouldn't have it, so they send me down to Kent, to this fucking shithole. Sorry Mrs. M. But you know what? I think I'm done here now. In fact I think I'm done with school, full-stop.'

Bart said, 'Well Raymond Feathers is definitely done here, isn't he? And Sophie Dean, she isn't done but she could have been.'

'Look,' Zack said, 'Your friend was nothing to do with me. And I'm sorry for Raymond. Of course I am. But he was who he was. He made his decisions.'

'So why did you kill him, Zack?'

Zack laughed.

'You know, I'm sorry. I thought we were talking about Lori.'

'Why? Did she kill him?'

He snorted.

'Maybe she did,' he said.

'You know what I think?' Bart said. 'I think that however you choose to cut it, Lori Cole has committed no crime here. And maybe she nudged you towards this mess and maybe she didn't. But Mrs. Malone has lost a grandson, you've lost a friend and, well I nearly lost mine too. No maybes about any of that, Zack. So let's draw a line under all of this. Let's go. Let's go and meet Lori. Break the circle, you know.'

Mrs. Malone swivelled in her chair and she said, 'I think

you should talk to your stepmother, Zack.'

And Lola touched his arm.

'Listen baby,' she said. 'Bart's going to have to tell the police about you and this place - he's giving you a chance here. A chance to do this on your own terms. He could have given this address over to my dad or the police already, but he hasn't done that. So I think you should go. Go and see Lori. And if you want to disappear afterwards, well, we can do that baby, we can go together. I'll go with you. I want to. Do you understand, baby? I want to be with you.'

Zack fixed Bart with a dark stare and he said, 'You're really going to tell the cops if I don't agree?'

'I'll tell them anyway,' said Bart. 'It's a question of when.'

'And it's just one meeting, yes? Just the one? No strings?'

Bart looked to the ground, head in his hands.

'Yes,' he said. 'Sure.'

38

Nestled under the long shadow of the seafront tower block, the pub was an extension of the railway buildings next to the station.

And Lori's R8 was parked outside.

It wasn't yet midday and the pub was near empty and Lori was sat by the window, at the far end of the lounge, her long legs stretching out across the carpet. She leaned back into the corner. Her hair was straightened and had been darkened again. Her drink was a rich red, clearing with the melting ice at the top of the glass.

Zack's limbs tensed and his looseness and his confidence left him. And for the first time Bart noticed that he was the taller of the two of them. Skinny boards spanned the ceiling.

When Zack pulled out a chair, Lori only half-looked.

'Hi babe,' she said.

Busy, on her phone.

And Zack said, 'Lori.'

He opened his wallet, handed Bart a twenty.

'Get me a lager. Whatever's there. And then whatever you're having.'

'Mr. Crowe, doesn't have to stay,' Lori said, and she looked at Bart and her mouth widened. She said, 'I'll transfer you a little something extra, okay.'

Zack said, 'Oh no. You know, I'm only here because of

him. I don't want to speak to you. And I want him to see you for what you really are. So Crowe stays.'

And Lori and Zack faced off. They fixed each other in a mutual death stare.

Lori broke first and she said, 'Well I don't suppose it matters.'

*

Lori moved her clasp bag as Bart placed the pints on the table. He squeezed in next to her, noticing the curve of her thighs in black jeans. She ignored him, speaking only to Zack.

'Well, I'm glad you're all-right,' she said. Her voice was deep and sugary. 'Your dad's been so worried. It has been nearly three weeks, babe.'

Zack took a mouthful of lager and wiped his mouth with his sleeve.

'Yeah. I got Dad's mail. Said the first thing he knew about it was when the police called him.'

And when Lori spoke it was just above a whisper.

'I was the one that told the police how to find him. And just so you know, he was going to cancel the tour. And in the end it was only thanks to Mr. Crowe here that he didn't.'

And her fingers touched Bart's shoulder, but she didn't turn and she didn't look.

'So is that what this is all about?' Zack said, 'You didn't want Dad to cancel the fucking tour? That figures.'

Lori smiled, knowing and defencive.

'Business first babe. You know that.'

Zack leaned back on his chair.

'So it's not that. It isn't just the tour. There's something else.'

Lori kept her gaze upon Zack and her eyes were big and sympathetic.

'If it was just business,' Zack continued, 'you wouldn't even be here, would you? You'd have just let Crowe track me until Dad came back.'

She reached out and she touched Zack's hand but he withdrew it.

A family were seating themselves at the next table.

And Lori said, 'Maybe I'm not as cynical as you think.'

Zack snorted.

'I know I'm pretty stupid and all. The wild child. Spoiled product of chaotic parents, yeah. All that. But you know that I couldn't give a shit about business. And you know how I feel about you. I'd destroy you if I could. And I'll never do anything you tell me, so why are you even -'

'I want you to come back to London, Za-'

'No you don't! You'd never say it if you did! You're only here because you want me to fuck up!' he hissed. 'You want me to get up and storm out of here. Make a little scene. Knock a few things over. Maybe get arrested. That's what you want!'

'Babe. I -'

'Jesus that's it, isn't it? That's actually it.'

The dad from the next table looked over as Zack drummed the table, lager spilling from his pint glass.

'You want to see me screw up. Get in as much of a mess as possible. Maybe even get locked up. And you? You'll be Miss perfect then, won't you? You even hired a detective to save me from myself. Fuck. Coming down to try and get me back into sch -'

'I'm sorry, Zack. But I can't keep listening to this. Excuse me.'

Lori tapped Bart on the knee. He moved to let her out and she passed behind him. She crossed her arms and when she spoke she was tearful.

'You think it's so easy, being a step-parent, don't you?' she said. 'Well I hope you have a try at it one day, I really do! I just - I need a moment, yeah?'

Bart watched her walk. She'd left her phone on the table. Zack was scrolling through the apps and messages.

'What are you doing?' Bart said. 'You can't just -'

'I thought you were a detective,' Zack said. 'Well I'm detecting. Now shut up and keep watch, all right.'

Zack's eyes scanned the screen.

Lori was taking her time.

'You don't think maybe you're being a bit -'

'Wait -' Zack said, '- wait - wait, wait - Oh shit, shit, shit! Yes! I knew it!'

Zack's eyes widened and Bart coughed and stood up. Lori was coming back. He held her seat for her. Her phone was in the middle of the table just where she'd left it.

'And what have you boys been talking about while I've been gone?'

She was renewed, refreshed and calm.

'Football,' Zack said.

'But you hate -'

'Football,' Zack repeated. 'United, doing great.'

Zack leaned back on his chair, and he exhaled theatrically.

'So,' Zack said. 'You're leaving Dad then?'

She stared at him for a little less time than Bart expected her to and she took her phone from the table.

'Have you been looking at my phone?'

The man from the next table looked across again and Lori turned to Bart.

'Didn't you stop him?'

Bart shrugged.

'What did you want me to do? Fight him? Here?'

Lori's nostrils flared and Zack leaned forwards, dark eyebrows raised.

And Zack said, 'You are! You're leaving Dad! Jesus! God, don't you get it good enough already? Jesus! You're going to destroy him, aren't you?'

'Don't be a drama queen, babe.'

'So it's true then?'

'I thought you'd be pleased.'

Zack frowned, his eyes rolling to the side.

'Well - I - I am - but shit, why are you even here, then? What do you actually want, Lori? What's the angle? Is it -' and he paused, head in hands, '- am I, like leverage?'

Lori said nothing. She sat back, something cat-like about her. Zack's eyes narrowed. The corner of his mouth curled downward.

'Oh man,' he said. 'You're going to use this, aren't you? All this shit with me and Raymond and the police. You're going to use me to squeeze Dad for every penny. You're a blackmailer.'

She looked up and tilted her head.

'Aren't we all, babe?' she said.

Zack swung forwards and he shoved the table with both hands. What was left of his pint toppled and washed over the table, over Lori and over Bart. They tried to stand but it was too late. The whole family at the next table were watching now. And the parents held their children close.

Zack's eyes narrowed.

'I wish you were dead!' he said.

And he formed an imaginary gun with his right hand. His thumb hammered out the imaginary bullet. He threw his arms in the air in a mock explosion and he stood. He kicked down his chair and he strode away. And he swept food and cutlery and condiments to the floor as he passed. The bar staff shouted and Zack gave them the finger. He stormed out of the pub and out across the road.

And his swagger was back.

Lori said, 'Walk. Don't look. Don't make eye-contact. And don't say a word.'

Fast and calm, Bart and Lori walked past the bar. And Lori looked at no one, ignored the shouting staff. But Bart looked. And he saw the barman's face, loaded with anger. He mouthed the word, *sorry*, and he did not look again.

39

The R8's V10 pushed into his back.

She said, 'You know, for a while I thought you weren't going to come through babe, but you know, I think there's enough here for a start. You did good. Maybe I'll send some more business your way.'

'Thanks,' he said.

'Just don't go quoting me on your website.'

She winked, and her whitened teeth gleamed.

And Bart's cheeks burned.

He looked at his knees and he said, 'Is it true?'

'What true?'

'That you wanted all this stuff on Zack - for a divorce. That you don't really want him back?'

Her expression hardened, but she wasn't angry.

'Don't ruin things babe,' she said.

'Because I can keep working,' Bart said. 'If you want me to. I think we could get him back, you know.'

She tapped the wheel and laughed.

'Oh Bart,' she said. 'You really think this parenting game is pretty easy, don't you?' And when he didn't reply, she said, 'It's okay. I'm sure I thought the same when I was your age. But one day you'll try it for yourself. Don't doubt it babe, you'll find it's not so easy as you think. Ten years I've been a mother to that boy - and Mickey too for that matter. And you know what? Mums get taken for granted. I bet you probably take yours for granted an all.'

Bart's hands formed loose fists.

'Probably,' he said.

'You wouldn't know this, babe, but listen. Mickey has affairs - like all the time. I know he does it. Well they're not so much affairs really, but he has a lot of sex.' And the word hung suspended in the air. 'But the thing is, we both know it's me he has to thank - for everything. And his career was in free-fall before I stepped in. Have you had any experience with addicts in your life, Bart?'

Bart thought he preferred her hair lighter.

She laughed again, and she said, 'Well, addicts aint easy either, babe. And I done what, fifteen years, sixteen? Mickey always used to be so grateful. Said I was his Guiding Star. Either that or he was just fucking horrible! But slowly you start to notice them saying the good things less and less, being horrible more and more - and kids do not help, Bart. They make it worse. Zack playing up like he did. Don't ever be a step-parent, Bart. You get all the responsibility but you don't get half the respect, or half the love. I was always the new girl. Except now. Now I'm Super-Bitch. I know what Zack says. But all I ever done was look after Mickey. And well Mickey looks after both of us, so-'

'My mum, I mean my step-mum. She left me,' Bart said.

Lori didn't say anything. She looked confused, as if this was one of those strange jokes that kids got but she did not. And then she saw he was serious.

'Sorry babe,' she said, and her hand tapped softly on his knee. 'You know, Bart, everything happens for a reason. Maybe it's for the best, in the end, eh?'

40

Roselawn Gardens curved into a cluster of emergency vehicles, uniforms clotting and clumping, luminous blots. Bart slowed as he sidled up to two police.
'What's going on guys?'
The two men ignored him.
'Is it like a heart-attack or something?'
The smaller officer turned.
'That's our business. Now you move on, son. Okay.'
So Bart moved on. He drifted across to the ambulance, tried to get a look inside, standing next to an old guy and an oldish woman who were also watching.
'The thing is,' the woman said, 'she put us all at risk, didn't she? Letting him in like that.'
'That's what happens in flats,' the old man replied. 'That's why we've got our own place. Thank God.'
A green suited paramedic kneeled beside the gurney. Mrs Malone under the cover. Bruised face. Pale, disorientated. One of the paramedics stroking her hair.
'Excuse me. But was there anyone else?' Bart said, loud and clear as he could, and he felt sick at his own lack of compassion.
The second paramedic gave him a dirty look, stepping in front of him, blocking his view.
'Sorry. I didn't mean - listen - it's just - was there a girl in

the flat? Has she gone? Have you taken her already?'

'This is an emergency operation, sir. Could you step away please.'

'Sorry but, listen, it's really important. My - my girlfriend - she was in the flat, and I need to know if she's all right.'

And the paramedic pointed. She didn't speak or smile.

Bart looked across the fracas, beyond the cars and the blue lights, and there, in her pastel blue coat with the swallows on it, Lola Golden leaned against a tree. She was talking to a woman police officer. The police officer was WPC Stock. She noticed Lola looking up and she saw Bart looking back. She made a note of something in her pad.

Bart crossed the grass, and when he reached her he saw the tears on her cheeks. Edging closer, her hand brushed his, and neither of them spoke. Then he embraced her. Her arms slid under his and she pulled him in. Her tears left silvery tracks on his shoulders.

They held each other for a clear minute without speaking, and then Lola said, 'He was wearing a mask! I just opened the door and I -'

'You let him in?'

'Yes! Yes, yes I did Bart. I let him in. That's what makes it so horrible! I just feel so - people get deliveries all the time - I just - I just -'

And she nuzzled his shoulder and she squeezed his back.

'You didn't know,' he said. 'Tell me what happened.'

'Oh Bart I've literally just told it all to the police lady - but okay - no questions though. Please, promise you won't ask questions?'

He held her tight.

'No promises,' he said.

And her grip eased on his back and the weight of her head lifted from his shoulder.

'He - ' she said. 'I mean - the man - he said he had a delivery to leave in the hall for upstairs. Said there was no answer from the bell. He had this dark skin, like tanned maybe, and this long hair sort of swept back. He had a package. He was wearing a cap and a black polo shirt. You know - he looked right! He said he needed a signature. And he had this weird accent, gruff and gravelly, cockney I suppose. But when I opened the door -'

Her voice trembled.

'Then what?'

'He kicked the door open almost before I'd unlocked it and he came at me and he grabbed me. He told me to get in the bathroom. He had my arms pulled behind my back. Mrs Malone tried to stop him, but he was just too tall, too big. She just bounced off him. He threw me into the bathroom and he hit her with the back of his hand - but like really hard! - and she just dropped. He tied my mouth and my hands and he took my phone and he shut me in the bathroom and he barricaded the door. I didn't see anything else.'

'But you heard things,' Bart said. 'Didn't you?'

She dipped her head, looking up under the heavy lids of her big blue eyes.

'Oh Bart,' she said, 'it was so horrible! And it wasn't what I heard. It was the silences - and the thumps - like working dough. And the silence again after each beating - horrible. The man wanted Zack's laptop. He kept going on about it. Over and over. The same. The same. And I could hear things being turned over, things being emptied and like, smashed. Threats and crying, and the longer it went on the angrier he sounded until he was just kind of making like animal noises. But I think someone in the building must have called the police because I heard sirens, and as soon as he heard them, he was gone. Didn't say a thing. And so I kicked at the bathroom door until - well - until I found her - Mrs Malone. Oh Bart, she was just lying there. And the sofa was turned over and the TV was cracked.'

'But the guy didn't find it,' Bart said, 'the computer I mean?'

'I don't know. I don't think so.'

She pushed herself away from him, looking over his

shoulder.

WPC Stock, was talking to a resident, but she looked at Lola, and she followed her gaze to a figure on the edge of the bend, a figure with a loose way of walking, arms like pendulums. More stagger than swagger, but there was no mistaking him. Zack Richards. And Lola left Bart where he was, walking quickly. Zack straightened, steadying himself, then he stumbled as she reached him. Lola putting her arms around him, kissing him on the lips. And Bart followed, not far behind, but Zack was already pulling away. His eyes swinging about wildly. Police. Neighbours. Ambulances. And the ambulance carrying Mrs. Malone drove past and Zack tried to free himself from Lola, but only stumbled, and he fell to his knees.

So Bart gripped him beneath his arms and he pulled him up and he hissed in Zack's ear,'Stay quiet, okay. You'll get yourself arrested.'

'I'm drunk,' he said.

'I know' said Bart.

'I'm drunk - and I'm stoned - I am as stoned - as a motherfucker, motherfucker!'

And he laughed, and then he coughed and his eyes rolled upwards. Lola leaned in, and she helped Bart to lift him.

'What's going on?' Zack said.

'Nothing's going on, baby' Lola said. 'Nothing at all. Come on. Let's get you out of here.'

And they steered him around, guiding him back up the street, the way he had come, away from the dissipating action. Three police officers stood at the edge of things and one of them looking their way. And WPC Stock began to walk towards them.

'Where's Mrs. M?' Zack said. 'What's going on Lola? Where are we going? Oh God - I am so fucking fucked!'

And Zack kept talking, a loose carousel of questions and swear words. And each time he spoke it was as if he couldn't remember what he'd said just moments before.

And WPC Stock was getting closer, but her colleagues

had paid them no further attention. Stock didn't call them. She was out on a limb, working a hunch.

'I could divert her,' Lola said, seeing Bart look over his shoulder again. 'Say I've left something in the crime scene. Something like that.'

Bart thought.

'It could work. But you know Lola, I've got him under control for now but I think he needs you here. He doesn't trust me.'

'I said, where the fuck is Mrs. M?' Zack interrupted.

Lola whispered in his ear.

'Where is she? Where's Mrs. M?' he repeated.

'I need you to keep walking baby. Stay with me, okay. Just keep -'

'Mrs M! Where the -' He wrestled himself out of Bart's grip and he staggered backwards and bumped against the fence. 'Where the fuck is Mrs M.? You - you fucking answer me now, or I'm not going - fucking anywhere!'

And Zack Richards wrenched himself away. He made his break for freedom. And he strode straight at WPC Stock. She held up her hand, instructing him to stop, but he barrelled right on past her. He shouldered her aside. Lola gave chase. And she called his name.

And then Bart knew they were screwed. And he put his hands in his pockets and watched as Zack strode on.

Stock had turned, following briskly at Zack's heels. She grabbed his shoulder but he batted her away. And now the other officers noticed, turning to face him, their big hands on their big hips. And they looked at Zack - his drunken lumber and his flailing arms. And a couple of them elbowed each other and laughed.

The pensioners and residents were shuffling awkwardly and backing away as Richards pushed through.

And Zack reached inside his Parka and he pulled out a gun. He waved the pistol in the air and he roared. The police officers weren't laughing now. They made for their radios. And one officer, a small, muscular looking guy, made a move. But Zack pointed the gun straight at him and shouted.

'Get back! Get the fuck back!'

He was in the middle of it now, surrounded by squad cars and police. And he swung his gun about, lingering on each of them. He grinned. Then he turned back, and eyes on Lola, he brought the gun back around, and he pushed the barrel against his own head, the muzzle in his ear.

And turning back to the cops he shouted, 'All right you fuckers! Look! Just look! You think you're the fucking law! You don't control a thing. You don't control a fucking thing!'

And he pulled the trigger.

The silence stretched out like a rubber band. The hammer of the pistol's mechanism clunked.

And then nothing.

Just silence.

The gun clattered to the ground and it cracked on the tarmac. And Zack Richards laughed. A loud and angry laugh that was as close to a cry as a laugh has ever been.

And the police were on him, and they crushed his face into the tarmac. And Zack Richards laughed and laughed and laughed.

DOCUMENT L

Text messages from Bartholomew Crowe to Sophie Heath: 21/11/19. 16:04 p.m.

[Dear Sophie. Good news. Bad news.]

[Good news - my client met Zack Richards today. So job done. Case closed. Getting a bonus too. The client wasn't exactly what I thought she was, but the job's done, chalked off, finito! I should be proud, I know, but I don't feel like I thought I would. You know, am I making a difference to anything? Yeah. Probably. I just don't know if it's a good one. That's all.]

[And now - in the bad news bit - I'm writing this from a police station. They're taking a statement from me - again!!! And Zack Richards is in the custody suite. I'm here with Lola - the girl from the gig - yes that one. There was a break-in where Zack was staying. And when Zack got back he pulled a gun on the police! Not at all smart.]

[So now the Police are talking about public possession of an imitation firearm and assaulting a police officer, resisting arrest. Could be a year in prison. Maybe more.]

[Note - the gun was an imitation - so not used in the murder or - you know.]

[Other news - sorry Soph, but your philosophy sucks. It sucks because there's already disorder EVERYWHERE! Just nobody WANTS to see it! I mean I used to do everything right before - school, university plans, career plans, family. So did YOU!!! And bad stuff still happened! So let's be clear. Chaos sucks. And it hurts people. And there's no escape. And no one's ever safe. And you can hide from it, sure, but chaos doesn't like that. It wants to be everywhere. And so we've got to fight it. It's down to us. For everyone. We can't just think about ourselves.]

[So anyway, I'm not coming home just yet. Not until I sort out who this gunman is. Because he's out there and I'm going to find him. And that's a promise.]

[How's that for A grade macho bullshit? Love to Noah, Bart X]

41

Simmonds parked on the jetty and looked out across the bay, rippling reflections on the water.

'And you're telling me you think this break-in guy is the Feathers guy is the Music Hall guy is the casino guy too. Is that right?'

'I think it's possible.'

'Anything's possible, Bart, but all right. I'll get the computer people to check the CCTV from the flats against that picture of yours. See if there's a possible match.' And Simmonds face took on a wry look. 'I'll tell you what. How about this? You give me your current theory. I like hearing it. Helps me to clarify my own thoughts, you know.'

'I'm not sure I have a theory exactly.'

'Humour me. Free associate.'

Bart pulled his beanie down over his ears and bounced the back of his head on the headrest.

'Okay - well - all right, so, what do we know? We know the photograph guy is a big man.'

'Like Zack?'

'Could be bigger even - Golden maybe.'

'He's got an alibi.'

'Well maybe the alibi's falsified or he hired some other tall guy to do it, Feathers let's say - Okay. So how about this? It's Feathers in the photograph.'

'So it's not the same guy then?'

'No. Whatever. I only said it was a possibility. Still is. But let's say for now it is Feathers, right. Zack gets a hold of the pic but through someone else. Like a small closed group or something. And Zack confronts Feathers about it. Feathers panics. He tells Golden, thinking his boss will clear everything up. Except Golden decides that actually the cleanest thing to do is have Feathers killed. So he sends someone - someone like Graham Cameron say - army guy - firearms experience - sweet temperament - and he has Feathers shot.'

Simmonds scratched his ear and said, 'Okay. So Golden solves the Feathers problem. But why on Earth does he need to continue? You know, why the shooting at the Music Hall? Why the break in?'

'Because, when Cameron turns over the squat at Athelstan Road he expects to find the memory card, but he doesn't find it. Golden puts the feelers out, tries to find out if Zack still has a copy - and of course Zack does have a copy! Plus Zack already knows about the connection between Golden and Feathers, and so Golden's been paying Zack off ever since, and he'll keep paying until he can find a way to kill him too!'

Simmonds stared hard at him and the stare lasted several seconds. He lifted an eyebrow.

'Wait. Just rewind there. Paying him off? Sorry, but have I missed something?'

Bart felt the heat rise in his cheeks.

'Yeah,' he said. 'I saw it, yesterday, at The Mechanical Elephant. Cameron left this package. Zack picked it up - like a drop off.'

Simmonds sighed through his clenched teeth.

'You know, I really would like to be friends with you, Mr. Crowe. I really would. But you're going to have to share these little gems with me a bit sooner, yeah. So let's just be clear. You've seen Zack being paid off by this Graham Cameron, so possibly Golden's involved. Do you have any other vital pieces of information that you'd like to share? You know, just while we're here.'

'No,' he said. 'Nothing else. Anyway. Sorry. That's it. That's my theory. I'm finished. By the way, Zack's gun. It was a dummy, right?'

Simmonds looked out across the bay to the lights of The Golden Arcade.

'Yes, it was a dummy. 8mm, Baikal. Russian. Very trendy, if you can use the word 'trendy' about a gun. Crooks get them converted, but this one was clean. The report says the gun used at the Music Hall was a 9 mil. So, not the same one, old boy, even if it wasn't a fake.'

'And Feathers.'

'Also a 9mm. Could have been the same weapon as the Music Hall, but you'd probably guessed that.' Simmonds paused and he milked the tension. 'You know there is one little problem with your theory, Bart?'

'Go on.'

'I can see how the gunman could have known that Zack would be at the Music Hall. Richards is the girl's manager after all. That makes sense. But, how did the same guy find out about the flat in Roselawn Gardens? I mean you are still making that link aren't you? And so soon after you found it too. Speaking of which, how did you find it?'

'I followed him home.'

Simmonds frowned.

'I never trust a short answer, Mr Crowe. But okay. Lola Golden - you didn't tell her the address in advance. So who else?'

Bart pulled his hat from his head. He twisted it in his hands.

'No one. I didn't tell anyone. Only Lola and my client and myself - maybe there's some other way - I just don't think Lola would -'

'Could it be your client, then?'

'She's not that stupid, Wayne. Anyway she's not involved in the rest of this stuff.'

'Were you tailed, then?'
'No.'
'Tracked?'
'I don't think so, but -'
'So it must have been -'
'Lola? No it couldn't -'

But Simmonds performed a drum roll on the steering wheel and said, 'Might explain why the attacker didn't give her the rough stuff though, wouldn't it? Blood is thicker than water, after all.'

Simmonds pressed the starter and the car lit up, headlights flaring on the waves.

'Come on,' he said. 'Time I clocked off. Where do you want to go?'

42

Eight o'clock, Friday, young men in skinny jeans filling the seats outside The Lifeboat pub, smoking, vaping, drinking beer, spilling out from the door in groups and huddling for several minutes, before filing back inside and into the warm, where middle-aged men squashed in at the bar, heavy built locals and Londoners in Crombies and DMs, women in twos and threes, voices slicing the background swell and sinking into it again, and at the back of the room, a blonde kid in a black sweater stood on a chair, forming a loud hailer with his hands.

'Hey buddy! Over here!'

Bart was the last to arrive. Zack and Lola were already there, Francesca De Souza too, in bright orange and teal, all had finished one drink at least. Lola's eyes met his and a thin silver pendant sparkled around her neck.

'Good to see you, man.' Zack waved a twenty in his face. 'A G&T for Lola, erm whatever Franny's having, an I'll have an IPA and a JD and Coke, and yeah like whatever you're having too, okay.'

Bart was ten pounds down when he came back from the bar. He brought the drinks back in two trips. He kissed Lola on the cheek. Francesca offered him her hand. He kissed that too and she grinned, and she winked at him as he perched on the edge of the bench.

Zack was beaming, and he slapped Bart on the back as he sat.

'Imitation firearm in a public place, buddy! That's it! Probably just a suspended sentence. Dad's lawyers are shit hot, man. Freedom!' He raised his glass, and he laughed as beer spilled over his wrist. 'So listen buddy,' his breath wet in Bart's ear, 'what do you make of my stand-in mother then? Piece of work isn't she?'

'Okay, she's no angel, but -'

Zack cut him off.

'She's a fucking bitch, man. Anyway, her people are coming to pick me up tomorrow. Take me home. Maybe I'll even go. Hey man, Lola told me about you, I mean what happened with your mum. She totally dumped you, buddy! That sucks.'

Bart's jaw tightened.

'Maybe it's for the best,' he said.

Zack stared at him, blank for a moment, and then he said, 'Whatever. Let's drink.'

But Zack's eyes were already floating, his head swaying. His body too. He lolled over, patting Bart on the back. 'You're all-right, man, you know.'

'Where'd you get the toy gun?' Bart said.

'What? Oh that! London. Had it a couple of years now. One of Dad's mates bet me he could get a real one in 24 hrs. Took him a week and he only managed to get me that fake! I love it though! Been carrying it everywhere. Gone forever now the cops have got it, though eh. Gutted!'

'Maybe you shouldn't have pointed it at them.'

A flash of irritation on Zack's face, but it was quickly replaced by something else, mischief and malice. His blonde hair flopped across his face and he lurched forward as he made a grab for Bart's cheeks. He wobbled them when he spoke.

'Come on, Bartholomew! Live a little!'

And then he slipped off his chair.

When he got up, he sat still for a while, head down and deep breaths. And Lola, who had been making small-talk with

Francesca about clothes and hair holidays, glanced over but she didn't look concerned.

'He's okay,' Bart said, and he turned to face her. 'How are you? Are you good?'

'I'm fine,' said Lola. 'Nice end to a bad day.'

And Bart said, 'Have you been to see Mrs -'

'Zack's going tomorrow before he goes back to London. He knows her best. I really don't want to think about it. So tell me, how are you now you've solved your case?' And Bart must have frowned because Lola said, 'Oh dear.'

'Oh I don't know. I know I should be happy,' Bart said, 'but it's like a pint of beer. I mean, I have it and I want it and I'll drink it all and be satisfied in a way. But then I'll remember that the world's just the same, except I haven't got a beer anymore.'

She smiled at that. She reached over and she ruffled his hair.

'Go home, Bart,' she said. 'See your friends. Get some rest. You should be proud. You did it. You're a success. You've got to take the positives -'

And then Zack's arm wrapped around his shoulder.

'Oh don't listen to her Bart! I still think you're a dick. Stay here. And don't forget that somewhere out there, there's a bullet with your name on it! So fuck it man, enjoy yourself! Plus, there's always more people to upset, right?'

Francesca squeezed out from her seat and she kissed Zack on the head and said, 'Your life's motto, isn't it Zack? Always one more person to upset.'

Zack snorted with laughter as Francesca made her way to the toilets. Lola laughed too, but Bart stood up, and he gathered up his coat and he said, 'I'm going. I made a mistake - You know, you guys can laugh about it, but Jesus, my best friend's back home with a hole in her side, and you guys aren't even worried? Seriously? Because I am! I'm terrified! I mean, maybe there is a bullet with my name on it. Or maybe it's got your name on it, Zack, or yours Lola, or even Franny's. So I'm not going home. I'm going to stay. And I'll do it because I want to stop this guy before he does it again, to any of us! So you guys laugh it up. I'll catch you later.'

Lola fixed him with a stare.

'You're overreacting,' she hissed. 'For God's sake sit down. Look, we're all worried, Bart. Of course we are. But think about it - what do you actually want here - you want to see us all shivering and cowering in a corner somewhere? Really? Is that what you want? And anyway it looks to us like that gunman was aiming at you. So maybe if you did go home we'd all be a lot safer.'

Bart pulled his hat down over his ears.

'Okay, Lola,' he said. 'So it's me he's after, is it? Then what about the break-in? Was that guy after me too? Because I don't think he was. And have you even thought about why you got off so easy? Why Mrs. Malone took a beating and yet you -'

A clumsy hand loomed up from beneath him, grabbing his collar, pulling him down.

'Don't you fucking upset my girlfriend, Crowe, you fucking dick!'

People were looking now. Lola touched Zack's free hand.

'It's okay,' she said.

Zack relaxed. He released his grip, and he gave Lola his hand which she locked in hers. Then she gave him his hand back, standing and slipping her arms into her pale blue coat.

'I suppose you had better come with me,' she said. 'Wait here baby. We won't be long.'

And she kissed Zack on the top of his head and threaded through the tightly packed drinkers to the door, Bart close behind.

They passed Francesca on the way out and Lola said, 'Franny?'

Francesca raised an eyebrow.

'Make sure Zack doesn't follow us, could you?'

Francesca winked.

'No problem.'

And Lola took Bart outside, down a side-street, away from the smokers and the passers-by, and she said, 'Okay, so you've clearly got some kind of a problem here, so -'

Bart took a swig of his lager. Then he put the glass down on the pavement behind him.

He crossed his arms and he said, 'I just wanted to know why you didn't get hit like Mrs. Malone? I mean, it's almost like the guy knew who you were.'

'Maybe he just knew who I wasn't.'

'If he didn't know who you were,' Bart said, 'I figure he would have found out, or he'd have assaulted you too? But he didn't even ask you your name, did he?'

She pursed her lips.

'Look, I really can't remember. I don't know, okay? Maybe I was next. The sirens disturbed him before -'

'And why didn't he try to use you to make the old lady talk?'

'Maybe he's just not as twisted as you are?'

She looked uncomfortable in a way he'd never seen before.

'Have you got your phone on you?' he asked.

She nodded, took it from the pocket of her coat and showed it to him.

'Lola. This is important. Did you tell your dad where Zack was hiding?'

She began to walk away but he gripped her arm and held her.

'Please,' he said. He released her arm. 'I do trust you Lola, but I need to know.'

She stopped, and she turned to face him.

'I didn't tell him anything! Of course I didn't!'

'Listen.' Bart breathed in. 'You need to give me your phone.'

She frowned, backed away.

'I am not giving you my phone.'

'Just think about it, will you? Just for a second. I get this anonymous text telling me you're going to be with Zack at The Turner. Your dad knew we'd met here last night. And then as soon as I figure out where Zack is hiding, your dad seems pretty keen to know that too. I don't tell him. I don't even tell you! And then, once you're there, suddenly someone knows. It's your phone, Lola. It has to be.'

She looked up, and her eyes were big and her brow furrowed. He took a step towards her. She backed away. But he pushed on.

'It's your dad, Lola. It's Glenn. He hires me to check on you. He pays Cameron to check on me. Of course he's tapped your phone. It's so his style - you've got to admit that. Give the phone to me, Lola. Please. Just for a day. My friend Noah, he's great with this stuff. Just let him look at it.'

She looked at her phone for several seconds, and her fingers closed around it and her nostrils flared.

'Just where do you get off?' she said. 'I mean where, exactly? Like, I've tried so hard to help you and - and I suppose I thought that you were a nice guy - but then you come out here, tonight, when I'm out with my friends, and you tell me that my dad is what, like some kind of criminal mastermind? That he hired that man who locked me in a bathroom and beat up an old lady? And you've got the nerve to say I got off easy! You think that was nice for me today, Bart? Because it wasn't nice at all. It was really, really horrible.'

Bart slapped the wall. His hand felt dirty and wet.

'I'm trying to help you, Lola! I like you for God's sake. I really like you. Okay? I mean I think you're beau-' And he paused, like a trolley on the crest of a hill with nowhere to go but down. 'I want to protect you, Lola. I - I just want to make sure that everything's okay.'

'Oh Bart,' she said.

She held her phone close in both hands.

A couple turned the corner with arms around each other's waists, and a man walked down from the other end the street.

Bart said, 'If you won't do it for me, do it for Zack. He's in danger, Lola. Real danger. Give me the phone. I'll go right now. I'll take it away and no one will find you here, at least not tonight.'

She looked at the ground and then back to the corner and the entrance to the pub.

'You guys got a light?'

The man was standing there. He was close to them. A big man with a long, dark coat, and shoulder length hair. He wore wayfarer sunglasses at night and he had covered his face with a scarf. His voice was a gravelly cockney.

Lola's expression froze. Only her eyes moved.

Bart said, 'We don't smoke.'

'That's a shame,' the man growled, 'cos the only light I got is this gun.'

And his arm wrapped around Lola's waist. She struggled but he dug his hand into her side, the gun into the small of her back. He wore black leather gloves.

'All right now listen,' his voice like an East-End hard man. 'Me and the girl ere, we're goin' on a trip. Now I aint gonna hurt her less you give me reason, right. But if you move from that spot in the next five minutes or if I'm followed, I'll shoot er head off, then I'll come back an I'll shoot you an' all. Plain-n-simple. Do you believe what I'm telling you?'

'You killed Raymond Feathers?' Bart said.

'Do - you - believe - I'd pull the bloody trigger?' the bearded man hissed.

'I reckon you're capable of pretty much anything,' Bart said.

'Oh I am mate,' the man said. 'I truly am.'

And he jabbed the gun into Lola's back and she made a sound of muted fear. She had closed her eyes.

The man backed away, and he took her back with him.

'At The Music Hall,' Bart said. 'My friend. The girl. You shoot her too?'

The bearded man ignored the question.

'We're going,' he said. 'Remember, I got no quarrel with you, or the girl. It's Richards I want. And he knows what else. I'll be in touch. Got it?'

Bart nodded.

'Yes.'

'Good. Now don't you move or I'll kill her and I'll be no worse off.'

The man nuzzled into Lola's ear and she winced, eyes shut tight. And he whispered into Lola's ear as he pulled her back up the street, back into the darkness of the car park. Bart was rooted to the spot, watching the girl he had almost called beautiful being taken away.

43

'What the fuck do you mean, *she's gone*?' Zack said.

'Okay,' Bart said. 'Listen. I'll say it again. Some guy - big man, big beard, black hair, semi-automatic pistol - sticks his gun in Lola's back and takes her. She's gone.'

Zack lunged at him. Francesca had a hold of Zack's arm, struggling to pull him back.

'If this is a wind up I swear to God -'

'Do I look like I'm joking?'

'So where did they bloody go?'

'I saw a car and a van drive away down the seafront. I didn't see Lola in either, but I've got pictures. I was hoping you'd be able to tell me something.'

Zack wobbled on his feet. The alcohol in his blood mixed with his thoughts and separated back out again. He moved his head back and blinked as Bart put the pictures in front of him - a white van and a green hatchback.

And Zack said, 'No. I don't know them. I don't know where they've gone.'

Bart said,'Have you still got the computer? Maybe there's something -'

Zack shook his head.

'Gave it to the cops, man. No choice. Had it stashed in the back of the Smart. And I lost the car too. Had it registered to Raymond bloody Feathers, didn't I?'

A grin flashed across Zack's face before he could correct it.

Bart said, 'What was on the computer, Zack? I mean, what was our bad guy looking for?'

And Zack's grin popped out for a second run.

'That would be telling, wouldn't it? I'll tell you what's not on it though.' He pulled a micro SD Card from his pocket, the same brand as the one that Bart had found in the squat. 'This!'

'So, what's on-'

'I'm not telling you what I've got, Crowe.'

'Will it help us find Lola?'

'It'll help me find her. You're going to fuck off back to where you came from. Remember?'

'I never said -'

'This is my business. Not yours.'

Zack shouldered Bart aside and he forged out into the crowd with Bart following in his wake, and making apologies to the many that Zack pushed aside.

Outside, the fine rain fell in a drenching mist and Zack held his phone to his ear as he crossed the road to the front. Bart and Francesca trailed behind him as Zack strode on, past the couples and drunkards, past The Mechanical Elephant and the bus stop, and on to The Golden Arcade. And he banged on the glass doors, pushing them open and barging inside, and taking centre stage in front of the CCTV.

'Come on out, Golden! Come out Glenn Golden, you spineless shit!'

And he turned and smacked the glass panel of a grabbing machine. A hundred stuffed Minions shuddered.

Bart followed him in, but Francesca remained outside. She shook her head. Her pink coat pressed against the glass door.

'Come and get me Glenn Golden! Come on you fucker!'

Bart looked back at the door but Francesca had gone.

Zack was still playing to the cameras. Bart stayed close but tried to keep out of shot.

And then the supervisor brushed past, a spotty lad, tall, skinny, early twenties, long, lank hair, dyed black. And he looked nervous, getting as close to Zack as he dared, leaning forward like a small bird looking for crumbs.

'Okay guys,' he said. 'I'm calling the police, okay!'

And when Zack looked at the lad, Bart saw ideas of violence flash across his face. He squared up to the young man and he raised his fists in the air, and then he turned, brought both fists down, slamming the glass of a first-person shooter, and then again, this time with both elbows. The glass thudded but it didn't break. And so he continued. Zack thumped and smacked on the glass as Bart headed to the door at the back of the arcade.

The crack of glass when it finally broke.

Bart turned around and Zack was grinning, and walking towards him, the supervisor following, protesting at every step.

Glenn Golden had made repairs to the door since Bart's visit that morning. He'd screwed wooden batons across the frame and a new padlock held it shut. Bart rattled the door, but it wouldn't budge. He began to scan the arcade for something he could use as a crowbar, but then Zack came in, cracking his foot against the door, over and over, an assault, battering and denting the skin of the door and testing the batons and rattling the lock. He was relentless. And once his foot had broken the skin the top hinge was wrecked soon after.

And the door banged and the door shook.

Bart crossed the arcade to the booth. The supervisor had left it open. There were keys on a hook beneath the desk and Bart walked in and took them. The skinny supervisor rushed back, tried to intercept him, blocking his way and grabbing Bart's shoulder. But Bart elbowed the young man aside and his head bumped against the door-frame. Bart was surprised at how light the lad was, now holding his nose, blood dripping down the back of his hand. He was crying.

Bart paused. He swallowed and he scratched his neck, not knowing what to say. Nothing he could say. He left the kid there and came out into the middle of the arcade. He spread his arms wide, advancing on the remaining customers.

'Okay you lot. Out! Arcade's closed. Yes, you too mate. Come on.'

And the supervisor shuffled towards the door with his hands over his face and blood dripping from his nose, and the remaining spectators herded out too. And they milled around outside with the crowds on the street. Bart kept his head down and covered the length of the building, locking the heavy glass doors as he went.

At the final door the skinny supervisor twitched. His mouth spasmed as he tried to find the part of his brain that made words.

'Uh can I uh - can I uh just get - my coat? It's just um - it's just it's - my wallet. It's just -'

He nodded towards the booth.

Bart pushed a fifty into the lad's hand.

'Get a cab and come back tomorrow. We won't touch it, okay.'

And then Bart pushed him back, locking the last door and turning out the lights. And he followed Zack Richards down the passage to Glenn Golden's office.

44

Zack lounged in Glenn Golden's office chair with his feet on the desk. He had helped himself to a cigarette and smoke clouded around him like thought. He leaned forward, nudging the packet to Bart.

'You want one?'

'No. Thanks,' Bart said. 'I don't. There's no one here, Zack.'

'There will be soon - if he knows what's good for him.'

'You mean Golden?'

'Who the fuck else? Of course I mean fucking Golden. Fuck.'

Bart moved to the window and peered out through the blinds.

'We should go. We won't be able to find her from a police cell.'

'I don't hear any sirens,' Zack said, tipping the ash from his cigarette onto the carpet. 'Relax man. Golden just needed a little shake. That's all.'

Zack smiled to himself as light squeezed in through the blinds. A car roared up on the backstreet behind the arcade. Its tyres scraped on the loose asphalt. The back door of the arcade rattled, and Bart jumped back as Golden's face appeared at the window. Golden rapped on the glass and the rain fell harder in the alley.

'I couldn't find the damned key!' he shouted. 'You'll have to come out through the window!'

Zack swung up from his seat. He crossed the room, dropping his cigarette on the carpet, and he put his face to the window inches from Golden's.

'Come on then, Crowe,' he said. 'Taxi's arrived.'

And Zack unlocked the window and he clambered through with an agility that belied his drunkenness. Bart was close behind but he was clumsier, and he fell on his hands in the street. And the two of them bundled in the back of Golden's Jaguar, rolling against the leather upholstery as Glenn Golden accelerated away.

They heard sirens and a police car passed them as they drove through a green light, heading South.

So you've got Sherlock with you,' Golden called from the front. 'Two toe-rags for the price of one eh? Special offer.'

45

It was a big place with grounds that sloped up to the road where tall ferns left crenellated shadows on the walls. An iron gate, remotely keyed, kept undesirables out. The gravel drive made white noise as they pulled in beside a modern, glass-fronted extension, and the back door opened onto a wide, open space, a curtain separating a lounge from a games room. There was a large settee. Covered in green velour. Probably antique.

Bart and Zack sat as Golden came back with bottles of Bud from the kitchen. His pale blue shirt was unbuttoned at the top and he was bare-footed, thick toenails with yellow ends.

'Little drinky for you,' he said. His tone was soft and he poured himself a whisky. 'You know boys, it's a shame I had to bring you back here really. I've got the keys to a - lock-up, I suppose you'd call it. And that would have been much more convenient.' And his tone changed, hardening. 'But I need to be here tonight, don't I? For when the bloody cops come round to tell me a pair of fucking idiots have broken into my arcade and made a fucking scene! He left the statement hanging. 'You know, I've got to hand it to you Sherlock.' And he raised his glass to Bart. 'You've delivered the goods my boy, in the end, haven't you? So let's hope it's worth it. So, what's the deal, Zack? After all, there's always a bloody deal, isn't there?'

Zack drank from his bottle and rested it on the arm of the settee.

'Where's Lola, Glenn?'

Glenn Golden puled a box of cigarettes from the mini-bar.

'I wouldn't know where she is any more than you would,' Golden said. 'First I heard of any of this was when you called. So you watch your tone, boy. And I'll remind you this is my daughter we're talking about.'

'Have you phoned the police?' said Bart.

'Not yet. I don't yet know the full situation yet, do I Sherlock? So is someone going to fill me in, or are we going to keep dancing around each other like a bunch of fairies?'

'Should I phone them now?' Bart said. 'The police I mean, so they can get started?'

Glenn Golden stood over him, all six foot three of the man.

And he snarled, 'You wanna push my buttons, do you Sherlock? Well, do you? Well I'll tell you what. How about you tell me everything *you* know, right now - or I swear I'll - you little shite!' And then he paused, and he breathed deeply. 'This is my house, you understand? My house. And in my house you do it my way or you can fuck off and see how far you get. My house. My rules. You got that, Sherlock?'

Zack looked at Bart and nodded, and Bart told Golden about the back-street. He told him about the tall guy with the black beard and the long coat and the cockney accent. He told him about the green hatchback and the white van and Golden listened intently.

And when Bart had finished he said, 'So, Sherlock, I suppose the first question is - who is this fella? Isn't it?'

Zack banged his beer bottle on the table.

'Oh for fuck's sake Glenn, come on! Stop playing games! You know who it is! I know who it is! Just stop all this bollocks man, and tell me where to go to pick her up. I'll give you the fucking files. No problem. Just make the call, let her go and we'll finish this shit. I give up, okay.'

Glenn Golden extracted a cigarette, and he looked hard at the two of them. Skinny lads with their slim brown bottles of beer. He snorted.

'Fucking children!' he said. 'Look at you both. You're kids. Got no responsibilities - either of you - and that's the trouble. You know when I was eighteen -' He lit his cigarette, dragged and exhaled. 'When I was eighteen. Well, it was a different world I suppose. We had responsibilities. You guys today, it's not responsibilities, it's choices. Choices, choices, choices. You choose this. You choose that. An' you make your fucking choices and you please your fucking selves and that's your fucking lot. And then, when you don't like the consequences of your choices, well, all you've got to do is *make another fucking choice and everything's supposed to go away, isn't it?* Not a jot of responsibility in sight. You know when I was eighteen I had to support my Mum and my brother and three sisters. And I give all the money I had to my mother. Because she needed it more than me. But you two. Fuck. Self-obsessed gobshites, the pair of you. You really think I'd kidnap my own fucking daughter - No, no, no. You see, unlike you, I understand what responsibilities are.'

He took another drag on the cigarette.

Zack said, 'Oh come on, Glenn! Lay off, will you? What do you actually want here?'

Smoke streamed from Golden's nose - he raised his head and his eyelids fell.

'What do I want? Well, let me see. What have I loaned you that eight grand for, again?'

Zack said, 'You haven't *loaned* me anything. Go fuck yourself!'

'Oh I think it was a loan, Mr. Richards. But anyway, what was the security on that loan, now? Oh yes, it was that little picture that was supposed to be on your computer - except that my friends in the police, they say that it's not there.'

Zack stood and he stepped closer to Golden.

'You're talking to me about loans and photographs when your daughter is missing? And you seriously expect me to believe that you don't know where she is? Bollocks!'

Glenn Golden smiled benignly and Zack moved across to the fireplace, taking a cigarette from Golden's pack and rolling it between his thumb and forefinger.

Bart leaned back on the sofa and he said, 'But you think you can find her though, don't you, Glenn? What with all that spyware you've put on her phone. That's why you're not panicking, isn't it? That's why you're cutting a deal. You think you can get what you want, then check the software, and go collect. Maybe Graham's already on his way to wherever, right now.'

Glenn Golden stubbed out his cigarette and he stared at Bart without speaking.

'Oh - my - God,' Zack said. 'The detective's fucking right isn't he? You're spying on your own daughter, you twisted fuck.'

Zack turned. He kicked the coffee table. And he kicked it so hard it toppled forward, Bart's beer falling to floor and draining onto the carpet.

Golden grabbed Zack's arm but Zack shook him off. He sat down at Golden's laptop with Golden behind him, pulling at him, muttering threats.

'You don't know what you're doing, kid!'

Gravel crunched outside as a car pulled up.

Zack tapped the keyboard and clicked on the mousepad.

Glenn Golden lunged for the machine but Zack swung a fist over his shoulder into the big man's throat, and Golden fell, holding his throat, rasping.

And Zack turned in the chair and he said, 'Do you want to start a fight with me? Now? Really? With the cops on their way here? I mean, do you? Because if you do, I'm fucking in!' Then, softening, 'Look man. This Microsoft shit is older than I am. I was born with this stuff okay. So shut up and leave me to it, yes.'

Bart got up. He helped himself to a whisky from the mini bar, and pressed his face to the glass looking for the car outside.

Zack turned to Golden and said, 'Okay, so I need your password.'

And Glenn Golden shouldered him aside as he entered the code.

And Zack said, 'Shit man! This thing has got like every text to and from Lola's phone. Some from me. You too, Crowe. Shit! Oh God! I'm sorry but Crowe, you are so sad.'

'Just click on the fucking GPS, will you,' Golden growled, and then he reached for his cigarettes.

Zack clicked, and clicked again.

'It's not working.'

Golden leaned over, squeezing the unlit cigarette between thumb and forefinger.

'Let me see.'

And he moved the mouse around and he tapped the keyboard harder as if he didn't trust the machine to do its job, and he put his hands behind his neck and walked towards Bart at the window.

Zack slapped the keyboard with the palm of his hand.

And Bart said, 'Her phone's switched off isn't it?'

'Yeah,' said Zack. 'It's almost like our guy knew what you were up to, Glenn.'

'Either that, or he's got half a brain in his head,' Bart added. 'I mean, would you really let a kidnap victim keep their phone, knowing what the police can do, now? I wouldn't.'

And when Golden turned he looked genuinely upset.

'You know what Crowe? You - are a fucking gobshite and a smartarse. And you are no fucking use to me whatsoever. I'm thinking you should leave.'

Bart looked about the room, and he tried to focus, to find something that made him necessary. But there was nothing. So he steadied himself and squared up to Golden.

Bart said, 'You know what, Golden. You're all show,' his chest swelling. 'You're the one with nothing. You're empty. And maybe you do know who's kidnapped your daughter. Maybe Zack knows too. Maybe. But the thing is, what good is that if you can't find him? This whole big man, Glenn Golden thing. It's all an act, and you're a sham.'

Golden clenched a fist and he said, 'You take a look at yourself, boy! You think *I'm* all show! Fucking little Sherlock. Who the fuck are you then? Answer me that, cos I don't bloody know? You're not a detective. Not a professional. Not like any that I've ever dealt with. And who's paying you for this? I'm not bloody paying you, I know that. And you owe me a grand. So that makes you a fraud as well, doesn't it? You're the only fake here, Mr. Crowe. Nobody wants you. You're not needed. So get out. Get out of my house. Get out of my business. And while you're about it, get the fuck out of my town!'

Bart looked to Zack for support but Zack gave him none.

Glenn Golden crossed his arms, and he placed his legs wider apart.

But Bart said, 'You two! You think you've got this sewn up, don't you? So confident. But you can't do it. You don't know enough. Well, do you? So tell me what you've got. I can help. I'll help you get your daughter back! You know, whatever this is, I'm already in it. Give me a chance, okay?'

Golden waited, evaluating, like a farmer at a stock market, and then he sneered and hot smoke streamed from his nose.

'Now you listen to me,' he said. 'You are nothing, Bartholomew Crowe. You're nothing. You're a lost little boy. Nothing more. So why don't you put your sorry little arse in your pretty little car and fuck off back home to your Mummy and Daddy, and leave the men to do their work, all right?'

Bart frowned.

'You're serious? You really think you can do this *by yourself*. You're such a big man, Glenn Golden. You know, while we're thinking about ourselves you might stop and think about *who really created this mess*? Because you know what? From what I can see, all of it, every miserable thing that's happened here, it's all on you, Glenn. You think no one's paying me? Well my best friend has a bullet hole in her side. She's lucky to be alive. So I say to you, I've got plenty to work for.'

At the back of the room, the curtains parted. Graham Cameron stepped in, and he hooked his thumbs into the pockets of his jeans. Glenn Golden poured another glass of whisky and he smiled without happiness.

'Sherlock, Sherlock, Sherlock. Such a simple fella aren't you? Someone to blame for everything. Always a cause and an effect. I bet you were really good at school. Always there, ready with an answer. Teacher's little pet I expect. Oh that's fantastic. Good for you, I say. And I'll tell you what. You need to get yourself back to that cosy little world. Get yourself off to a posh university. Get a cosy little job somewhere. Be a doctor. Be a lawyer. You'd be good at that. All neat and tidy, cause and effect. Of course I'm not from your world, Mr. Crowe. Where I come from the only thing that matters is getting the right result for yourself and for those closest to you. And you know why? It's because the rest of the world is doing exactly the same fucking thing.

'Now I wasn't great at school. I've not got any of them qualifications you modern lot stack up. And my dad didn't have any neither. No, my dad worked in a paper mill and drank like a sailor. And he'd come home and he'd hit my mother when he was pissed. And Mum was a boozer too. And sometimes he'd give her no money at all. And she would have to beg for booze from the neighbours and from family and that - and maybe she'd get some food as well. And I was on the streets all hours back then, on the lookout for cash. A bit of shoplifting here, a bit there. Always plenty of older lads'd pay me to steal to order. Clothes and shit. Some of them would give me little packets to take places. And every time I picked up or dropped off, I saw these guys with wads of money. Tens and twenties. And girls too. Pretty girls. And I thought I'd have me some of that one day. And so I started selling as soon as I could. For others at first and then for meself. Pretty quick I was making good money. About your age I was. And I was earning way more money than my Dad ever did. And I let him know it too. I gave money to mum and it was my house then. I came and I went as I pleased. Mum couldn't do enough for me. I brought mates back, and girls, and Mum and Dad never raised a finger. Dad just stayed out later, getting more drunk. It wasn't legal, what I was doing then, and it wasn't right. But it felt good and I did it, and I'd do it again. So tell me Crowe, who was to blame for all that? Me? Or not me?'

Bart shifted uncomfortably. Golden's eyes widened and his mouth hung slightly open, showing the tips of his yellowed teeth.

'Anyway that's how I learned my numbers. Not in some schoolroom with grades and fucking stickers. I drank and smoked and dealed and fucked. And pretty soon I came to realise that most of the lads I once looked up to were weak. No work ethic. I saw 'em getting caught and arrested and stabbed and shot. And I started to make sure some of them did get arrested - or otherwise dissuaded. But you know what, Mr. Crowe, a crook can't be a crook forever. My little kingdom could've crumbled with a single knock at the door. And that was no good. I needed something that would offer me protection in law. Insurance if you like. And that's when I discovered property. Legitimate income. So I bought places and I rented them. It wasn't instant, Mr. Crowe, but I made money. And it was easy. Money for old rope. And it wasn't thieving or dealing or any of that stuff, but the principles were the same. And that was my education. Problem was, once I was legit, I couldn't stay in Birmingham any more. Too many people with too much to say. So I looked around until I found Margate. It was cheap back then, and by the sea, and there was government money to be had. So I bought big houses and turned them into care homes and kids' homes, or bed and breakfasts for DSS. And then there was my casino, and my arcade. All little vanities.

Little profits. But you know, I'm a gambler, Crowe. I like a flutter. But good gamblers don't lose, do they? So I never do. I do what I have to and I take what I can. And you can hate me if you want. And you can try and bring me down. But can you blame me? Truthfully? Because I don't blame myself. Never. Because what was the alternative? Poverty? Depravity? Death? Dependence? No, no, no. I do what's necessary. And right now, Mr. Crowe, it's necessary for you to leave. Graham will take you where you need to go.'

Bart looked from Golden to Zack, and from Zack to Graham Cameron and not one of them offered him hope. Zack was leaning forward in his chair, waiting to see what Bart would do. His expression was unreadable.

'You know you're wrong, Glenn,' Bart said. 'I mean - you say everyone else is doing the same as you. but they're not! They're just not! You know why? Because the moment they do, you're screwed! We all are. So you know what, I'll go. Okay. I'll get out of here. And you can do what's 'necessary' and you can go to Hell, and I'll do what's right. You coming Zack?'

Zack Richards flicked his hair and said, 'You'd should go, buddy. It's for the best.'

And Bart could feel his stomach churn.

And Golden's pale eyes gleamed and his chest swelled.

'Okay.' Bart said. And he finished his drink and he placed down the glass so that it made a loud clink. 'But you better open those gates for me because I'm walking out of here alone. I think I need some air. It's all a bit close in here.'

And Graham Cameron glowered as he passed.

46

At the water's edge, the calls and shouts of the dying night disappeared into the ripples and mist. He pulled down his beanie and held the phone to his ear and the November chill tickled his cheeks.

'You're going to need to report this through the proper channels -'

'I know,' Bart said. 'But I'm telling you, we've got to take action - do something - tonight - or there's going to be a mess. God Wayne, I don't know what to do - and I - well - I think I trust you.'

'I wish I could say the feeling was entirely mutual, but all-right. Go on. Talk.'

'Right, well, the kidnapper - it has to be the same guy that beat up the old lady today. That's obvious, right? Too many similarities.'

'Such as?'

'The accent. Maybe it's real, maybe it's fake, but both the same. Then the long, dark hair. He must be the same guy, he must be. And the guy tonight had a gun, and I can't be sure but I've been looking on the net and think it was a Heckler and Koch. That's a 9mm. Could be the same gun from the Music Hall shooting and the Feathers murder. I mean, how many people in this country have an automatic pistol? And then there's Glenn Golden. He knows something. I don't know what it is but it's something, and he's planning to act on it, whatever it is.'

'Okay Bart. So let's say Golden does know something, and let's say that Richards is in on it. What exactly do you think is going to happen between now and tomorrow?'

'Golden was ready to torture me to get to Richards. And now they're working together. That's a pretty dramatic turn around. Golden's daughter is missing, and he knows about it but he's not reporting it. There's already been a murder and a shooting and, God, I just know someone else is going to get hurt, unless we step up and we stop it.'

'All right, all right, slow down. Look, let's be honest. We don't actually know what's going to happen. So the real question is, how do we find this girl?'

'Well, I've got the plates of vehicles that left the scene straight after the snatch. I can mail you the pics. You guys can track the vehicles and identify owners, can't you? And that has to lead us somewhere, right?'

There was a pause. Wayne Simmonds let out a long breath.

'Bart - if you report the crime we can look at that, yes. But I can't just run number plates on a whim. Do you have anything else?'

His arm dropped and the phone hung loose at his side, the waves lapping at his feet.

'Bart? - you still there? Hello?'

'Hi. Look. Okay. Listen. I just need - God - tomorrow - it's going to be too late. I need your help now, Wayne! And I need someone to believe what I'm saying. Someone who believes in justice like I do. Someone who's going to make the world a better place. So no. Okay. I've got nothing else. I've got nothing except you. That's it. You're all I've got, okay.'

No one spoke for a second.

Simmonds said, 'You know, it sounds as though you're asking me to be proactive, Mr. Crowe. You do know we don't work that way.'

And Bart breathed in and salt air spiked his lungs.

'Maybe they don't,' Bart said. 'But I'm hoping you do.'

A protracted sigh.

'Send me the plates,' Simmonds said. 'Go on. I've got nothing better to do. Just sleep. And who needs sleep, right? I'm going to hang up now. When I call back don't answer. I'll leave a message. I'll tell you what to do about reporting the crime. Listen to it. Act on it. Then delete it. Got that?'

'Listen. Act. Delete. Yes I've got it. Hey, thanks Wayne. I've got to tell you -'

The phone beeped twice and the line went dead.

47

Bart shone the flashlight through the bars of Golden's gate. He could see the tail-light of Golden's Jaguar. No sign of Cameron's BMW. The garden wall was high, but he figured he could do it. He backed into the road and took a run at it. It took a couple of goes to get a good grip on the top of the wall. But as he pulled himself up, his phone vibrated and he slipped back, landing on his arse in the road.

He cursed at the phone as he swiped the display.

[We're heading over to the school. Don't tell police. Really important. Come over. Witness us at scene. Could help if things turn nasty. Attached pic speaks for itself. Z.]

There was an image attached. Bart tapped it. The picture of the man in the door from the night of the fire, except that it wasn't. It was the same pic all right, but it was clearer, and when he zoomed in on the face it was recognisable.

It was the face of Steve Hasland.

*

Bart got out of the taxi and he pulled up his collar. Cameron's grey BMW was parked across the street, up the hill from St. Stephens. He peered in through the tinted glass. In the footwell were scrunched up bags of McDonald's. They'd eaten en route - hardly a sign of panic.

He photographed the car and he headed down to the gates.

The paths around the dorm were tarmacked so he had no problem moving about quietly. Everyone was in bed. Just a couple of night owls with reading lights on. But there were lights behind the curtains of Hasland's house. He stood on the step and he rapped on the door with his fists. The lights went out and the house was silent. No one came. He knocked again and he spoke through the letter box.

"Hey guys. You know sooner or later someone is going to notice me out here, and erm, well, I'm not the one in someone else's house without permission am I? Just saying.'

There was a scuffling, and the door opened and clunked against the chain.

'Oh look,' Cameron said. 'It's the proverbial bad penny.'

But he unhooked the chain and Bart stepped through.

In Steve Hasland's front room identical sofas had been overturned. Their undersides ripped open. No dirt in the spaces they'd left. Photos had been separated from their frames and scattered across the floor with current issues of fitness magazines.

A voice from the kitchen.

'Hey, Graham. I found some more files and papers, buddy.'

It was Zack.

Cameron pushed Bart into the corner of the front room. 'Sit there!' he said. 'Stay!'

Bart went along with it. He sat.

Zack was pulling out papers and boxes in the kitchen.

Cameron went to look and he said, 'Leave them boxes with me. You head on up the stair, okay?'

Sitting on the floor Bart noticed something black and glossy. It was tucked under the TV stand. His fingers were edging towards it when Zack wandered back into the room.

He was carrying a large photo album. On the front cover, a white sticker - 'FAMILY #2' written in felt-tip. And Zack flipped through its pages. One page forward. Back. Forwards again.

And then he stopped turning.

Zack looked over at Bart but he was distant. And he returned to the album, his eyes fixed on a single image.

'Hey, Zack?' Bart said. 'Are you okay? Have you found something?'

And Cameron appeared at the door to the kitchen.

'What've you got there, son?'

'Photos.'

'Oh ay, anything good?'

Zack didn't answer.

Cameron crossed the room and leaned over and Bart edged along the wall, close enough to see.

In the album were pictures of Steve Hasland at sixteen or seventeen, a strong and healthy lad. He was with a small woman, a pale woman, with a lined face and straggly hair. She shared Steve Hasland's grey-green eyes, except hers were paler, as if they had been drained or diluted. Another man was in two of the pictures, slightly older than Steve, mid-to-late twenties. A man who carried himself with confidence. And there was something familiar about him. In one picture the three of them posed together, the woman - Hasland's mother? - standing between them - and the two young men behind her.

'They've got the same nose. Look,' said Cameron. 'Sorta hooky.'

'Aquiline,' said Zack.

'I'll stick with hooky, okay?'

'Is that other guy Hasland's brother?' Bart asked. 'He looks like -'

There was a silence and Cameron shrugged.

Then Zack said, 'He looks like my fucking dad!'

Bart looked again. Zack was right. They were looking at a picture of a teenage Steve Hasland standing beside a thirty year old Mickey Richards, and they did look like family. Bart didn't know what to make of it. Co-incidence, or?

Zack was silent.

Cameron said, 'Are you gonna snap out-a-this, Richards? Or am I gonna have to finish this thing on my own?'

Zack gave him the finger.

There more photos of Steve Hasland in the album. More of the skinny woman. But no more of Zack's dad. But the back of the album was filled with magazine clippings, all of Mickey Richards.

'What do you make of it?' Bart asked.

Zack turned the page back, and he was squinting, staring at the page as if the photo had more to give.

'Dad was adopted,' he said. 'He told me about it one time. Said he'd found his natural mum. Said she was an addict. Said that must be where he'd got it from! Like addiction is genetic or something. He told me he'd paid to get her cleaned up but it hadn't worked out and they'd drifted apart. Never mentioned a brother though.'

Bart put his hand on Zack's shoulder.

'Are you okay?'

'Yeah buddy. I'm good.'

'So, I guess this makes Mr. Hasland your Uncle Stevie!' Graham Cameron announced, grinning. He looked at Bart. 'An I thought I told you to stay in the corner, Crowe. So I think you'd better get back over there, hadn't you?'

Bart held up his hands. He shuffled back to his place in the corner, but a little closer to the TV this time. Slipping his hand beneath the TV stand, he hooked out the glossy black object that had caught his eye and he slipped it into the pocket of his coat.

It was Steve Hasland's Filofax.

DOCUMENT M

Text messages from Sophie Heath to Bartholomew Crowe: 22/11/19. 01:15 a.m.

[Dear Bart. This is a late one. And I'll be honest. I've been putting off writing it. CRAZY DAY!]

[You probably know - well you do know - how Noah stuck around in Margate during my incarceration - big word BONUS! - in the QEQM - that's the hospital, remember. You went there once. Well - I haven't told you that Noah came to see me there. He's been here today too.]

[He's said some very nice things about you to Mum and Dad. So that's good!]

[We've been hanging out playing video games and stuff. He even reads to me! I know it sounds corny but he's really good! He reads from one of the books you bought me. It's about this wizard who like goes to New York with all his magic. Everyone falls in love with him and all these couples kind of all fall apart cos they love the wizard so much, except that of course they're all going to hook up with each other later. It's just that they were with the wrong people at the start.]

[Whatever. That's just how stories go I guess?]

Geoff Smith

[Anyway, tonight when he's finished reading he leans over and he kisses me. I mean PROPERLY kisses me!!! And at first I was like - WTF are we doing this!? Seriously? And then I was like - I guess we are doing this - AND WE KISSED!!!! I'll be honest. I don't even know if it was nice or not cos Noah's elbow was right beside me and his forearm was pressing near the wound. Only lightly, but, honestly, when Noah kissed me, it was all I could do not to cry out or swear! I know that sounds horrible. And it was actually pretty nice of him really. I mean it was sweet. He meant it nicely if that makes sense.]

[I don't think this means we are a thing or anything. It has to happen like three times to be a thing, right?]

[So anyway... that happened.]

[Back to the small stuff - you know - like being shot. I literally can't move without being in total agony and most important, I AM SO BORED!!! Missing school so much it makes me sick thinking about it. Then I think how weird it is to think like that about missing school! So, in short, everything's a bit rubbish.]

[It's great that you got that boy back with his mum. You did it! You should be proud! I mean it. My little Bartie - the macho P.I.!! Well I'm proud of you anyway, that's all. And you didn't say anything about the gun in your texts - which I assume means that it's not a match??? Am I right?]

[But this is what I don't get. WHY HAVEN'T YOU COME HOME!?!? WHY!!!! All this stuff with guns! It scares me - obvs. I told the boys about it - of course!!! - and Connor says he's going to come back down there and sort out whatever mess you're in. I don't think he means it and I know it's all bull - but I kind of secretly like him when he's like that. For God's sake don't tell him that tho! And I don't mean 'like him' like him ok!]

[Anyhoo that's all for now. Except I will ask you again. Bart please don't go chasing after gunmen. I'll be okay and the police will get the truth out of it sooner or later. They know what they're doing, *and there's lots of them.]*

[Seriously tho Bart. Come back. We need you.]

[Big love Sophie x]

48

The ball of paper arced across the room and bounced off the side of Zack's head. Graham Cameron grinned.

'Wake up, sleepyhead!'

Zack had been looking at the picture again. But now he stood up, the album close to his chest and the paper ball at his feet.

'Okay,' he said, 'I'm done.'

'Okay. Right enough.' Cameron picked up Hasland's computer and iPad. 'Let's go. We'll get what we can off these gizmos and see what his plans are.'

Zack flicked hair from his eye and fixed Cameron with his cold dark eyes.

'Sorry Graham,' he said. 'I don't think you understand. When I say I'm done, I mean I'm done - with you. So run on back to Daddy and you tell him Zack doesn't want to play anymore. Bart, you're coming with me buddy.'

'No no no son. You're no goin' anywhere. We agreed.'

Cameron stepped forward but Zack was already half way to the door, and Bart said, 'Looks to me like he's unagreeing.' He held up his hand and gave Cameron a wave. 'See ya.'

The stocky Scot followed as they walked up the street, laptop and iPad under his arm.

'Richards!' he hissed. 'You're bein stupit! Jesus man, you two got nothing. Got no hope of ever gettin nothing. No to fuck. What you gonna do, eh? Where you gonna go? So where? Answer me that.' Then he stopped and he pulled a gun from his jacket. He said, 'I think yous guys should turn around.'

Zack looked round, then sighed and kept walking. But Bart did stop. He turned to face him. Graham Cameron. Another gun. Another man trying to control him with the threat of violence. Bart unbuttoned his coat and he held it open wide.

'Go on,' Bart said. 'Shoot if you want. Look. It's easy. But think about it Graham, do you really want to do that? I mean here? In a residential street? And me with a picture of your car saved to the cloud, the last picture I took before my death? Hardly seems worth it, does it? So maybe you should put the gun away, okay?' And Bart held out his hand. 'Here. Let's shake. You can wish us good luck. And I'll wish the best of luck to you. You know how it goes.'

Bart held out his hand. Cameron sneered, but he put his gun back in his jacket. He took Bart's hand. But then his grip tightened, and he yanked it down and he pulled Bart close and he swung his other fist around, and he punched Bart in the side of the head and left him sprawling on the floor.

And then Graham Cameron kneeled down beside him.

'Fuck you!' he whispered. 'Fuck yous both!'

Then he stood and he spat and he crossed the street and climbed inside the BMW, revving his engine and pulling away.

Zack offered Bart his hand.

'Shit buddy,' he said 'You're a crazy man! You know, if anything's going to make him shoot it's a stuck up little prick like you telling him to do it. Fuck it, I'd shoot you myself if you did that.' He laughed. 'My God, you've got guts buddy!' And he patted Bart lightly on the side of the head, just where Cameron had hit him. 'You're fucking stupid but you've got guts.'

Bart grinned and he let his head bump back on the pavement, and he breathed hard and said, 'And this is from the kid who's blackmailing an arsonist with a faked photograph.'

DOCUMENT N

An email from Bartholomew Crowe to Colin Crowe: 22/11/19. 01:58 a.m.

Dear Granddad.

I've got loads to say and not much time so sorry in advance for what I miss. Things are getting scary and if anything happens to me I want you to forward this on to DS Wayne Simmonds at Kent police.

So this is it.

Lola Golden was kidnapped tonight and we think it's a guy called Steve Hasland. It looks like he burned the casino - 95% he's the guy in our picture - he may have killed Raymond Feathers too. Plus I think he was the gunman that night at The Music Hall.

And before you ask, yes, I have reported it.

I'm in my car now and I'm outside a supermarket. It's two in the morning. I've got Steve Hasland's Filofax and I'm waiting for Zack Richards. Don't quite know how it happened but somehow we're working together to find Lola.

So Hasland's our bad guy - but somewhere there's Glenn Golden behind it all. I think that Golden paid Hasland to burn the arcade and Golden's been paying Zack to keep the picture away from the police. What makes no sense to me though, is how a school teacher ends up working for Golden on a cheap crook's job like the one at the casino.

In other news, it seems that Steve Hasland is related by blood to Zack - his uncle - so Steve's motives - if it is him we're dealing with - are doubly unclear.

Anyway, if we're right and it is Hasland we're looking for, then Zack and I are going to find him before he makes his move. We'll use the Filofax and hopefully be able to narrow down some possibilities.

So tonight we're on the hunt for a gun toting kidnapper.

I'll keep you posted.

Bart.

DOCUMENT O

Text message from Bartholomew Crowe to Sophie Heath: 22/11/19. 02:22 a.m.

[Hi Soph. Sorry for the late text but this is important. I know who the gunman is. His name's Steve Hasland. He's a teacher at St. Stephen's school. He's kidnapped Lola and now he's hiding out. I'm going to figure out where he is and I'm going to get him arrested. And as soon as the police have got him, then I'll come home. I'll text again in a couple of hours - I'll try not to do anything too stupid before then! Love you guys. Bart xx]

49

'Any luck getting hold of Richards?' Simmonds asked.

The car's interior lights faded and the two men were draped in darkness. A flashlight cut its narrow beam across the bonnet of the dark Mondeo. Bart covered his eyes.

'No, and I'm worried. I'll admit it.'

'Do you know what address he's at?'

'I know where he's going first.'

'So - if there's still no response we check that next.'

'Okay. Look Wayne - can you turn that thing off, please? I thought we didn't want to be seen.'

Simmonds deactivated his flashlight and their eyes strained to adjust. They had driven out beyond Margate and Minnis. There were no streetlights and there was no traffic. No light at all. They floundered a few steps in the blackness before they gave up and used the dim light of their screens to guide them. Twenty metres up the road they found it, a bungalow. Muted lights behind the curtains and a light coloured van on the drive.

'Check the plates,' Simmonds said, 'just to be sure. And stay off the stones if you can. I'll see who's in.'

Bart ducked behind the hedge as Simmonds walked down the drive. The curtain stirred and a light went off. Simmonds stood on the step and pretended not to notice. Then the lights came back on and the door opened. A tall man, middle-aged and well groomed and in good shape in pyjama bottoms and a vest. He and Simmonds spoke for a moment. Then another man appeared, and looked over the shoulder of the first.

Steve Hasland.

And then the three men went indoors.

Bart clambered through a gap in the hedge and crept across the grass, hoping the two men would be distracted enough by the strange policeman, that they might not notice a misplaced footfall or broken twig. When his phone vibrated in his pocket he nearly jumped out of his skin. Simmonds. He pressed the green button and he hurriedly turned the ringtone down to silent.

The first voice he heard was Hasland's.

'No, no. I've been here with Tony all night. I did pop into town for some wine a little bit earlier - No - No sorry, I don't remember the exact time. I think it was somewhere around nine though.'

The other man was deep-voiced and well-spoken.

'Honestly officer, Steve, he was gone for like an hour, tops, so I really don't think we can help. I was out at the time, in the car, visiting a client. We were discussing some plans she had for her garden. I can give you the number if you'd like to check but really I'd appreciate it if you'd wait until the morning.'

'That won't be necessary thank you, Mr. ?'

'Sullivan - Tony Sullivan. Sullivan's landscapers.'

By now Bart had snaked round the side of the house to the white van. The light of his screen glowed against the number plate. The van was a match with the photo. The same van he'd seen earlier when the man took Lola. He tiptoed onto the gravel, and he tapped at its panels.

'Hello?' he whispered

He tried the handle on the back of the van. It was unlocked and so he opened it. The inside of the van was empty. No Lola. No anything. He climbed in and used his flashlight to light up the van's interior. A drawing of a stick man on the plywood lining. A smiling man holding a shovel and the word 'uncal tony' scrawled above it. He sighed and shuffled back towards the back of the van. Then he heard gravel crunching behind him. In a panic he pulled the van door almost closed, shutting himself in. He put the phone back to his ear.

'It's right around here you say Mr. Sullivan.'

'Yes it's just here. Hang on. That's weird. Looks like it's -'

The van doors squeaked open and the three men all shone their iPhones onto the face of Bartholomew Crowe.

'Who the hell -' said Tony Sullivan.

'Mr. Crowe!' Simmonds said, feigning surprise. 'Now fancy meeting you here. Mr. Sullivan, Mr. Hasland, this young man is Bartholomew Crowe. He's a private detective who's been following me around of late. I've told him to stay away of course but - young people, they never listen, do they - you'd know that of course Mr. Hasland. Come on Crowe. Out then.'

And Wayne grabbed Bart by the collar and pulled him roughly from the van. He twisted Bart's arm up behind his back.

Steve Hasland was shifting his weight from foot to foot, looking back towards the house.

And Simmonds noticed his nervousness.

'Are you all right, sir?' he asked.

'Just cold,' Steve said. 'Look, maybe you should bring him inside. Sort this out back in the warm.'

And he hugged himself and he stamped his feet.

'Why is your detective in my van?' Tony said.

'Well,' Simmonds said, 'I imagine he thought there might have been someone else in here before him.'

'You too -' Tony said and he looked at Steve and his eyebrows raised in the middle.

'Who did the picture, in the van?' Bart asked. 'It's you isn't it?'

'What that? That's just my niece. She likes to play in there sometimes, when I visit.'

*

Back in the bungalow, Bart sat in the leather armchair, Steve and Tony on the sofa. Simmonds stood by the fireplace, inspecting the ornaments, the photos and trophies.

'You're proud of your business, Mr. Sullivan?'

'I've worked hard. Look, Officer - really - do you think we could do this tomorrow? It's getting on for four in the morning.'

'I'll be brief,' Simmonds said. 'So as I was saying before, a girl went missing at approximately nine o'clock last night and your van, Mr. Sullivan, was seen at the scene immediately afterwards. Now, Mr. Hasland, would you like to change your story about the off-licence? I can check the times of any transactions of course.'

'No, Mr. -'

'Simmonds.'

'No, like I said before, I was in town to buy wine. And no, I didn't keep the receipt but I'm happy for you to check of course.'

Bart raised his hand.

He said, 'Sorry everyone, I need the uh - you know - sorry.'

Simmonds nodded at Tony.

'End of the corridor on the right,' Tony said.

Bart pulled the bathroom door closed without going in. Instead he turned left into the bedroom. On the floor by the bed was a blue holdall. It contained neatly pressed clothes. A black shirt, dark jeans and underwear. He slid his hand down the side of the clothes. Underneath them was a large wash bag. He removed it and carefully released the popper.

A dark wig.

A fake beard.

A pair of Wayfarers.

And a 9mm Heckler and Koch automatic pistol.

A rush of blood, a rising in the stomach. Bart refastened the popper and slipped the packet back beneath the jeans and the aftershave.

Coming back into the living room, he silently cursed himself. He had forgotten to re-open and re-close the bathroom door. Forgotten to pull the flush. He shivered and he whispered into Simmonds ear as he passed. 'I found the gun.'

Simmonds tried not to react but he straightened slightly, the slump of his shoulders lifting like a topped up inflatable.

And then Hasland was walking towards them. Simmonds' chest expanded as much as a skinny man's chest can expand, and he moved his legs slightly further apart.

'Please sit down, Mr. Hasland.'

'Sorry Sergeant Simmonds, but if I'm not under arrest I want a beer. I'm going to the kitchen. Would you like -'

Simmonds stepped aside.

'No. Thank you,' he said.

And Hasland disappeared into the kitchen. They heard the whump of the fridge door.

Tony said, 'Look Officer I'm not being difficult, honestly. But I think we've told you all we can.'

A drawer opened and a bottle top popped.

'Just one or two more things I need to clear up,' Simmonds said. 'I do appreciate your time Mr. Sullivan.'

A clink, a bottle top landing on the tiled floor.

'Okay,' Tony said. 'Shoot.'

And Steve came from the kitchen with a bottle of beer. He had put a denim overshirt on over his t-shirt. As he passed Simmonds he let the bottle fall. A black bladed knife slid out from his sleeve. He caught it, and, hooking his left arm around Simmonds' neck, he swung his right arm upwards and plunged the black blade into Simmonds back. The blade like a shadow. And Simmonds' breathing stalled. His eyes widened, glazed with shock as the blade jammed in.

Tony clambered over the settee and he crouched

against the back wall.

'Christ! Fuck! Fuck! Fuck!'

And Hasland's eyes were fixed on Tony as he stabbed Wayne Simmonds a second time and then a third. And the policeman shuddered with each thrust of the knife. Then Hasland let him fall. He came towards Bart, slow, and swaying like a tiger, a cool predator. Blood dripped from the blade, from his knuckles and fingers.

'Okay,' Bart said. 'Calm down okay, Steve. I'll do whatever you say all-right. Just calm. You don't need the knife for me - okay? Okay?'

Hasland feinted left and he jabbed to Bart's right. Then he stood tall, and he smiled broadly. It was a smile of exhilaration. He spread his arms wide and he took deep breaths. And when he spoke he was almost friendly.

'Okay then. On the floor, guys. Lie down. Both of you.' And he pointed the knife at Tony. 'Come on, Tone.'

Hasland pulled cable-ties from the pocket of the overshirt and he knelt between them. He bound Bart's hands behind his back and bound his feet together. Hasland left him there and fetched two chairs from the kitchen. He sat Tony in the chair and he bound his arms to the chair. And then he lifted Simmonds into the second chair. Bart looked at the tall policeman. Still breathing - at least for now. And the sergeant's head lolled forward and Hasland had to double tie his arms to the back of the chair to keep him in place. Then, he leaned in close to Tony, and he cupped the other man's face in his hands.

'Whatever happens now, Tone, always remember I loved you, all-right,' he said, 'more than anyone else. Anyone ever.' And he kissed him on the lips.

And Tony shook with fear.

On the floor, Bart tried to move but Hasland had pulled the ties so tight, it hurt to stay still! Then, wrapping an arm around Bart's stomach, Hasland pulled him to his feet and then he clapped a pungent cloth over Bart's mouth.

50

His vision blurred under the weak electric light. Angled struts. Chipboard. And then himself, bound up like a worm, his body numb. There was a dead-weight in his head and a burning sensation in the back of his throat. His phone was gone. His wallet. His watch. There was something glittery in the haze, and his eyes worked to bring it into focus. Pale ankles. Sequined shoes.

'Lola?' Bart said. 'You're here.'

'Hello,' she said. 'You're here too.'

She didn't sound like a girl afraid.

'I like your shoes.'

'Thanks.'

Bart said, 'I thought you'd be, like, you know, like upset, or something?'

'Oh I've been here for hours, Bart. And, you know, until you got dumped up here, nothing at all has happened. Fear gets boring really quickly.' She took a sip of wine. 'Listen okay, Steve - all he wants is this photograph, and a memory card or something? And he says he has to talk to Zack about it. Look Bart, Steve's a bit crazy but I can handle him. I promise. I'll talk him round.'

Bart's saw Lola's ankle was cuffed to a bench. The bench was built in, bolted to the floor and to the struts. But her arms and her other leg were free, and she had a small table with two open bottles of wine. She had a glass and it was half-full.

She took a sip.

Lipstick on the rim of the glass.

'He's treating you well.'

'Well apart from taking my phone and cuffing me in a loft,' she laughed. 'Look, he's really not a monster, Bart. Really. I don't expect you to understand.'

Bart twisted up and around until he was kneeling before her, and he almost told her about the policeman who was bleeding to death in the lounge downstairs. But it felt somehow childish and mean.

'I seem to be a little more restricted than you,' he said.

'I suppose he doesn't quite trust you yet,' she said and she offered the wine glass up to his lips. But Bart turned his head away.

'You do know what Steve did? I mean, you know he burned your dad's casino?'

She stroked a hand past her cheek and rested it on her neck.

'Oh I know,' she said. 'He told me, you see. But Bart, he's had a life you could never know. And anyway, if I hate Steve for what he did, well then - that could get a little awkward for me.' She took another sip of wine. 'Turning into quite a night though. You sure you don't want some?'

'Actually yes. I will. Thanks.'

So Lola leaned forward and she tipped the glass. Wine dropped into his mouth. It felt hot, and it soothed his burning throat. A little stream of red trickled down his chin.

'So about Steve?' he said. 'I mean, you were saying?'

'Listen Bart, Steve and my dad have known each other since they were kids, okay? My Dad would look out for him, and sometimes pay him for jobs - the kind of jobs that he doesn't really do anymore. So, when Dad wanted the casino done Steve agreed like he always has. I think he feels like Dad and me are family in a way. I'm kind of like his unofficial niece I suppose. It's weird, okay. I'm not going to say it's not weird, but it is actually pretty nice. And he really does care about me. More than Dad does sometimes. And you know Zack really shouldn't be doing what he's doing anyway. Because my dad can take it, but it's really hurting Steve. He's more sensitive.'

'Could I have some more wine?'

She leaned forward and poured more wine into his mouth, more of it dripping down his chin.

'Listen, Bart,' she said. 'If this thing goes right, I mean tonight, everything could get sorted out, like that. If Zack hands over those images, well, then Steve can go back to living a normal life again - he can marry Tony - Dad can get back to his property portfolio and his dumb arcade, and Zack will be done with this whole mess and Steve and Dad will forgive him, because they'd know he was giving the whole revenge thing up for me. And Zack will see that -'

Her lips pursed and her eyebrows narrowed.

Bart said, 'What will Zack see?'

'He'll just see,' she said. 'That's all.'

'And Raymond.'

'Raymond? What about Raymond?'

There was a metallic creaking sound and Hasland's head pushed up through the hatch. Seeing Bart trussed up and kneeling in front of Lola, he grinned.

'I would say get a room,' he said, 'but - I've already taken care of that one, haven't I? Honestly, it's a shame to disturb you two, but we've got to move.' And his hands pushed through the hatch and he pointed the gun at the pair of them. 'So - let's just do exactly what I say, all right - unless you want to argue with this - and I think by now you know that I'm quite serious about that, don't you Bart?'

51

Lola walked ahead of him, past the wooden shells of old slot machines. Her hands were bound but not as tightly as his own. Hasland had one hand locked around Bart's collar, and the barrel of the 9mm pushing into Bart's back with the other.

The storeroom took up the whole of the arcade's first floor. There was a box room on the far side of the space. It had thin, board walls and single-glazed windows. It may once have been a staff room but now was dusty and neglected. There were cushioned chairs facing each other on both sides of the room and Steve shoved Bart onto one of them, cable-tying Bart's ankles and wrists to the chair's chromed frame. Lola sat opposite and Steve bound one ankle to the chair. There was a filing cabinet in the corner. Hasland rattled it open. Green tea cups, a tray and a couple of spoons.

'So who fancies a cuppa?' he said.

And he left them there while he went downstairs, cups clinking on the tray as he walked.

*

And Bart said, 'My God, Lola, doesn't it scare you to see how relaxed he is? How relaxed you are? Because, my God, I've got to tell you, I'm not relaxed at all.'

She frowned then, and she looked almost angry.

'I told you. It'll work out. Zack will come. Everything will get sorted out. Just you wait and see.'

And Bart kicked his legs but the binds wouldn't budge.

'For God's sake Lola, listen, Steve just stabbed a police officer - at the bungalow - and he did it three times! A police officer! And I'm sorry, but picture or no picture, he's not going to be able to sort that. And you can see how happy he is! He's left two witnesses to a murder, and one of them is me! He's going to end us tonight Lola, you have to see that?'

Lola's shoulders hunched. She leaned forward.

'You're making it up as you go along,' she said and she twisted away from him.

'Oh come on. You think I'd lie about something like that? I'll tell you what. Why don't you just ask him? See what he says. Because, you know what Lola, if you're in on this, you'd better start getting yourself out of it.'

And then Hasland was weaving through the slot machines with a plastic tray, three cups of tea and a Heckler and Koch self-loading pistol.

'There we go,' Steve said, placing the tray on the cabinet. 'You know, this little get together is actually quite nice under the circumstances, isn't it?'

Neither Bart nor Lola spoke. Hasland sat opposite Bart. He tasted his tea and his face contorted before he dribbled it back out into his cup.

'Urgh look at that. I forgot the bloody sugar. My own bloody cuppa as well!'

Lola laid a hand on his leg. She said, 'Let me go get it for you, Steve. I know where it is. You can trust me.'

They looked at each other.

Then Steve drew the combat knife from his jacket and held it in front of him, gazing for a while at the subtle inflections of light on the matte-black blade.

'All right but -' And he stroked the blade of the knife against Bart's cheek. 'if you're not back in three minutes -' He pressed the point against Bart's nose until he drew blood. 'This Crowe's going to lose his beak.'

And Lola said, 'I won't let you down, Steve.'

Steve breathed out, long and slow as if in meditation, and he blinked a few times, and he looked deep into Lola's eyes for several seconds and said, 'All right.'

He cut the tie from her ankle and Lola stood. She leaned down and she kissed Steve on the forehead. The big man slumped back into the chair as she left for the stairs, lost in thought, turning the blade.

Then Bart said, 'Why did you burn the casino, Steve?' And Steve sat up, tensed and alert. His lip raised up on one side and his cheeks tightened as Bart continued. 'Because that's what this is all about isn't it? The casino, I mean. The one you burned. Like, I feel sorry for you, Steve. I do. You did the wrong guy a favour, and you had some bad luck. But what I don't understand is why a guy like you would do something like that. I mean, I don't know how much Golden paid you but-.'

'I didn't do it.'

'Yes you did. And you killed Torin Malone in the process.'

And Steve's tight-lipped tension became a smile, and it was a smile to club you to death with.

'Bart,' he said. 'I like you, right. I really do. I've always liked you, but you need to be careful here. Because if you're not careful you'll annoy me.' He brought the knife close to Bart's face. 'And if I get annoyed I might cut off that nose anyway - or I might kill you.'

A shudder ran through Bart's body, the blood drying tight at the corner of his nostril. But he steeled himself and he said, 'So I think we're all here because Glenn Golden hired you to burn down a casino for him. He's known you for years. And maybe he's got something on you. So you did it. You burned his casino, just like he asked. Except it all went wrong for you didn't it, when a young man - someone who knew you - snapped you at the scene and died. So when you found out that

Zack Richards - who you already hated - had the picture and was blackmailing Glenn Golden with it, you had to act then, didn't you?'

Steve tapped the end of the knife on Bart's nose. Then he stood and stretched. He had a powerful frame. Gorilla-like. A silverback.

Bart said, 'Except when Raymond Feathers broke into Zack's room and stole the photo. He put the squeeze on you direct then, didn't he? So Golden gave you the address of that squat the guys were dealing from and you went over there - and maybe you just wanted to end it, to get the memory card and move on - but Ray was more determined than you thought he'd be. He wouldn't talk. So you shot him, didn't you?'

And Steve lifted the pistol from the coffee table, spinning into a gunfight pose, James Bond or Jason Statham, and he pointed the gun at Bart's head.

'Bang!' he said, and he laughed out loud. Then he looked at his watch and said, 'Looks like you're losing that big, beaky nose of yours Crowe.'

'You didn't find that photo though, did you?' Bart said. 'But I did. I found it. And when you heard about that through Lola you decided to take me down. And so you went to The Music Hall, hoping to catch me on my own, but then, when you were behind the hall, and it was so secluded and quiet, it was just too tempting, wasn't it? You took a shot at me and you put a bullet through my friend. But then, after all that, you found out that Zack still had a copy of that picture as well. That must have made you like insane! So when Golden fed you the address of the flat where Zack is hiding with Mrs. Malone, you figure you have nothing to lose. But Zack's not there, and you wonder if anything will ever go right, so you turn the place over anyway, rough up the old lady. But you come up short - again. And of course you don't attack Lola because -'

They heard Lola's feet on the stairs. Both men stopped for a moment.

Bart said, 'Did Lola know you were coming to Mrs

Malone's place? Did she know about you? About all of this?'

And then Lola was there. She put down the tray and she hopped over Hasland's legs.

Sitting next to Steve she said 'Sugar?'

'Ah you're a good girl,' Hasland said, transformed and grinning, all sweetness and light. He checked his watch. 'Two minutes and forty seven seconds. Down to the wire eh Bart?'

He reached out and he wobbled Bart's nose between thumb and forefinger.

And Bart looked at Lola and said, 'Did you know that Steve was the guy in Mrs. Malone's flat?'

'What?' she said, her eyes widening. 'Are you serious?'

She sounded convincing but Bart was not convinced.

And he said, 'I am serious. What about you, Lola? Are you serious?'

And Lola looked at Steve.

And Steve said, 'She knew who I was. But she didn't know I was coming. Anonymous tip off. I was expecting to find Zack.'

Bart rocked his body towards the tea tray and Steve raised an eyebrow.

And he said, 'My lord, where are my manners?' And he reached out with the knife, cut Bart's right hand free, and he passed him a cup of tea.

The tea was lukewarm. Over the rim of the cup, Bart looked at Lola, but she was avoiding eye contact.

And then something clunked - noises downstairs.

Steve reacted quickly.

'Sorry sweetheart,' he said to Lola. 'It won't be for long.' And he fastened cable ties round both of her hands and both of her ankles. Bart's free hand retied, the half-drunk tea taken away.

'We have guests, guys,' Steve said, 'so let's get ready.'

He took ball gags from his holdall and he pushed them into their mouths. He fastened them and grinned.

'Always pays to be prepared,' he said. 'So I'd love to stay

and chat but uh - no rest for the wicked.'

And Steve tied cloths around their eyes.

And then he was gone.

Pushing on the gag with his tongue and wriggling in his seat, Bart tried to shift the blindfold, rocking his body in the chair. But he only managed to scrape the skin from his ankle and to bruise a finger.

The world darkened. Steve had turned out the lights in the main storeroom. The fluorescent tube still lit the small room where they sat. He and Lola would be clearly visible to anyone coming up the stairs.

*

Two voices. The first a gutsy, London female, and the second male, smooth and sophisticated, just the hint of affected estuary.

'This place is filthy! No offence.'

'Be quiet will you? You're going to get us killed. I'm serious, Franny. Wait. Look!'

'Is that Lo-? Oh Jesus Christ, look at that. What a perv!'

'I said - oh shit. Whatever. Just listen. You'd better stay here, okay. Seriously. It's safer. I'm going in. If you see anything weird going down, you run, okay? Get the police, all that shit.'

'Go on. I got your back babe.'

'This is serious, Fran.'

'I know. I know. Seriously. Now go. Go.'

And Francesca De Souza watched as Zack Richards moved through the maze of games machines and slots, between the fruit machines and pinball tables, towards the lighted room where Bartholomew Crowe and Lola Golden sat bound and gagged. And as Zack got closer, Steve Hasland began to uncurl from the husk of a first-person shooter.

*

Ten metres from the lighted doorway, Zack kneeled and

watched. The perspex windows were patterned with cobwebs and dust. Behind them sat Lola and Bart, tied up and blindfolded and gagged. He looked back the way he had come, back to Franny, standing at the stairs, her clothing bright in the grey shadows. And something felt wrong. He scanned the room, looking for movement, sounds, but he saw nothing and he heard nothing.

'Hey, guys,' he whispered. 'I'm going to get you out, okay.'

And Bart and Lola turned towards his voice and they made noises, trying to tell him that Steve Hasland was here, that he was hidden and dangerous, but with the gags on it meant nothing, just noise. Zack saw their panic and he took it as a warning. Perhaps a trip-wire or a sensor. He ran fingers up and down the sides of the door-frame. But nothing. No wires. No sensors. And so he took a chance. He stepped into the room.

No bomb, no wires, no sensors, no nothing.

*

And at the back of the arcade, Steve Hasland had slithered out from his wooden box. He felt good, and strangely natural, like the years he'd felt at home, crawling out from under the dining table. He crouched on his knees and he hugged himself. And then he stretched. He reared up like a cobra. He loosened the muscles in his neck and he breathed deep, filling his lungs.

Hasland's hand clapped across Francesca De Souza's mouth. She jolted and struggled in his grip. Then she felt the knife-point pricking the skin of her neck. She saw the blade.

And Steve hissed, 'Make a sound and I'll slit your throat right here, and I'll send you off to Hell without a second thought, all right?'

And she quivered and her breath was shallow. Steve moved the knife slowly, down, down to her belly and he clapped her head tight to his chest, and then, half pushing, half carrying her, they moved across the space and towards the lit room.

*

Zack removed Lola's blindfold. She blinked hard at the sudden return of light, and her eyes were wide. He unbuckled the gag, pulled it down.

'He's here, baby,' she said. 'He's here! He's here! He's got a gun! Get out. Go! Go now!'

But Zack wasn't listening. Instead he hacked at the cable ties with his keys until he snapped her hands free, and he pulled hard on the remaining ties until the last one gave.

'And I'd stop right there if I were you.' Steve Hasland was at the door and he held the knife to Francesca's throat. 'I mean if you want to have all your friends alive for breakfast. Sit down Zack. It's lovely to see you by the way. Oh, and if you could stick that memory card of yours down on that tray while you're about it, will you?'

Zack held up his hands.

'Okay,' he said. 'Okay. Stay cool. I'm going to put my hand in my pocket now. And here's the card. Look. See. No more copies. All gone.'

He placed the card down on the tray.

'Now sit in the chair,' Steve said.

Zack sat next to Bart.

'Sorry buddy.'

And Steve dropped a bunch of cable ties on the floor.

'Tie him down, Lola,' he said. 'Do it quick! Or I cut this bitch, right here.'

And for a moment it looked as if Lola might tell him to go fuck himself, that he could kill them all if he wanted. But she didn't. She kneeled in front of Zack and she pulled the ties tight until he winced, and Steve nodded at her work. When she was finished she looked up at Steve, and at Francesca, shaking, with the knife at her throat.

'Do you want me to tie her up too?' Lola asked. 'I think I'd enjoy that.'

'Oh dear, oh dear,' Steve said to Francesca, and he twisted the knife against her neck. 'Looks like we've upset somebody.'

Then he lowered the knife to Francesca's stomach and pulled her back by the hair.

'Why don't you hit her?' he said to Lola. 'Go on. Just give her a smack and tell her exactly why you hate her.'

Lola looked at him and her eyebrows were raised.

'What?'

'Do it. Hit her. Just a slap. It does have to be hard though. Just to see how it feels.'

'For God's sake let her go!' Zack shouted. 'She's got nothing to do with any of this.'

But Lola loosened her shoulders. She wound herself up, and she hit Franny with a stinging slap.

'Boyfriend stealing bitch!' she said.

*

Blindfolded, Bart didn't see what happened next, didn't see the knife being raised back to Franny's throat. He did hear the fizz of slicing flesh, and he heard the clumping beat of the body falling to the ground and he felt the floor vibrating through his feet. He heard Zack screaming and swearing and rocking on his chair. He heard Lola murmuring, 'My God, my God, my God.' Over and over and over. And then he heard Francesca, gurgling and spluttering. And he heard Steve clapping slowly and loud.

And then Steve said, 'That's one score settled, isn't it? And now that's been taken care of, we can all have a nice orderly chat, can't we? About the rest of our business. Take that blindfold and gag off young Bart, Lola. We don't want him missing out now, do we?'

And Lola leaned over him. She released the buckle of the gag, lifted the blindfold. And she whispered, 'I'm sorry. So sorry. So sorry.'

52

The white Corolla stopped at the gate, and its horn sounded again and again, honks that merged into a pulsing blare. A grey figure emerged from the big house at the end of the drive, small at first, but becoming taller, broader.

The horns stopped. The car door opened. Its hinge squeaked, and brown brogues slid out onto the tarmac. Grey pressed trousers and a knee length suede coat. The man stood beside the full-beamed lights with his hands in pockets and his legs parted.

The approaching figure stopped three feet from the gate. His skin glowed orange in the light. He covered his eyes with his forearm. Light flared on the heavy band of his watch.

He said, 'What the fuck are you about?'

'I want my grandson. I want Bartholomew Crowe.'

The figure's lip curled up at one side. He checked the pocket where his cigarettes should have been but there were none there. His expression changed, cold as iced whisky.

'Never heard of him. Now fuck off before I call the police.'

'You're lying to me. I know who you are Glenn Golden. I know all about you and I know you've got hell to pay, I can assure you of that. I've seen the photograph.'

Glenn Golden stood tall and he pushed out his chest.

'Listen fella,' he said. 'I'd be very careful about what you say next if I were you. I say I don't know any Bartholomew Crowe. And you can please yourself with your fucking photograph, you daft old git. Now fuck off.'

The hook of Granddad's nose brushing against the damp iron gate.

'Listen to me Mr. Golden. I'm retired. And I've got time. Lots of it. This is a day out for me. And I know people too, police people, insurance people. I can be quite irritating. And maybe you're not bothered by that right now but I promise that you will be. Now, are you going to tell me where my grandson is, or should I get back into that car and sound that horn until I get arrested? Of course, when I do get arrested, I'm going to make sure that they write down the reasons why I'm here. Now I'm asking you again. Where is Bart? Where's my boy?'

Glenn Golden moved closer. Their faces almost touched. He took in the other man for the first time, this skinny guy, bearded, average height, and older than him, straggly hair. And Glenn said, 'Crowe left here five hours ago. I threw him out. I don't know where he went.'

'He went looking for your daughter is what I hear. Nice to know someone is, isn't it?'

Glenn curled his lips into a sneer and he snorted, and he said, 'All of a sudden everyone knows my bloody business. You leave my daughter to me Mr. - Crowe, is it? And don't you worry yourself. When it comes to my daughter, I will get the right result.'

Granddad narrowed his eyes and his brow furrowed.

'The *right result*! I don't want to hear about your *right result*. You can keep your *right result*. Because people like you, you're steeped in blood, aren't you? The next *right result*, it's all you've got, well that and washing yesterday's blood from your bloody hands. So you keep your *right result*, Glenn Golden, *because* I don't believe you know what *right* means, and I don't care how successful you are. So how about you do something useful and help me find my boy?'

Glenn Golden raised an eyebrow. He rechecked the empty pocket for cigarettes.

He said, 'I see where Crowe gets his self-righteous streak. Look, I'd love to help you, old fella, but I don't know where Crowe is. And you know what? I don't care where he is. But I do care about my daughter and I care about what's mine.'

'Of course you do. So all right then, let's go find what's yours, shall we? Let's go and find your daughter, and maybe we'll find my boy too. Come on then, Golden. The engine's running.'

A glow from Golden's coat pocket. A phone vibrating. Glenn turned his back. He held the phone to his ear.

'Yep?'

DOCUMENT P

A phone-call from Graham Cameron to Glenn Golden. 22/11/19. 06:15 a.m.

GOLDEN: Yep?

CAMERON: We've got a problem. *[PAUSE]* Richards has gone. *[PAUSE]* Are you still there?

GOLDEN: Yes, yes. So there's someone with me right now, so if you could just uh -

CAMERON: Just talk?

GOLDEN: Yes.

CAMERON: Okay, okay, I got it. Right - well you'll remember that I had that run in with Crowe up at the house. Well, I got myself down to the car park at the Travelodge and I got lucky, cos Crowe pulls in and he drops Richards off. And then Richards got unlucky because he met me. And that's when I sent you them pics of the Filofax with the circled addresses, right? So I was just gonnae sit tight in the room til Hasland made his move. An ah shit. Okay. This is embarrassing but - there was this knock at the door and it was like cleaning services or some shite. So I opened up and there was this girl standing there, pretty, dressed all bright, sort of foreign looking. And she says, 'Zack?'. And I say 'I think you got the wrong room, darlin'. Maybe it's the next floor you're wanting?' An' she says, 'Oh it's just that I've got something for him.' An' I shouldda clocked then but I didnae. And she pulls this tube out her bag and she maces me in the face! An' ah Glenn, I never been maced before. I got to tell you, it's fucking shite, it's like snot city. And the pain! Jesus Christ! It's a killer. It shouldnae be legal. Anyway, the girl pushes past me, and she sets Richards loose. An' before I know it he's on top a me, and that kid's a tough little fucker. Boy I'm gonna get in a few shots myself next time I see him. I can tell you that.

GOLDEN: I see. So what's next?

CAMERON: They were talking about what order they were gonnae do the addresses. And it was like they thought I couldnae hear them, or something. Or they didn't care about me hearing. And I'll be honest, I couldnae recall the order exactly but I remembered they mention that Bart was away at the Minnis address first. So after I don't know, ten minutes, I'm comin' back to myself and they've tied me up with sheets. I got outta that, nae bother. So I drive up to the Minnis address, and the place turns out to be a bungalow, and outside it there's like polis and a medic car and a Mondeo parked down the road apeice and I'm pretty sure it's polis too but -

GOLDEN: Intriguing. So what about our clients?

CAMERON: No sign. I walk back up to have a look, but the cops had marked the place off. An' I tried playing the nosey insomniac neighbour, but they were pretty tight-lipped. Fucking professionalism, eh - it's not what it was you know.

GOLDEN: Hang on a moment.

[No one speaks for a few seconds. Golden taps his pocket, looking for the cigarettes that aren't there.]

So how are we moving forward?

CAMERON: Sorry Glenn. I'm afraid I don't know . I could try again, get a bit more assertive. An' maybe they'll arrest me but - I'm sure I can get something.

GOLDEN: No. I think we leave it for now. Keep control at our end. Why don't you head down to the office, and we'll see how we can move forwards from there.

CAMERON: Got ya boss. I'm ay on my way.

[GOLDEN hangs up. He puts the phone in his pocket. There is a man in his mid-sixties, COLIN CROWE, on the other side of the gate.]

GOLDEN: All right then fella. You drive. I'll tell you where to go. You're looking for your boy and I want my little girl. I suppose it makes sense. Plus it will shut you up for a while.

53

Steve Hasland clicked the SD card into the port on his phone.

'That's me all right,' he said, and he leaned against the door-frame, pistol in one hand, phone in the other. 'I tell you, that friend of yours, Torin Malone, God rest his soul, he caused me a lot of trouble with that little snap. And I didn't even want to do the job, not really. Good picture under the circumstances.' He shook his head. Zack looked at Bart. 'But there we are. Dee-leted. Done. I know we don't have any wine glasses or anything like that, but I think we should raise a little toast - to Torin Malone!'

And Steve swept the gun around the room, pausing on each face, then he raised the gun in the air and gestured.

And they all said, 'Torin Malone.'

Only the corpse of Francesca Da Souza was silent.

Steve had lifted her up and set her on the chair next to Lola. Her head had flopped back to expose the bloody slit across her throat. The flow of blood had more or less stopped but her left side was drenched, and Steve's whole front was red from moving her.

Zack straightened in his chair.

'The picture's not gone,' he said. 'It's not deleted. I mean it's still out there. You've got the card, but the picture's still out there, in the cloud. And I've got it scheduled to go out on all my social media. Totally automatic. Midday today. So don't you even think about killing us, because I can stop it. And I'll delete everything straight away if you let us go now. So, what do you say, Uncle Steve?'

The grin was still stretching out across Zack's face when Steve's fist smashed into his right eye. Zack righted himself. Cut cheek. Bruised ego.

'Bullshit,' Steve said. 'You've not had time. And what exactly d'you mean by calling me that? Explain now, or I'll smash you again!'

He pulled his fist back for another hit.

Zack was still woozy so Bart said, 'There was a scrapbook, at your house. There were pictures. You and Zack's dad.'

And Steve turned on Bart, and he grabbed the lapels of his coat.

'What were you doing in my house, Crowe? That stuff's private.'

Bart clamped his jaw shut and he braced himself for a blow that didn't come.

Instead, Steve stood and placed his hands behind his head, turning, and lifting the gun up high. Then he brought it down, slowly, the end of the barrel inches from Zack's face. Then Lola reached out, and she touched Steve's forearm. She came to him and she looked into his eyes until Steve gave in and looked back.

He backed off then, dropped the gun to his side.

'Sit down Lola.' He spoke quietly, calmly, slow. 'Sit back down, or I swear it. I will kill him.'

Lola sat. Steve squatted down in front of Zack Richards.

'Right then,' he said. 'Let's talk family.' And he stroked Zack's hair. 'So Zack, how's your mother? I expect she's still struggling with that big ranch in Argentina? All those staff, eh? Must be tough, I mean with her being out of it all the fucking time. That's what the papers say, isn't it? Been out there much? Last Summer maybe?'

'You don't know what you're talking about,' Zack said.

'Oh I bet it's lovely riding over your own land in the sunshine. Just you and the gauchos. Lovely.' And he looked from Zack to the gun, then back again. 'So anyway, now that's done, let me tell you about my mother. I know you didn't ask but - um - she's dead, actually. Overdose. Heroin. Your mum probably likes a bit of that too, doesn't she? Heroin. Except that my Mum's stuff was cut with some crappy extra shit. You know, like they do now, elephant tranquiliser or some shit.' He tapped the gun on Zack's knee. 'I don't suppose you have that problem, do you? You probably get the good stuff. The very best. But there you go. My mum's dead and yours isn't. And it's funny too, because though my mum never met yours, the one thing she did love as much as heroin was your dad. All the time talking about him. Her famous son. Adopted and made the big-time. And you know, when your dad came down to the estate and found her that day, all those years ago, that was the best day of her whole miserable fucking life, and all because your dad turned up with a bit of fucking money and a red fucking Bentley and a big fucking smile. And from that moment her eyes would light up at the mention of his name on the telly or the radio. And she talked about him all the time. Never talked about me like that. Never. Never proud of me. Not me, the kid who achieved at school and kept up on all his work and was no trouble to no-one despite having a druggie for a mother and a piss-head of a stepdad, and two psycho fucking step-brothers. Never fucking proud of me, was she? Like I didn't fucking exist. But in comes your dad, the king of rock and roll, two months and a wad of cash - he's the second bloody coming.

'Didn't last though. Your dad got bored, didn't he? She wrote him letters you know? Every day. Well every day she wasn't wrecked. Dirty, pleading little letters. Fawning, sycophantic, sniveling things, they were. And you know what your dad did? Fuck all is what. He just disappeared. The coward's way. We heard nothing, not for a full fucking month. Then a single letter arrives. All typed and legal. I never got to read that. She burned it over the sink. You know, she'd already got herself into debt thinking there'd be more money coming. And she took a hit that night. A big one. And then another the night after. And the night after that an' all. And one night, about a month later, she took a hit, and she never fucking woke up.

'So the way I see it, your dad killed my mum. He stole her from me. He broke that woman with her own fucking dreams. My big brother! The famous fucking Mickey Richards. So you know what, you can call me Uncle Steve if you want to. But the way I see it, your dad owes me a life. And I've decided to take yours.'

'Steve!' Lola said. 'Steve! You said -'

She came towards him but he batted her away with the back of his hand. She cried out in shock.

And Steve said, 'I'm going to kill you, Zack Richards. So, you know what? I don't give a shit about your faked fucking photo or your fucking cloud. A son for a mother. And that's poetic justice right there.'

He moved the gun in a mock firing action.

Zack Richards flinched in his chair.

54

Sweat beaded around the muzzle of the gun that pressed into Zack's forehead. Zack began to shake and Lola jumped forwards. She lunged for the gun. Steve was too focused on Zack to react quickly, but his grip tightened on the gun and his finger tightened around the trigger as Lola pulled the barrel away.

And the whole room shook.

Board rumbled and perspex rattled.

And the roar of the gun faded. Zack Richards' was screaming, loud and loaded with swearing. Bart, who had flinched at the gunshot, now winced at the screams. He looked down at his jeans spattered with blood, and then across. A part of Zack's right shoe was missing and blood spilled out of the hole and onto the bloody floor.

And Zack shouted.

'Shit. Shit, shit, shit! Look what you've done. You fucker! My God! Look at it! You crazy, fucking! Fucking Christ!'

And Lola looked like she was going to be sick.

'Oh God,' she murmured. 'Oh God, oh God.'

Steve was pointing the gun at her, shaking it in her face. He pushed her roughly down and he sank to his knees. He re-tied her ankles and he made a sound that was somewhere between a growl and a cry.

Lola was breathing hard and Zack's swearing sank into

a syncopated mutter. Then Steve Hasland stood and reshaped his hair.

He said, 'All right. I think it's time we'd got this party started.' And he stalked out into the storeroom and left them.

From their chairs they heard a series of loud clanks and splashes. Wanting to see, Bart craned his neck. Steve was out there, swinging a jerry can around amongst the machines.

Bart turned to Lola and said, 'We're not getting out of this. You're the daughter of the guy that's made him a murderer, Zack's the son of the man who killed his mother, and I'm, I'm a dickhead of a private detective who doesn't know what's good for him.'

But Lola wasn't listening. Her eyes were fixed on Zack's bleeding foot. And Bart turned to see the sweat stream down Zack's face.

'Come on,' Bart said. 'You don't want him to die. Lola. We've got to get out.'

And when she looked up Bart saw a panic in her eyes that he had not seen before.

She stammered out, 'He - won't - kill - us.'

'Christ Lola. What is it with you and him? Are you guys like a thing?' Bart asked. 'Is that it?'

And Lola laughed. It was a cold and tiny laugh. And she shook her head.

'You're ridiculous,' she said.

With his head tilted back, and gazing at the ceiling, Zack breathed heavily and said, 'So - what is he - like a big brother or something?'

Lola glowered.

And Bart said, 'Come on Lola! There's something going on here. So what is it? Is it revenge? Against your dad or something?' He nodded at the corpse of Francesca De Souza. 'Against her, maybe? You know Lola, if I'm going to die today, I kind of want to know why.'

Her cheek twitched, just once.

'It wasn't supposed to happen like this,' she said.

Outside, the clanking and the splashing stopped.

Steve was listening.

Then there was a whoosh, and orange flame lit the far corner of the storeroom.

Lola turned to Zack.

'Okay, so I knew about you and Fran,' she said. 'And I was jealous. Of course I was jealous! But that's only because - look I - I didn't want - I didn't want - any of this, okay!' She paused, calmed herself. 'I just thought - Oh God - I just thought that I want - look, I love you, Zack. Okay? And I mean like - I properly love you - I - I thought I could help.'

Zack tilted his head and he forced his eyes open.

'Lola,' he whispered. He was almost smiling. 'I think you -'

'You think she what?' Steve said. He swung in around the side of the door-frame and hung from the crossbeam, a broad smile on his face. 'Go on then. Spit it out, Zack. You think she what?'

And Bart said, 'He thinks if Lola asks you nicely, maybe you'll let her go.'

And Steve bore his teeth like an angry ape, bending down, his gaze charged and calculating, and Bart saw the knife, sheathed and balanced precariously in the back pocket of Hasland's jeans.

'You think so, do you?' Steve said. 'Well she can always ask. Maybe I will say yes, eh?' And no one spoke, so Steve continued. 'Well then. I'll ask you, detective. Do you think I'll say yes, you know, if she asks me?' He brought his hand close, and he palmed Bart full in the face and he laughed. Warm blood trickled down Bart's upper lip and Steve leaned to inspect his work, drinking in the pain and vulnerability. 'You're a bit of a joke, aren't you Crowe?' he said.

And Lola looked at her feet and her sequined ballet pumps that were soaked in her boyfriend's blood and in Francesca De Souza's blood. She began to shake. Steve turned to her and he stroked her hair, and when Lola didn't move, he rubbed her arm and he whispered in her ear, and he took her hands in his with real tenderness and he pulled her gently to her feet. And Lola Golden shook with tears and Steve pulled her to him and put his arms around her waist.

Lola Golden laid her head against Steve Haslan's chest and she wept.

'Shit man, this is so fucked up,' Zack rasped.

And Steve's lips curled down at the edges and his eyes closed, as Lola's blonde hair draped against his chest, a tear on his cheek and the combat knife in his back pocket, while out in the storeroom, twisting totems of smoke spiraled to the high ceiling and the flames moved closer.

And when Steve released his hold on Lola, she shuffled back and brushed the hair from her eyes. Still looking down, her eyes moved faster, recompiling the events of the last few hours. And when Steve stepped forward and touched her shoulder she pulled back.

'Okay. Okay,' Steve said. 'Stay there. Can you stay standing? I mean are you strong enough to stand?'

Lola nodded. Steve dropped to one knee and the knife fell from his back pocket and thudded softly on the bloody carpet.

Steve said, 'Lola - Okay, okay - Lola - Oh Jesus! I thought this would be easier, you know. I've literally planned this speech so many times and now I - okay - right, I'm ready - Lola, I need your forgiveness.'

And she backed away until the frame of the chair dug into her calves as outside another pool of petrol caught light with a whump.

'Listen - Steve,' Lola said. 'Please - you don't have to -'

Steve said, 'It was me! It was me that did it. That's what I have to tell you.'

And Lola didn't move or respond but Zack leaned forward, straining to hear.

'It was me,' Steve said again. 'I took your mother from you. It was me! I shot her. I shot her with this very gun!'

And he pulled out the pistol and he held it flat in his palms as the flames rose up and rattled the perspex windows. And it was as if they were roaring in applause.

And Steve said, 'It was me. I kept the gun. In 2010 - when I first came down here - this gun - it was waiting for me. Your mum was out running. And I hid on the beach. And I ran up behind her. And I shot her. Point blank. I shot her twice. And I left her there to die on the sand. It was me. I did it.'

Lola gripped clumps of hair in her hands as the peaks of flame rose higher. Her mouth was open but she couldn't and didn't speak.

DOCUMENT Q

Text messages from Sophie Heath to Bartholomew Crowe: 22/11/19. 07:01 a.m.

[Dear Bartie Boy - ANSWER YOUR BLOODY PHONE!!! I rang like six times. I left a message like twice.]

[So I got your text!!!! There hasn't been another one. That means the police don't have this Hasland guy and it means I don't know if you're OK.]

[And you've broken your promise cos you haven't text me like you said.]

[I rang Noah. At least he answers his phone when I call! He offered to drive me down there. I mean, right now. He just offered! So kind. And I'd go too - you know - if it wasn't for the bullet hole - it just hurts too much. Even thinking about it hurts and I don't want to make it worse.]

[Listen. I know you want to save this girl. And I know you want justice - for me or for yourself - but I want you to promise me - do not try and talk to this Hasland guy. DO NOT GET CLOSE! Don't put yourself in danger. The instant you find him, CALL THE POLICE okay. Please. I mean it.]

[You know I will get over this bullet wound thing - probably -

mostly - eventually. And you know what else? Deep down, I could probably get over losing you - probably - mostly - eventually! - sorry!!! But that would be REALLY HARD AND I DON'T WANT TO! Bart don't make me do it. I DON'T WANT TO LOSE YOU!!! So promise you'll be good and stay alive and CALL ME WHEN YOU GET THIS OKAY!!!]

[I'm phoning the police in 1hr. Sophie Xx]

55

Tongues of flame danced beyond the perspex sheeting. Steve was looking down when he spoke.

'I knew your dad when I was a kid back home in Brum. But you already knew that, right? And he'd pay me to carry stuff for him. I carried a lot of packets but even then I never did it for the money. You know when you're a kid, you're happy hanging out in any kind of crowd really, it's like you're part of something isn't it? And it was brilliant actually. I was everyone's kid brother.'

He smiled.

'And you know, sometimes the lads would try to get me to take some of their stuff, bit of grass, bit of ganja or LSD, all that - and I don't know if they were always serious - but I always said no - I didn't want to be like Mum, you know. And sometimes I actually fought them off physically. But that was okay. Showed them I was tough didn't it. Made them nervous, see.

'And it was during that time I noticed that Glenn was like that too. I mean he smoked fags and a bit of weed and that but never more, and he'd always pick me for jobs you know, over the others. Knew I wouldn't get stoned and fuck it up like the rest of 'em. He was smart, your dad, anyone could see it, and I wanted to be just like him.

'So I did a lookout job or two. ID-ed guys for him. Whatever, really - but I never took no drugs no matter what. And when I got bigger, I got a lot bigger and Glenn started me in with a bit of the rough stuff. But I wasn't a thug about it. I was organised, and I was patient, and I never got caught. And when I hurt people, I never felt anything you know. No guilt. My step brothers and their mates, they'd done some horrible stuff to me. And nobody ever gave a shit about that. Not Mum, and definitely not my step-dad. Not my teachers. Not the social services. Not bloody anybody. So I knew pain. I still know it now. Every moment is soaked in pain, sort of like breathing.

'Anyway, I was organised like I said, and because I was organised I did pretty well at school - out of trouble for the most part - and hiding the truth about my car-crash of a life. And nobody ever helped me. Not a soul. But I made it - school and uni and teacher training - and all on my bloody own too. And you know what else? At the end of the day it was easy! All the other guys at uni moaning about assignments and deadlines and shit. I was just like - fuck, I slept under a dining room table for four years. This is a fucking holiday!

'So, anyway, after uni I moved back to Birmingham and I got a teaching job at my old school. Got married. Got divorced soon after, but - well, that didn't work out - but I still had my mum, and I looked after her as much as she'd let me. And that was when Mickey Richards came by, and Mum thought she's saved - saved from bad gear. And I even thought that maybe having this new brother proves I'm special too.

'But it turned out that Mickey Richards got bored real fucking quick. And that's the thing about addiction isn't it? It's fucking boring. It bores people. So anyway, Richards fucks off and two months later my mum is dead. And the shithead doesn't even go to the funeral. Now she's three crappy pages in his autobiography. I don't even get a fucking namecheck! And Mum wasn't much but she was all I had. I went fucking crazy. Not drugs. But sex. Hookups and prozzies, S&M, men and fucking women. Fucking everything. I did all of it.

'Then when Glenn contacted me on Facebook, it was

exactly what I needed really - the old family from the old days come to bring me back from the brink. Something real you know. Something human. My mum was dead and I was having these empty, emotionless hookups. And I knew pain, and I knew death. It didn't seem such a leap to kill somebody really. And if I'm honest, the idea excited me. Another taboo to check off the list. So I did what Glenn wanted and I shot your mother.'

Lola closed her eyes and she rested her chin on her thumbs.

'Why?' she said. 'Why did Dad want her dead?'

'Oh it was money. Pure and simple really. They were getting divorced you see, and she was being difficult. Glenn figured he'd sold his soul to the devil long ago. He'd paid his price for what he had, risked his freedom, so why should she have half of it, you know?'

'But what about me then?' Lola said. 'What about custody of me? I was nine years old! Was it about custody too?'

'No pet. It wasn't about you. You were always going to stay with your dad. But I only got one side, remember.'

Lola looked into Steve's grey-green eyes. And Steve reached out to her, to touch her shoulder, but she shook her head, dusted his hand away.

'No. No, sorry. I can't forgive you, Steve,' she said. 'I don't forgive you. Not for any of - this. I can't.'

Rumbling flames, black smoke covering the ceiling, and Steve had to raise his voice over the fire.

'I understand,' he said. 'I do. But remember Lola, I was in a bad place then. Fuck me, I'm in a bad place now! But I want you to know the truth, because Lola, I'm gonna let you go. Now. So that's it - you're free. So go. Before the flames take hold. Go home.'

Lola looked at Zack, then at Bart.

And she said, 'I won't go.'

Zack rocked his head forwards and he smiled at her through his pain.

But Bart said, 'Go! For Christ's sake, at least one of us has to get out of this alive! You've got to go now, Lola!'

And Lola looked at Zack. Poor drowsy Zack, on the edge of consciousness and she shook her head.

'No,' she said. 'I won't.'

Steve said, 'Lola, I took your mother's life. Now I'm sparing yours. You need to go now, sweetheart.'

Zack, grinning drowsily, moved his head towards the door and said, 'Go, babe.'

A tear slipped down Lola's cheek.

She mouthed the words 'I love you.' And she turned to Steve and said, 'Can I have my bag please? I want to clean myself up.'

Steve pulled Lola's grey-blue hand bag from his holdall and Lola sat in the chair next to the corpse of Francesca De Souza. She studied herself in her compact and she dusted her face with brushes and pads.

Steve walked to the door. He looked out into the flames and the blackening smoke. And while his back was turned, Lola picked up the combat knife from where it had fallen under the chair. She walked up behind him, the knife behind her back.

'Okay,' she said. 'I'm ready.'

Steve turned. He rested one hand on her shoulder. And the muzzle of the gun touched her neck.

'I know you can't see it now, but I hope one day you can forgive me, Lola, for all of the badness I've done to you.'

'Can I say goodbye to the boys please?'

The flames crackled and snapped. Something fell and something smashed and Lola smiled softly. Steve nodded and he turned back to watch the flames and smoke.

And Lola knelt close to Bart, and he felt the point of the black blade prick his skin as she pinged through the cable tie and squeezed the knife under his forearm.

'It has to be you, Bart Crowe,' she whispered and she kissed his forehead. Then she spoke loudly so Steve could hear.

'I'm so sorry Bart. You're a good person, okay? And if there's a heaven -'

'Thanks Lola,' Bart said.

And she kissed him on the cheek and she stroked his hair.

Zack was struggling to focus, but even in pain his eyes were dark and intense. And Lola's lips quivered as she held him to her chest, and she kissed his head and his nose and his cheek. She kissed his lips. She held his head in her hands as his eyes strained to find hers.

Their eyes met. Unspoken words hung like threads between them.

Then there was Steve, pulling her away.

'You have to go now,' he said. 'Before it gets too dangerous.'

Lola wiped her eyes. She stopped at the door and she looked back to see Zack looking back at her. Then she left them, weaved her way to the stairs, past the flames and debris, her pale blue blouse blending into the grey of the smoke.

Steve sat opposite the boys, next to the corpse of Francesca De Souza, in the seat that Lola had left. He let out a long sigh and he said, 'So, I guess that's that then. You know what, Bart, I really thought it was a shame that you and Lola didn't - you know. And it's a real shame because if you had've done, I would've let you go too.'

Bart looked at Zack. The grimace of pain. And he hoped his friend could stay conscious a few minutes longer.

'I did try,' Bart said, 'but, well, that's life I guess.'

Steve snorted.

The flames were brighter outside and the heat tickled their skin, and puffy black clouds padded the ceiling like the down of dark swans.

'They have a pastor at the school you know? A service and a sing-song every day. And you know, when you think about it, all this here, it's all a bit biblical, isn't it? Sins of the father and all that.'

And Bart said, 'If you think you're God's agent here, I'm putting in a complaint. I mean, Zack here, he's not blameless, but - what about Francesca? What about me?'

Steve tapped the gun, and his eyes began to scan the ground.

'Where you're going wrong there, Crowe, is that you're seeing living as a right and I'm really not sure that it is. There's sin in us all. No-one free of it. We're all to be judged in the end.'

'And what about Glenn Golden then? Who's going to judge him?'

'I've got no quarrel with Glenn.'

And Bart craned his neck around and he looked out into the store room, and then he snapped his head back to look at Steve.

He said, 'Glenn Golden paid you to kill Lola's mum. He paid you, Steve. It was his crime. He's as guilty as you are. More guilty -'

And Bart looked to the side again, out into the storeroom, making it as obvious as he dared.

'That's the second time you've looked - What the fuck is it you're looking at? Is there someone out there?'

He glared through the smoke. His head jerked about like a hungry bird. He gripped the neck of Bart's shirt and he shook him.

'What did you see? Who's out there?'

Bart grinned and Steve butted him in the face.

The impact burned.

His nose throbbed.

Blood welled on his upper lip.

And Steve shouted, 'What the fuck did you see?'

Still woozy from the head-butt, Bart wasn't prepared for the punch that crashed into the side of his head and he could only half focus as Steve lurched up towards the door and stood there for five clear seconds, looking out over the storeroom.

Sensing his opportunity, but still giddy from the blow,

he lifted his hand and he gripped the knife tight. He sprung his left hand and he reached down to his ankles and sliced off the ties. And he stood and staggered up behind Steve, the knife in his hand. His whole arm shook and his legs quaked. He pulled his knife arm back. And he paused.

The knife.

If he could do it without the knife, without killing.

And he threw himself onto Steve's back, and he wrapped his arm, the arm with the knife, around Steve's throat. But Steve had a hold of his wrist, and he smacked Bart's hand against the frame of the door until the blade fell, its sound swallowed by rumbling flames. Steve elbowed him in the gut and Bart doubled over, stumbling back as Steve's big fist wheeled and crunched into his jaw. Bart fell, fell to the floor. And he saw the sole of Steve's foot growing larger. He rolled away, deflecting Steve's stamping foot with his forearms and shifting sideways and back to his feet. And he hopped onto the chair, twisting to avoid the powerful arms that grabbed at him.

Then there was a tug on his jeans and two big hands clamped on his leg. They yanked him off his feet and he fell back. His body left a dent on the insulating board on the back wall, and he slid down, landing on the coffee table. The edge of it jabbed into the small of his back and he cried out. But then Steve had a hold of his collar and his hair. He twisted him round and dumped him in the bloody carpet. And Steve dropped his whole weight down, pinning Bart's arms under his knees, and his forearm pushed against Bart's neck.

'You're nothing, Crowe,' Steve said, panting, a broad smile across his face. 'You're fucking nothing. You're nothing now, a couple of hours you'll be nothing still. So it doesn't really matter if you die then or if you die now. Do you understand me?'

Wheezing, Bart said, 'Can't - talk -'

Steve pulled the automatic pistol from his inside pocket and jammed the barrel into Bart's ear.

'How about now? Can you talk now? Does that fucking help? Do you fucking get it now, Crowe? You're nothing at all. You're a sideshow. You're a sad, pathetic nobody.'

Bart nodded. He tried to say he understood but he couldn't find the breath he needed for the vowels and his consonants rattled like keys on a fob.

The flames were tapping at the door and the smoky ceiling descending. The window nearest the back wall cracked with the heat and the perspex fell inwards. And, in the corner, next to Zack, a tall, fake pot-plant wobbled. Leaning, slowly at first, almost imperceptibly, like the first moments of a toppling tree. And then it fell. And it fell towards Steve and Bart, and as it came down, Steve twisted. He tried to bat the thing away, swinging his pistol hand, shifting his weight, and Bart was suddenly able to pull his legs back, and so, with everything he had, he rammed his feet into Steve Hasland's gut. And Steve was caught off balance. Twisting and writhing, he fell sideways as the plant came down and the gun flew from Hasland's hand. It flew through the air and it clanged against a metal chair and dropped, onto Francesca De Souza's lap.

Both of them saw it.

Steve lurched forward. He gripped Francesca's calf, pulled her leg and her body slumping in the chair. And Bart moved too, grasping at the semi-sheer fabric of her blood-soaked orange top, grasping, reaching hand over hand, like a man dragging himself from a pit. And the gun was there. Hasland's hand close to it, but Bart was closer, and then - he had it.

He had the gun.

And it felt unnaturally heavy.

And when Steve saw that Bart had it, his small eyes widened. He froze. And then it was Bart who came down on top of him, knees pressed across Steve's shoulders. And Bart had the pistol in both hands and both hands shook. And the room shuddered in the heat.

Only Steve's eyes remained steady.

And Bart had to shout over the roar of the flames.

'Okay right - You're going to stand up - and - I'm going to bind your hands - and - we're going to get out of here - okay!'

And Steve shouted back, 'No! No fucking way, detective! No fucking way! I'll fucking kill you. An' I'll kill Richards. It's what I am. It's what I came here to do. I've come too fucking far to fucking compromise!' The gun shook in Bart's hands and Steve said, 'So go on. Run if you want to. Go get help. You can try. See how far you get. Or you can put that gun into my mouth and you can blow my fucking head off and you know what, Bart? Either way is good with me. So come on then, detective. Make your choice.'

Above them, the tube light flickered and died and the room darkened.

Bart's knees shook as he tried to steady the gun.

'Do it, Bart. Do it if you're a killer like me. Do it now, if that's what you are. I'll not fight you.'

And Zack said, 'Do it, do it, do it! For fuck's sake. Shoot the psycho! Fucking shoot him!'

And Bart lowered the gun and Steve opened his mouth and Bart pushed the barrel inside.

And he squeezed the trigger.

Steve's eyes were wide, shaking his head and trying to speak with the gun in his mouth.

Bart pulled the gun back and Steve said, 'You've left the bloody safety on, you lummock. On the left. No, the left. Yes, there. Don't push it all the way down. Just to the middle.'

Zack screamed with frustration and he choked and he coughed.

And then Bart brought the gun back down and he rested the muzzle on Steve's temple. He squeezed on the trigger. The cocking action clunked. And then, when the gun fired, the crack of the shot was muted by the roaring flames, like a thunderclap in a down-pour. But it was the kickback that shocked him most. He fell back and the pistol writhed from his grip, and he fumbled, trying to keep a hold, as fragments of skull and of brains spattered his face and his coat.

And then Bart stood over the body of Steve Hasland, and he was not fully able to comprehend what he'd done. It was horrific. His red hands, the gloss of blood that covered the pistol. He let the weapon fall and he looked at his hands and he shook off some of the blood, wiped his hands on the back of his coat. And the gun landed on the chest of Steve Hasland's body. And the flames roared and windows cracked and black smoke filled the room.

And then there were sounds of sirens wailing outside.

Bart scrabbled around in the bloody mess on the floor, and when he found the knife, he cut the ties on Zack's wrists and ankles. Then he hoisted Zack from the chair. He fumbled as he tried to loop Zack's arm over his shoulder, his friend slipping, falling to his knees before Bart could steady him.

'I'm going to lift you up again okay?'

'Yeah.'

And Bart lifted, feeling the strain in his hamstrings. And Zack slipped down again. This time Bart gripped Zack's wrist, heaving him up, and the two of them swayed in nervous equilibrium. Bart stepped forwards. He slipped, losing his footing on the blood covered floor, losing his hold on Zack's wrist. And as Zack slipped down a figure appeared at the door, emerging from the smoke, a man. And the man pushed his arm around Zack's waist. And as Bart took Zack's arm back, the man took the other arm. Brown suede coat and brogues. And Bart looked across at his Granddad, standing beside him, helping him save his friend from a burning building. And neither of them smiled. They took what air they could from the smoke-filled room, and they looked straight ahead, and they focused on finding a path through the flames. They stepped. They stepped again. And step by step through the fire and smoke.

56

The back-street behind The Golden Arcade was dotted with police officers and firefighters, more arriving. Granddad was pulled away and the two young men were quickly surrounded.

Bart sat down against a wall, looking across at the older man with medics and police, as an officer patted him down. A paramedic kneeled next to him. She clicked her fingers in front of his face. He looked round and feigned a smile as she checked his pulse and his breathing.

'You know, we're going to have to take you in because of the smoke - I'm sorry but I can't give oxygen to the three of you at once,' she said.

The three of you...

Did she mean Granddad or -

Scanning the scene frantically, too many people, too much to take in, and then there she was, Lola Golden, sliding out from the back seat of the medic's car, coming towards him, tears on her cheeks.

'You know these boys?' the paramedic said.

'Yes,' Lola said, and she looked into Bart's eyes, her voice trembling as she blinked away a tear. 'I knew you wouldn't let me down.' She widened her mouth and she sucked in her lips as she stroked Bart's hair.

And Zack was wearing the mask, hungrily sucking oxygen into his lungs. And when he coughed and choked, and his eyes moved rapidly as he came back into himself. He pulled the mask away, and he coughed again before he could composed himself.

And then he said, 'Hi.'

'Hi,' Lola said, and she held out her hand.

'Okay kids,' the paramedic said. 'I'm just going to talk to my colleague for a mo, okay? I'll be right back,' and she walked down the road to speak to a good-looking police officer who was leaning against his car.

And Zack held up his hand and he and Lola connected, their fingers and thumbs, interlocking them, clamping them tight.

Lola said, 'I love you, Zack.'

And Zack said, 'Yeah? Well, somebody has to.'

And Lola kissed his forehead as Zack slipped the mask back on, and then the paramedic was standing over them.

'Okay -' she said and she raised an eyebrow, '- so I'm really sorry guys, but there's a couple of ambulances out front waiting to take you away. And the fire people, they really need to get another engine down here, so if you guys could hop into the car -'

Bart got to his feet and he touched the paramedic's upper arm as Lola Golden and Zack Richards held each other in a tearful embrace. 'I'll sit up front, if that's okay.'

DOCUMENT R

The Kent Clarion Online
22/11/2019. 11.38 a.m.

Fire destroys Margate seafront amusement arcade

A fire has destroyed an amusement arcade in Margate.

Firefighters were called to the incident at The Golden Arcade on Marine Terrace, just after 7 am on Saturday.

The fire, which is being treated as suspicious, is being seen as a major blow for the resort which has experienced something of a revival in recent years.

'The fire crews have been incredible'

The blaze broke out just before 7 am but took hold with incredible speed.

People gathered on the beach to watch the fire with many commenting favourably on the speed and scale of the fire services' response.

Colin Crowe, 68, who was in Margate to visit his Grandson, was one of the first on the scene and one of the many who reported the fire to the authorities.

He said: "The fire and ambulance crews have been incredible."

Over 100 fire-fighters were at the scene during the course of the blaze.

'We are all devastated'

The amusement arcade, which forms part of an Edwardian terrace, partially collapsed within an hour of firefighters being called out.

Fire crews have now subdued the blaze, but damping down and checking roof voids is likely to continue well into the afternoon.

A spokesman for Kent Fire and Rescue said: "Firefighters have fought hard to restrict damage from the fire on the first and ground floors of the building and have been largely successful in restricting damage to neighbouring properties."

Police have stated that four people, a woman and two men, all eighteen, and an older man, escaped the burning building and that they have been taken by ambulance to hospital in order to treat them for the effects of smoke and other toxins.

A police spokesman said: "The cause of the fire is currently being treated as suspicious. Work is ongoing to ascertain the circumstances of the incident and whether, indeed, there have been any casualties."

The arcade forms an important part of Margate's seafront attractions and was due to be refurbished in the new year.

The owner of the arcade, Glenn Golden, 52, was also one of the first to arrive at the scene. He said: "We are absolutely devastated. The arcade is a real attraction and is tremendously popular with visitors to the town and provides work for a number of local people."

57

Bart was squeezing dirty washing into his rucksack when the envelope fell to the floor. A thousand pounds in used twenties. Glenn Golden's money. The notes looked scruffier than he remembered. He picked it up and stuffed it back into his coat pocket. And, looking around the dusty room one last time, he slung the rucksack over his shoulder, pulling the door closed behind him.

Barbara Feathers shuffled out to meet him at reception. She looked tired and she wasn't trying to hide it. She produced a bill that exceeded his calculations, just as he thought she would. But he paid without complaint. Barbara didn't thank him and she didn't say goodbye. Instead, she returned his card and his receipt, disappearing back into her flat with little more than a word, and then she was gone, back to the safety of her comfy settee, back to the safety of daytime TV, and the solace of the bottle.

Bart reached over the desk. He took a thick looking pen and pulled the envelope from his pocket. He wrote, 'To Mrs Feathers. For the future.' And he tucked it under some papers she had on the desk, protruding just a little. He pulled open the heavily sprung door and walked out into the morning light.

*

In the midst of the city with skyscrapers and office blocks high on all sides, many of them made for the nearest doors, looking to hole-up quickly. But most, like the three boys, wanted to score high. They continued to the centre of play where the tracers zipped in erratic grids across their screens.

Noah said, 'Left, left left! Keep running!'

They crossed the square to the grand hotel.

At the entrance Bart had turned to looked back as Noah's screen flashed red. Shot by someone. No idea who, or where from. But his friend made it inside without another hit. And the red flashes stopped. Just a stray bullet perhaps. The hotel foyer was grey-brown and dark, but light streamed down from the stairs. Connor led the way, running fast, and they all climbed up through alternating spells of darkness and light.

A flash of blue.

Bart turned.

'Behind!' he said.

Noah and Connor doubled back to see there were three of them, three blues and Bart had hit one. It was a headshot, but not an instant kill. Red marks on the soldier's ear. It would be an easy kill from here. But Bart didn't fire, didn't finish him. He just stopped, standing on the lowest stair, an obvious target. His screen flashed red, flashed again. Connor and Noah could see the first soldier was recovering and knew that Bart would soon be in his sights too.

So they opened fire with everything they had.

'Die Blue scum!' Noah shouted.

Sophie snorted derisively from across the room.

The first soldier was hit again, this time in the arm. He looked to be finished. Connor and Noah engaged the enemy as Bart's screen cleared. But the two Blues had regrouped. His screen flashed again. Red and red and red.

Bart dropped the controller on the carpet as the image

froze.

Game over. Option to restart.
Noah and Connor focused on the two Blues. With Bart having drawn their fire they were able to finish them quickly.

The danger gone, Noah looked round at Bart.
'Come on bro. Hop back in. You know where we are.'
But Bart had put down the controller.
'I've been thinking I should go and chat with the guys downstairs for a bit,' Bart said. 'You guys play on. I'll be back up in a couple of minutes. Okay?'
'Hey. That guy downstairs with your granddad,' Noah said. 'He's really that cop that got stabbed, yeah?'
'Yeah,' Bart said. 'He is. Three times in the back. He's called Wayne, and he's a good guy. You should come and say hello.'
'Looks like something out of the nineteen-eighties,' Connor said, still focused on the screen. 'Mental tache though. I like it. It's cool.'
And Bart said, 'I'll tell him.'
And he lifted his hand and ducked his head as he opened the door.
'Hey, Bartie?'
'Yes Soph.'
'We love you!'
At the door, Bart turned and he smiled. Connor and Noah didn't speak or look up, but Soph did. Of course she did. They were back in the game. All of them. He knew it and she knew it too. He felt that they loved him and his mouth widened into a broad smile.
'I love you guys too,' he said.

*

Skeletal trees lined the road into Lower Slaughter and idyllic, stone-built cottages lined the banks of the river Eye.

He passed slowly through the village, parking the Mini in front of a heavy double gate and gathering his thoughts. He got out and opened the boot, carefully lifting a large bouquet of white oriental lilies. The plastic wrapping crackled and he felt a bit sick. Still, he held them close to his chest and he walked the two doors down to the house.

The sound of the bell made his heartbeat race.

And when the door opened there was Julia.

She looked well - Breton-striped top and linen trousers - she looked really well. She was wearing her glasses on her head and her face looked strained from smiling. She'd had her hair done too. Shorter, feathered, blonder than before.

'Hello,' Bart said.

There was giggling from the lounge, but when Julia recognised him she put her glass of wine down on the sill, and her smile was gone.

'Bart. Look, you really should have let me know -'

'It's okay,' he said. He pulled the beanie from his head and stuffed it in his pocket. She hated him wearing it. 'Listen -' he said, his brain still wanting to call her Mum. 'I just wanted to say thank you.'

'Bart -'

'No M- Julia, I mean let me - I want to say you were right - I mean back when we met. I was so angry back then and you did help me through it. You really did. And you want to find your own path and I just want to say that's cool. And thanks. Okay? I mean, sure. I'm still looking for my path but - okay - I just wanted to wish you - I mean I wanted to say good luck. You look happy.'

'I am happy, Bart.'

'Good. That's good. Okay. So - well - you won't be seeing me again - I mean unless you choose to - but I do love you - and yeah - so that's it. Cheers.'

And he pushed the flowers at her and they crackled as she took them.

'Thanks,' she said. 'They're pretty.'

'Yeah.'

And he turned and he walked away. He was stiff and awkward and he walked too fast. Julia didn't close the door. She watched him walking away like that, like an over-wound clockwork soldier, and she waited and she watched as Bart pulled away and disappeared around the bend in her erstwhile husband's weekend car.

And the grass on the path was green and cold and the November light shimmered on the surface of the river. Julia removed the card from the envelope on the bouquet. Pulling her glasses down, the words came into focus.

You can go your own way.

Much love,
Bart.
X

AUTHOR'S NOTES

If you've just read 'Burning Crowe', I thank you. It's my first novel and it's been a few years in the making (three I think). I hope my next book will be much quicker!

As I said 'Burning Crowe' is my first novel and it's been a long old road, trying to figure out a style and to build an online presence. Being honest folks, I've wasted a lot of time, done a lot wrong, and a few things right.

So, now I'm going to continue. I'm going to keep on going. I'm going to write more books. I've got a few ideas - some hardboiled crime, some not - but whatever comes next I'd love to share my journey with you, as I take my writing forward.

Join my list and get my collection of short stories for free here.

Finally, if you enjoyed reading 'Burning Crowe' it would be great if you could leave a review on whatever platform you bought it from.

Find me online:
Twitter: @geoffsmithbooks
Blog: geoffsmithbooks.com

THANKS

This novel is dedicated to all the people who inspired me to write it and helped it become what it is. So thanks to my incredible author/readers Kenneth George, Tom Steer and Finn Bell. Guys, I did my best to take your ideas on board, and thanks for being my friends. Thanks to Elizabeth Hall, whose feedback came first - the only person who has suffered or will ever have to suffer reading the very first draft. Thanks to my dad, and to my Father-in-law, Chris, whose detailed error spotting and broader feedback was so insightful, and to Kurt Ellison for the once over. Thanks to Kurt and Justin at the Point Blank podcast whose insight into the hardboiled genre is second to none. And thanks to everyone in the Point Blank Goodreads group too. And finally, thanks to Scottish genius writer, James Kelman, for bringing me back to reading in my twenties. Thanks to Raymond Chandler and Cormac MacCarthy and Patricia Highsmith for blowing my mind with great writing. Thanks to RFExtreme, whose album '84 Minutes' provided the soundtrack to the first draft, and to Paul Teague whose podcast 'Self Publishing Journeys' and 'Paul's Podcast Diary' kept, and still keeps, the dream alive.

Printed in Great Britain
by Amazon

29261344R00182